Oathbound, the Suffering of Others

David Giles

Cover design by Kye Ottley

First Published October 2022
by
Budding Authors Assistant
www.help2publish.co.uk

Cover design by Kye Ottley

ISBN: 9781739121549

THE NECROMANCER'S APPRENTICE SERIES

Oathbound; the Suffering of Others (Book 1)

Prologue

The last embers finally stopped glowing, leaving the last unburnt remnants of the small border village of Mori's Respite, or just Respite to those who had lived there, illuminated by the slight slither of silver moon that dared, bravely or callously, to show itself in the cloudy night sky. Normally such a conflagration would have taken a full day to cool, but the early winter night had been particularly cruel such that ash would perhaps be mistaken for snow at a distance. A little over twelve short hours ago, as evening set, the village had been vibrant and lustrous yet soothing and tranquil in its people. Now all that remained was the near-skeletal framework of a few half-charred buildings amidst the ash. And the gallows; the so terribly full gallows.

The slim trace of a moon just beginning to wax slowly traversed the starless sky, the only sounds the creaks of the gallows as the corpses swung in the wind; that was perhaps the first sign that something unnatural was at work beyond the hideousness of mortal cruelties, no carrion birds disturbed the slow precession of the nooses' occupants.

Slate grey eyes watched from the forest, apparently content to watch forever as they waited for even a trace or glimmer of life and tragically finding none. As the sun slowly crept up past the horizon, lighting up first the warming ochre, orange and yellows of autumnal canopy and then blackened timber, pale, grey ash and cracked, baked earth, dawn descended upon the village.

Normally people would be about their daily

business already, not the loud bustle of life in full flow, but those early risers who by habit or occupation wore dawn as a cloak as they did those small tasks that needed doing before the real work of the day could begin, the contrast was a dagger in the kidneys to that terribly calm and unseen gaze. Fortunate perhaps that it was unseen, for there were cracks in that level observation, smouldering ruins of a rage that had been hammered and bent upon the anvil of its bearer's self-control. There would be a reckoning for this, but not today. Today was for mourning and recrimination.

Satisfied at last that Respite was unguarded in truth rather than in guise, the watcher stepped out forth from the treeline, its choice of sable attire rendering it almost a silhouette even in broad daylight as it proceeded to what was once the village square. In the ensuing hour, the dead were cut down, and the beginnings of a mass grave dug, the watcher working tirelessly well past the point where mortal muscle and endurance would have forced a break for water or sustenance, doing the work by hand and handling each body with something if not quite reverence then at least akin to it, guilt perhaps.

He could have done it faster, arcane means would have rendered the task the trivial work of an hour, he could have gone so far as to have the dead bury themselves even, but such thoughts were anathema. This had been his failing, his fault, and the burden to care for the empty shells of what had been good friends fell to him and him alone. It was a small selfishness and he knew it. Even now, time he could ill afford to spend was being wasted, but that burden too was his alone. Until it wasn't.

A slight cough from within one of the burned-out

ruins caught his attention. Without any visible motion from its owner, a blade released itself from the bottom of the watcher's staff, clicking and locking into place fourteen lethal inches of supernaturally sharpened steel, the weapon held guardedly in front, wicked point aimed roughly at what would be the throat of a human, ready to stab forward or block an incoming strike. Nothing could have survived the blaze of the previous night, or at least nothing fully human.

The dry cough came again; there was a faint movement in the ash and debris. Cautiously the staff was reversed, and the movement poked gently with the blunt end, a flawless ebon facsimile of a skull. Another cough and a faint groan of pain, the staff was discarded, rolling to a stop as the blade got lodged in what was probably once a fireplace, about three inches of solid stone cut clean through. Carefully the survivor was picked up, a boy just on the verge of his mid-teens, rendered invisible in the dirt by the thick layer of grey and black ash covering him. With infinite care, the watcher wiped the dry dirt and crumbling grey powder of his erstwhile home from the child's face, revealing pink and healthy skin impossibly unmarked by the savage flames that had ravaged his home the previous evening.

"Well kid, I guess you're coming with me."

CHAPTER 1

Alec awoke. The first thing he was aware of was a stabbing pain in his back where he was lying on a particularly pointed stone no bigger than a knuckle yet entertaining delusions of knifehood. Sitting up, he found himself covered by a thick and rather scratchy grey cloth of some kind, not wool or any other fabric he could put a name to. Slowly he rose to his feet, surprised to find his knees wobbling and unsteady, blinking furiously as his eyes strained to readjust to the gloom.

It was a cave of some sort, exceptionally dry; the only sign water had ever once existed here were the small stalactites and stalagmites, almost vestigial, the diminutive structures forlorn and time-worn relics of an era before man's ancestors had pondered the pros and cons of standing upright. Ignoring the muted majesty of the structures around him, and barely able to see them in the dim light, Alec zeroed in on the light source which was just visible deeper in the cave. It did not flicker or, if the temperature was anything to go by, provide warmth, but projected a clinical white ambience that carried far, though by the time it reached Alec, white had faded to a dismal and murky grey.

Advancing cautiously and using the stalagmites — at least those few large enough — as cover, he approached, stopping still at every slight clack and click of his boots upon the stone until finally, the light source came into view.

On the hard, rocky floor, a black-robed figure sat, cross-legged and back ramrod straight, gazing at what had to be one of the most beautiful sights Alec had ever laid eyes upon.

A perfect sphere, almost two feet in diameter, floating and apparently transfixed roughly ten feet off the floor, the sphere glowing so brightly that he had to look at it out of the corner of his eye or risk being blinded.

"Beautiful isn't it?" the robed figure asked softly, disturbing the heavy silence of reverence that had overtaken the cave. That said, he got to his feet and bellowed out into the cavern, his voice echoing back at him in a fading baritone, "Ente! Come forth so that you may be taken back to the place you once called home. Come forth from death's embrace, your vigil is over, fellow magi have found your work. Come forth."

Alec took a step back involuntarily, realising he was either in the presence of a sorcerer of the darkest magics or a madman, and, if the stories were to be believed, potentially both.

And then a voice answered back out of the darkness.

"You claim to walk knowledge's path. What proof have you?" It was a faded, reedy and rasping thing, more the idea of words really.

"When has the pursuit of knowledge required proof?" the robed figure countered.

"For a thing to be known to be true it must be observably true, you should know that. Now demonstrate your knowledge, you wear the black robe, summon me forth. By your power and craft, summon this old ghost or leave me to rest," demanded the voice.

There was the barest hint of a chuckle from within the robe before he sketched a symbol in the air with his hands. Alec could not truly describe what he'd done, there was no glowing script, nor impression in the air, but somehow he could see the rune the necromancer, for that was what he had to be to commune with the dead so, had sketched. And then a struggling Ente stood before him, his body, for lack of a better word, just a translucent blob of colour, barely even humanoid.

"Time has been harsh on you," the robed figure observed softly.

"Not so harsh I cannot defend my work," the ghost stated firmly.

The necromancer sighed before speaking, each word careful and measured. "I regret to say that the Tear must be destroyed."

As soon as the words left him, the ghost surged forward, its shape becoming more defined, its colour stronger and sharper. Instinctively Alec knew this was an indicator of the ghost's strength; Ente had been feigning weakness.

The necromancer was unperturbed by this assault from beyond the grave, the old ghost simply coming to a halt mere inches from its target no matter how it swung and clawed and raked at whatever invisible barrier kept the man from joining his attacker in the hereafter.

"Bastard," Ente declared angrily to the impassive face holding him at bay.

"Technically incorrect, I knew my father, in fact he and I were on good terms until the day he died, and even now we talk from time to time. Still I can appreciate the sentiment," the necromancer said in the same too level tone. "I am sorry Ente but paladins are closing in on this cave, I can't allow them the Tear. It would prove… disruptive."

The ghost sighed, seeming to collapse into a defeated slouch. "Is there no other way?"

"None," the necromancer said firmly. "But I have brought a ghost jar. I may not be able to save the Tear but I can at least bring you home. Let them have their small victory, for what is the Tear compared to the mind that made it?"

"My thanks," the ghost answered, terribly weary and fading once more, whatever strength it had had burned away in its desperate attack. "Long have I wished to go home, it's just a pity my life's work must die."

The dark mage quietly got to his feet and moved over to his backpack, like the rest of his ensemble it was as black as a midday shadow, and removed a small transparent crystal the size of Alec's thumb, each facet a polished octagon, the teenager was almost disappointed, as gems went it might as well have been glass.

There was another hand gesture, almost a grabbing motion, and then Ente was gone, the gem glowing ever so faintly azure before it was hidden in the voluminous depths of the magician's pockets.

"Rest well."

With that done, the necromancer knelt back down to pick up his staff. A time-polished shaft of dark wood topped with a black gem shaped like a human skull, and the same size as well, very much in keeping with the necromancer's gothic appearance. It should have been unwieldy in its weight, a hideously top-heavy act of artifice, yet going from how its owner held it, the balance was perfect.

With a mild sense of ceremony, he pressed the gem to the Tear, the light fading from within until finally, power either spent or drained, the orb fell, plunging the cave into darkness as it shattered upon the ground into a blizzard of glass shards which bounced harmlessly off of Alec and the necromancer, presumably a spell of some kind.

"Stay close child," the mage intoned, a small flame appearing in the palm of his hand, "this cave is more than vast enough to lose you beyond even my abilities to find you."

Alec jumped slightly at being addressed, presuming his presence forgotten.

"W-why have you kidnapped me?" he asked, not quite managing the presence of will to make it a demand now he was no longer entranced by the events around him.

"I would more call it a rescue than a kidnapping," the barely visible figure replied softly, utterly failing to answer the question. "Now follow, it wouldn't pay to get lost here."

"I want to go home!" Alec declared, loud, defiant and just a little bit petulant, if understandably so, his voice echoing around the cave.

"Keep your voice down," his rescuer/kidnapper hissed urgently. "If they've found this cave already then they'll hear you."

"Who are they?"

"Paladins," the kidnapper answered, almost inaudibly.

"Paladins?" he breathed, relief coursing through him as he inhaled deeply to yell.

He never got the chance. A thin, gloved hand moved over his mouth; he'd barely seen the necromancer move.

"Don't be an idiot, Alec. They'd kill both of us in a heartbeat."

That said, he removed his hand. The beginnings of

a scream died on Alec's lips as his eyes rolled up into his head, the only thing keeping him from slumping to the floor in unconsciousness the iron grip of his kidnapper.

The necromancer sighed, knocking out the child had been distasteful but necessary.

With another monumental sigh, he hoisted the boy over his shoulder, then, at the same time as hooking the unused arm through a strap on his pack, picked up his stave before heading for the exit.

Chapter 2

When Alec finally awoke from his magically induced slumber, it was night. And he was tied to a tree.

"Sorry about this but I thought it best to explain things before I gave you free reign of the camp," his kidnapper said kindly, sat opposite a small fire, the man no more than a silhouette in the dim flickering firelight.

"What do you want?" Alec spat, words harsh as he could make them to disguise the fear in his voice.

The man took a deep calming breath as he steepled his fingers, apparently deep in thought. "I want to atone for my mistakes, which is impossible. So I'm going to do the next best thing, saving your life."

"By kidnapping me‽" Alec exclaimed furiously.

"I will admit circumstances are not what I would have wished but I hope in time you will come to understand," he answered solemnly.

"Not bloody likely," was the less than encouraging response.

"Now I'm going to cut you loose and, if you're wise, you won't run," he warned quiet but firm. That was one thing Alec had already noticed, the necromancer was always very softly spoken.

"And what will you do if I ignore your advice?" the teen enquired, an undertone of anger in his voice; if he'd had the free use of his hands 'advice' would have most certainly been given air quotes.

"Try to prevent you from being eaten." There was a slight chuckle. "Foolish boy, there are far more dangerous things than a mere mage in these woods, why do you think your own village — the very frontier of human civilisation — was built just two miles in? And surrounded by walls besides."

"So what's so dangerous?"

"Well for starters there's the arach, which grow unusually large in these parts, the walking woods that make navigation a hazard at best, then there's the carnivorous plants. Underworld above, even the dryads are known to be malevolent at times," the necromancer's voice trailed off, though whether this was because he didn't want to scare his reluctant charge or that he'd run out of creatures to name only he knew.

Alec gave this due thought. "What do you mean *was*?"

The necromancer winced, damned from his own mouth, "Ah. I'd rather hoped to wait to tell you, Alec."

"Tell me what?" was the suspicious reply.

Another sigh, one hand massaging his forehead to try and drive away a headache, "Respite's dead Alec, every man, woman and child."

"Y-you're lying," Alec protested, starting to try and struggle free from his bonds.

"I wish it were so but I'm sorry to say that I buried the bodies myself, only you survived," the necromancer said softly, solemn and sincere. "Do you honestly remember nothing of last night?"

"Stop lying! They can't be dead."

"Alec, believe what you will of me but I am telling you the truth."

"Liar," was Alec's obstinate reply.

There was a mirthless chuckle. "I can't make you believe me, nor would I try. Perhaps a compromise?"

"Like what?" the teenager demanded.

"Next time we pass near your hometown, I'll return you to it," he promised. "My solemn vow upon it."

"And how long is that likely to take?" Alec inquired with all the chill venom of snake and spider ice cream, fully aware that the offered deal had a major loophole.

The necromancer shrugged, "Presuming I'm not ordered to do otherwise? Probably a year. Is that satisfactory?"

"No but I don't really have a choice do I?"

"Not really. Still I have given you my word, dubious though it's value may be to you. Now try not to move," he instructed, moving over to the boy, cutting his bonds with a slim hunting knife.

Alec collapsed to the floor like a puppet whose strings had been cut.

"Need a hand?" his kidnapper offered, reaching out an arm.

Swallowing his pride, Alec accepted, allowing himself to be helped to a log so he could sit down and start massaging the blood back into numb arms and legs.

"The feeling will return to your limbs in a few minutes," the necromancer assured. "Now, if you'll excuse me, I need to organise safe passage for us through the forest." With that said, he stood and walked off, swallowed by the trees in seconds, leaving Alec alone with his thoughts.

After a few minutes, as promised, he found his arms and legs weren't aching as much. With difficulty, he got to his feet weighing the pros and cons of running.

The necromancer had yet to do him any physical harm, though he was still confining him against his will, which, going from the stories, wasn't typical necromancer behaviour, then again, nor was letting him live. There was also the dangers of the forest to consider; after all, the place had rather earned its name of Forest Von Mori, which he'd been reliably informed meant Forest of the Dead in one of the elder tongues that had passed from this world, though if he'd never seen any of the dread creatures hidden within its many trees.

All in all, it was probably safer to do as he was told in this case.

Having reached his decision, Alec allowed himself to sit back down upon the log, staring vacantly into the fire. He hoped his parents were okay, the necromancer's lies, for that's what they must be, troubling him nonetheless.

His thoughts were interrupted by his captor's return, the mage returning in a swirl of black cloak and robe as he emerged from the treeline, quickly sitting down beside the teenager.

"My… contact will be here soon, try not to say anything," Alec was informed coldly, the necromancer's change in demeanour quite worrying.

Barely had he said it than a quiet came over the forest, the muted sounds of birdsong dwindled, the insects fled or perhaps died, and even the wind seemed to hold its tongue. With bated breath, the two watched vines extend from the base of the trees, slithering serpentine across the leaf-littered floor, noticeably skirting round the fire before all meeting in front of the log, forming a writhing ball of plant life.

The vines receded, leaving behind a woman but like no woman Alec had ever seen. For starters, her skin was a vibrant and botanical green, and she was dressed in decaying leaves, a long flowing dress that extended to the floor while petals of all colours made up her hair.

"Nice entrance," the mage commented blithely.

The woman gave a shallow bow. "Thank you necromancer, from one of your order that is quite the compliment," her words were melodic and soothing to the ear.

"You are too kind, Lady Dryad," was the mildly bashful reply.

"Lady Von Mori," the dryad corrected, though not harshly.

"My apologies, I was unaware I was talking to such a distinguished dryad, though I am honoured that you view my plight worthy of your attention."

The dryad smiled, "You are courteous; I had forgotten how skilled your people are with words." There was something stilted to the compliment as if she were reading off of a script she wasn't quite familiar with, and an echo of that same slight wrongness in the necromancer's words too.

"The better to offer comfort to the bereaved, Lady Von Mori," the necromancer claimed solemnly.

"You don't need to explain yourself to me," Von Mori said with a warm smile, though there was a look in her eye that Alec was less than comfortable with when her gaze swept over him; it put him in mind of a hunting falcon preparing to dive on a squirrel caught in the open.

"My thanks. Does this mean you will allow us safe passage?"

Von Mori sighed, the sound like the rustling of autumnal leaves in the breeze. "Normally I wouldn't hesitate to grant your request but if death is your fate it is not my place to save you."

"My fate?" the necromancer queried, not having to feign confusion.

"I am not ignorant to how the peace is maintained. If your order has chosen you to die then I will not intervene for I value this peace too much," her tone was kind and consoling yet portrayed great sadness.

"M'lady you wound me greatly, I am a research mage, they would not see such as I led, like a lamb, to the slaughter."

"The paladin said otherwise," Von Mori stated flatly.

"Of course he did, Lutan is nothing if not a skilled liar. I have my credentials here if you would allow me?"

"Of course." The dryad nodded, "I would be glad if your tale is true."

The necromancer nodded back, lowering his hood to reveal a youthful face, barely out of his twenties, though with an unnaturally pale complexion. He then reached into one of the many inner pockets of his robe and withdrew a small bead of black stone, handing it to the ancient dryad without hesitation. "As you can see my licence to practise magic in paladin lands has not been revoked."

Lady Von Mori smiled, handing the stone back, "So I see, my apologies for doubting you, Erebus. I take it this means that this paladin has broken the Treaty?"

"Yes, now let us speak no more of it, the boy has yet to be inducted."

"Ah, that can be dealt with…" Von Mori said darkly.

"I would rather you did not, I have invested a lot of time and energy into keeping Alec alive, m'lady," Erebus said, voice still soft yet with an implacable hardness in the undercurrents.

There was a chuckle from the dryad, ethereal yet lighthearted, "Necromancers and their apprentices, always so protective."

Alec went to protest only to be silenced by Erebus' glare.

"Alec is not my apprentice," the necromancer replied in even tones.

"But he has-" Von Mori began, only to be silenced by one of the necromancer's hand gestures, the dark mage sweating from the effort to restrain such a powerful creature.

Outraged, Von Mori howled in silence, her anger washing over them like a forest fire as the roots and branches of the forest began to reach for the unfortunate Erebus and Alec alike.

"P-please m'lady. If if you wish to sp-speak of this th-then let us go out of earshot of the boy," Erebus rasped. Even from metres away, Alec could see the veins and arteries of his face and neck throbbing as the necromancer struggled to keep the dryad's attack at bay, the psychotic flora coming to a furious halt a few scant inches from the mage, lashing and cracking against a barrier of pure will, though they never got within feet of Alec.

Scowling fiercely, Von Mori ceased her assault, jerking her head to the side to indicate where to go.

Silently the two departed the clearing, leaving Alec alone once more. Tempting though it was to try and eavesdrop on the two, a sense of self-preservation was telling him that the tree spirit was sincere in her threat upon his life. Not that he was going to waste his time, instead using it to compile a small list of unanswered questions.

What was the black stone the necromancer, whom he now knew was called Erebus, had given the dryad? What was 'the Treaty'? And perhaps most importantly, he realised belatedly, how did the necromancer know his name?

Meanwhile, outside the clearing, the two supernaturals faced each other, the friendliness from earlier rather lacking.

"You had better have had a good reason for shackling me, necromancer. For your sake," spat Lady Von Mori.

"The boy is paladin raised, he would not have appreciated knowing he had the gift," Erebus explained patiently, unperturbed by her anger.

"You bound me, the dryad of this forest, for a mere child's sensibilities?" came the outraged reply.

"Surely there are few reasons that can compete with that?" the necromancer began, only to prove his question rhetorical by continuing. "However no, I had other reasons as well. The 'Lord Protector' of this region, the paladin Lutan, has done more than just betray the Treaty of Gerlun, I could have coped with a mere attempt upon my life, he also massacred the village of Respite in its entirety, though their only crime was to offer me shelter, unknowing of my nature."

"I see. But how does this equal a reason to render me mute?" Von Mori demanded, not yet appeased.

"Oh calm your wounded pride, it was merely the quickest way to organise a conversation alone," Erebus exclaimed, briefly losing his softly spoken persona.

"How dare you-" Von Mori began before realising such an outburst only proved the necromancer's point and calmed herself. "Very well, what do you wish to discuss?"

"I am headed for the Necropolis, the council need to know what Lutan has done."

"And what do you need from me?"

"Anything that is yours to give," Erebus stated, almost pleadingly.

"A steep request, do you know what you ask?" the dryad enquired, shocked at the temerity.

"I would be a fool if I did not," the necromancer

said with a sad smile. "Alas the situation is that grave, Lutan is ambitious and vengeful, mostly vengeful, he will not stop until magician and paladin make open war once more."

"Can the treaty be saved?" was the now anxious reply.

"If I can warn the council before Lutan can sow his own version of events to fester," Erebus responded. "Also, just in case I should pass from this life before I reach them, I would ask you to ask any other mages you might meet to pass the news on to their respective council members."

"Very well, I will do what I can." And with that, the venerable dryad simply melted away in a flurry of blossoms, evoking a slight smirk from Erebus, who then returned to the clearing to sit beside the troubled Alec.

CHAPTER 3

By the time Lady Von Mori returned, and it was very much Lady Von Mori, only a fool would refuse her the title, the fire had burnt itself to ash, the last embers had cooled, and the first hints of sunrise to made themselves known. Alec lay asleep, the necromancer's dark cloak wrapped around him, a kindness which regrettably had had to be applied after the young teen had slipped into slumber.

This time the dryad entered without the theatrical flair, walking into the clearing with a girl of around Alec's early-teen years, at least in appearance, at her heels and clutching a branch of wood to her chest. Of course, upon closer inspection, the girl was also a dryad, albeit not quite as obviously or grandly as the lady of the forest. Her hair was probably the biggest giveaway, waxy and red, while the girl's nails were almost talons.

"This is Holly," Von Mori said in the way of explanation. "She has agreed to accompany you through the forest."

"I was hoping for a dryad out of their first century." It was probably as close as Erebus ever got to an outright complaint.

"She was the only volunteer," was Von Mori's chilly reply.

"And has she been made aware of the consequences?"

"Indeed she has."

It was only now that the necromancer addressed

Holly directly, voice still hushed to avoid waking the sleeping Alec. "You don't have to do this."

"I know." Holly replied firmly.

"It's probably not my business, but why did you volunteer?"

"How else is a dryad supposed to see the world?" she replied as if it were obvious.

That actually earned a brief smile from Erebus, "Very well, I only hope that hindsight does not find the price of your wanderlust too high."

"Only one way to find out," Holly stated blithely.

"Very well, return to your tree, we will join you shortly," he commanded quietly, with Holly gratefully complying, to be this far from her soulbound plant was a strain despite her mother's aid.

"Doubts, necromancer?" Von Mori asked once the young dryad had disappeared.

"I would have to be an unusually cruel monster to not," Erebus replied quietly.

"True," the elder dryad observed. "But this was your idea."

"Desperate times call for terrible ideas," Erebus said with a shrug of his shoulders.

"Your paladin is closing on this clearing," Von Mori declared suddenly, her gaze now sightlessly focused on the middle distance. "Wake the child, we must move."

"How do you know?" the magician asked, though moving to wake Alec regardless.

"This is my forest, I know everything that happens within it, though I know not how he has our location, the trees had led him on a merry chase these past hours yet now he makes for us as a bloodhound upon a scent. I wonder what changed," she mused aloud.

Erebus shook Alec's shoulder none too gently.

"Wake up boy! Wake up."

Groggily by the third such shake the boy complied, throwing his protector's cloak off of him as soon as he was awake enough to notice it. "Wha- what's going on?" he asked, the last word modulated by a titanic yawn whilst he stretched.

"We need to move, fast. Von Mori says that… a predator is closing in on the clearing. If either of us is to see the dawn then we must go now!" The urgency in his tone spurred Alec to wakefulness; anything that could scare such a dread creature as a necromancer could probably scare and kill him.

The necromancer grabbed his cloak and pack, shrugging them on before kneeling down to pick up his staff. "Now we run," he said softly, following his own advice.

As the three made their way through the forest — technically two as Von Mori was the forest — Erebus found himself with the surprisingly arduous task of keeping up with the dryad whilst also ensuring that the young Alec was not left behind.

Fortunately, Holly's tree proved a mere mile away, admittedly with ample opportunity to get lost along the way, their path speeded in Von Mori's wake, miraculously cleared of the byzantine snares and tripwires a forest floor became at any speed above a walk. Despite the disparate paces, they all made it safely to the tree, a young holly unsurprisingly.

"What's the lifespan?" Erebus asked with even greater seriousness than usual.

"Most I've ever seen a holly manage is five of your centuries, but most don't even reach one," Von Mori said boredly, not seeing the point of the question.

He sighed heavily, "A pity. I can only offer her two

hundred years, you see I'm not lich material." There was the barest hint of a wry smile at the last bit.

"It is longer than she would expect," Von Mori snapped coldly.

"Considering I am literally about to rend soul from flesh I think I owe her more than under half her potential lifetime," Erebus remarked, voice full of ire, if not anger. His expression soon changed as his gaze fell upon Alec, from grim determination to a quiet thoughtfulness. "Tell me boy, what does the Order teach you about dryads?"

Von Mori nearly lost her temper. "We don't have time for this!" she almost screamed, just managing to remember to keep her voice down.

"There is always time for rational discourse," Erebus said calmly. Von Mori went to argue only to stop as he held up a palm for silence, achieving easily with authoritative body language what he had almost failed to achieve with magic. "I will be brief."

"You'd better be," the forest spirit grumbled, folding her arms. "Time is against us, your 'predator' draws near, though at least he appears uncertain of the path."

"Well Alec? Answer the question," Erebus ordered as kindly as he could.

"Uh well… they're tree spirits, nearly every tree has one and uh… if you cut down their tree then they die. Forest ones don't like people but they usually won't hurt you unless you're lighting a fire or carrying an axe, I think," Alec managed, struggling from being put on the spot.

"Better than I expected from paladin teachings," Erebus admitted, "Though mildly inaccurate." The mage paused, clearly mulling something over in his mind. "This tree's dryad has offered to guide us through the forest, but to do that I'm going to have to hurt her very badly," he began, trying to put the process into words that wouldn't come over as too eldritch for a person who had spent their entire lives under the paladin yoke.

"Why would you want to do that?" asked Alec, looking confused.

"Because…" A brief pause as he chose with care the words he'd use, "Because it's the only way to allow a dryad to move so far from its tree. Now I need you to do something for me if you're willing. To move away from her tree, a dryad needs to be bound to a person, much like how they are already bound to their tree." Another sigh from Erebus. "If I bind her to me then she'll be forced to spend the rest of her life in musty libraries, cold stone walls and colder caves, which is why, with your permission, I'd like to bind her to you."

"Huh?" was the shocked response.

"Snap out of it Alec, normally I'd demand you both take months to make such a decision but we don't have anything like that sort of time. The monster I mentioned will soon pick up our trail, yes or no. Decide."

Seconds trickled past until the teen broke the silence. "…yes.

"Okay." Erebus put his pack down and fished out an axehead and a small handle. With a mechanical click, he slid the axehead into place then pulled the base of the handle down, the steel periscoping out until that too provoked a click as it locked into place as well. "Hold this."

Alec complied nervously.

"Now, when I tell you, I want you to drive the axehead as hard as you can into the tree."

Alec nodded.

Erebus grimaced, "Then let us begin." Closing his eyes the necromancer began to chant, placing his palms on the trunk.

Minutes dragged by; it was as if the entire forest was holding its breath, and, going from Von Mori's tensed form, maybe it was.

Finally there was a noticeable effect. The axe adopting a fiery glow, red, orange and yellow dancing along the cutting edge, next came Holly, despite her earlier bravado, dragged kicking and screaming from her tree. Alec was so shocked that he nearly dropped the axe.

Erebus continued to chant; the words were of no language Alec had ever heard, though he'd be amongst the first to admit he wasn't exactly well travelled. A faint whisper filled the air, a thousand voices echoing the necromancer until, at last, Holly was fully extricated from her home.

The chant stopped. "Do it now."

The hatchet swung round and impacted on the bark. In the hands of the young teen it should have barely grazed the wood at such a bad angle; instead, it embedded right to the handle, cracks spread across the trunk, an intricate spiderweb of destruction slowly spreading through the young Holly, then two things happened at once, the tree caught fire and Holly let out a single soul-rending shriek before collapsing to the ground - a puppet with its strings cut.

Silence descended once more, if only for a few moments. Erebus was the first to recover, surveying the pale drawn faces of Von Mori and Alec.

"First time observing a sundering?" he asked the elder dryad.

Von Mori shook her head, "First that I've been party to."

"It doesn't get any nicer," Erebus stated before gently placing his hand on Alec's shoulder. "What about you, are you okay?"

"Uh I- I think so… maybe," the boy stammered, staggering slightly.

"Evidently not," the necromancer mused with a slight chuckle. "Can you walk?"

"Yes," Alec weakly answered before proving himself wrong by losing his balance, propping himself back up on a tree.

"Again; evidently not. Lady Von Mori, I hate to ask but can you carry one of them? I doubt I can manage both."

"I am no beast of burden necromancer, I may be sworn to give aid but I am not some servant to fetch and carry for you. Now if you'll excuse me your hunters are upon your trail once more. I will delay them for a time and then consider my oaths fulfilled in this matter, good luck young Erebus."

The dark mage tried to reply, perhaps protest, but she had already disappeared in a hurricane of leaves. "Always with the dramatic exits," he grumbled. Then, with a grimace, he tied his staff to his pack and hefted both Holly and Alec — with much protest — over his shoulders and set off at a run. The pair would be rather bruised and sore by the end of it, but, in Erebus' opinion, it would be a small price for their joint survival.

CHAPTER 4

It was a sombre morning; the light was dim beneath Von Mori's trees while the gaps in the canopy, though somehow too small to allow mere photons through, allowed just enough of the dawn's cold drizzle past it to put a dampener on such concepts as happiness and comfort.

Poor Erebus had run for three hours, magic doing what his muscles could not, and now came the toll, Von Mori was unusually hard for mages to traverse, sapping the magic from them with every step.

It wasn't much; most would barely notice, but if forced to use magic constantly, the toll became readily apparent to even a master magus, and thus the fatigued necromancer lay dead to the world, not even the drizzle and dew soaking through his robes had stirred him from his slumber; giving Alec and Holly little to do but get to know each other; so far it wasn't going well.

"How do you humans stand it?" exclaimed a shrill female voice.

"What is it this time?" Alec asked, exasperated beyond measure.

"Being so fragile."

"How am I fragile?" the human demanded; he certainly didn't feel fragile.

"Can't you feel it? Your heart, what if it times the muscle wrong, it could rip itself asunder, or what if it stops or goes too slow or-"

"It has gone this long without a problem," Alec

interrupted grouchily; being carried at a full run hadn't been restful.

"For now, and that's just one organ. What about your lungs, or your liver or-"

"I do get the point," Alec stopped her again. "But I would like to point out I've probably got a good thirty years of life ahead of me if I'm lucky."

"Thirty years?" Holly stammered, looking horrified.

"You volunteered for this," the boy pointed out fairly.

"I was expecting to be bound to the necromancer," she snapped, folding her arms in front of her, in what Alec assumed was a sulk until he heard the sobbing.

Instinctively he moved to comfort her, but a firm grip on his collar prevented him. The boy startling; he hadn't noticed the necromancer move.

"Walk with me a while," Erebus said, it wasn't a request.

As soon as they passed out of sight of the clearing, the necromancer called a halt. "Wait ten minutes so she can get some of it out of her system, then go to comfort her, she will be angry, likely hit you. Do not retaliate. Understood?"

"Wha- why?" Alec exclaimed in shocked annoyance.

"She is going to be the closest relationship in your life, closer than your wife, should you marry, closer even than your children, should you have them. Two bodies, one soul. Well one and a half."

Alec went to protest only to be cut off.

"I'm not saying you'll fall in love with her, just that no one will ever know you as well as she will, so do you really want her hating you?" Erebus asked gently.

"I guess not," Alec admitted, looking thoughtful.

"Indeed. Now, if you'll excuse me, I must return to my slumber." And without another word, the necromancer returned to his flattened patch of grass, appearing to fall asleep in moments.

He definitely wasn't how Alec had grown up expecting a necromancer to be. Instead of the bloodthirsty butcher of childhood fairytales, Erebus appeared to be a gentle and compassionate soul who, more than anything, reminded Alec of a wandering monk who stayed yearly in his village from late autumn through to the end of winter. The monk had been a kindly if shrivelled and wizened old man possessed of that strange vitality of the old and carefree. The village had seen to it that he was provided with food and shelter, and, in return, though without asking and at his own insistence, the monk had added greatly to the sparse education the village had to offer.

Adis, the carpenter's wife, had done her best, of course. All the kids knew their numbers and their alphabet, though letters weren't much use when there were just three books between the entire village, or at least there had been until a few years ago when the monk had arrived slightly later than usual. The man had usually arrived like clockwork, midday on the autumn equinox; that year, he'd been two days late and presumed dead. Instead, he'd arrived with a satchel of books over his shoulder, though why eight books had delayed the old man two days had remained unclear.

Alec was interrupted from his musings by a noise, or rather the lack of one. Holly had finally run out of tears, albeit her shoulders still wracked to dry and silent sobs.

Silently as he could, Alec walked over to the young dryad, sitting down beside her with a weak smile, which Holly either ignored or completely failed to notice.

With mounting dread Alec placed a hand gently on her shoulder, fully expecting a razor nailed hand of misdirected vengeance to come sharply in contact with his face, which it did.

There was a gasp, more out of shock than pain, as Holly raised a hand to her cheek then took it away, examining the sap there, the blood of trees, oozing from four long cuts on her cheek, exactly where she'd left an identical wound on Alec.

This provoked another bout of tears as Alec, ignoring the dripping blood and slowly gathering pain of his own cuts, put an arm around the weeping dryad's shoulders and, in a show of surprising tact and insight, just held her close until once more the tears ran out.

Only then did he speak, his voice calm and understanding, his own anger and irritation put aside in the face of this emotionally fragile creature. "Do you want to talk about it?"

"Yes," was Holly's uncertain reply.

"Why are you so upset?" he asks as tactfully as he can.

"I… don't want to die," the dryad informed him hesitantly.

"I'm not sure anyone actually does," Alec mused for her benefit, which showed a rather limited worldview.

Holly giggled slightly before returning to her mournful state. "Doesn't it bother you? Knowing you'll die?"

"I'm not viewed as an adult yet so I've never taken the time to think about it, still… yes I suppose," he shrugs, the motion surprisingly expressive for such a small frame. "But, the way I see it, everything dies eventually, it's what you do before that which matters."

Holly frowned, "Surely it's how long your life lasts that's more important?"

"Doubtful," came the voice of their eavesdropper.

The two started like frightened rabbits, looking around to see no one.

"Too easily frightened," whispered the voice, heavy on the air and coming from all directions. "I mean you no harm."

"Who are you?" Holly asked, still turning in search of the disembodied voice.

"It's just Ente," Alec assured her before declaring imperiously, "What do you want ghost?"

"Just a little conversation," the ghost promised, still unseen. "It gets rather lonely in my jar with no one to talk to. You'll want to work on limiting that bond if you want to stop sharing wounds."

"I'm sorry but who is Ente?" Holly asked, her brow wrinkling in confusion.

"A ghost Erebus captured, an old necromancer or something," the teen answered vaguely.

"Necromancer or something?" came the affronted reply of the ghost. "I was the preeminent researcher of my age!"

"How long ago was that?" Alec asked, mildly inquisitive despite his strict paladin upbringing.

"I don't know, it's hard to keep track of time in a cave," the ghost admitted, "best to ask Erebus when he wakes."

"So what were you saying earlier?" the boy asked, "about it not being about how long you live?"

"People can go their entire lives just living day to day, but there comes a time where surviving simply isn't enough, your life means nothing if it doesn't give something to those around you," the ghost philosophised slowly.

"And did you?" Holly snapped.

"I'd certainly like to think so," Ente replied with utter solemnity.

"Holly leave the ghost alone. He's done nothing to you," Alec ordered quietly, though with a surprising authority. "Sorry about that, she's hurting right now," he said, paraphrasing Erebus.

"I heard… is there any chance of getting my jar out of the young necromancer's pack? I'd like to be able to see my surroundings, I mean sensing the life force around me is nice but after who knows how long in a cave I'd like to see the sun," Ente requested quietly.

"How can a ghost see?" Alec asked perhaps a tad insensitively, but it was understandable, and the ghost understood; the curiosity of the young was very hard to restrain. Admittedly Ente's definition of young was anyone under three hundred, but the theory still stood up to reasonable scrutiny.

"I don't *actually* know," Ente admitted with little hesitation. "It was still a mystery in my day, I would be quite interested to see if they've solved it."

"Oh. Okay," Alec said quietly, "Any idea how long until I can ask?"

"At least another three hours, and that's presuming he has exceptional recovery, now… sorry to nag but, could you please take my soul jar out now?"

"Of course, Holly could you pass me Erebus' pack please?" Alec asked cheerily.

"Get it yourself, I'm not your servant," the dryad snapped.

Alec sighed, doing just that. Sometimes it just wasn't worth arguing. Best to wait until such a time as the ears may be receptive to one's words. It was one of the monk's sayings, and as always, it proved useful.

He untied the string around the top of the pack, reaching inside to pull out the small gem that contained the old ghost. Unlike last he saw it, the gem was now giving off a pale ethereal blue. "Is that better?" Alec asked.

"Much, thank you, could you possibly put me on top of the pack? A slight elevation will give the best view," came the disembodied voice.

"Sure," Alec said cheerily, placing the gem down with surprising care and respect, enough so that Ente couldn't restrain a question, albeit disguised as an offhand comment.

"Hard to believe you're paladin born, though perhaps things have changed since my day," Ente said, carefully drawing the teen into a conversation.

Holly sighed quietly; no one had asked about her past, not that there was much to tell. The only hint of excitement in all of her years had been Alec and Erebus travelling through the forest near her tree, and in a moment of insane wanderlust, she'd signed her soul over to the young teenager. In retrospect, she'd clearly acted irrationally. Holly jerked from her brief moment of self-deprecating introspection as Alec took the proverbial bait Ente had so carefully laid.

"Your day?" he asked simply, clearly fascinated by having access to a (metaphorically) living link to the past.

"Yes my day, back then paladin and necromancer would have killed each other on sight yet you show little hate towards anything, though I suppose that's because you are both young and fearful," the ghost mused.

"How am I fearful?" Alec asked with sudden nervousness.

"Your mannerisms boy, you're as tense as a coiled cobra, constantly second-guessing your own choices, words and actions."

"I suppose there is some truth in that," Alec admitted. "Though I do have one question, if I may?"

"Of course boy, despite the teachings of the Order, curiosity is no great sin, though in perhaps some cases, it is a mild one. Ask your question," Ente insisted. The boy, in his opinion, showed great promise and surprising understanding of philosophical discourse for one brought up in a society that had, in his time, viewed curiosity as a sin worse than murder. In fact, a lot of murder had been committed to try and prevent such perverse and disgusting behaviour as curiosity. Thus he held unusually high hopes for the insight the boy was hopefully about to display.

"What's a cobra?"

If ghosts could sigh, then the sound Ente emitted was a sigh, though he answered all the same; after all, curiosity was to be rewarded no matter how much it failed to meet expectations.

"A particularly venomous type of snake with a hooded appearance found in a place far to the east of here," the ghost imparted.

"What's a snake?"

"A snake is uh…" Ente stopped for a moment, trying to figure out how to explain the creature. "It's a reptile with no legs, broadly speaking."

"What's a reptile?" came the insistent questioning.

Ente floundered. "Well uh… they're… I'm not sure how to explain to be honest," the ghost finally admitted.

"…Oh, sorry," Alec apologised uncertainly.

"A word of advice boy, don't apologise for things which aren't your fault. It shows great empathy on your part but too easily can it lead to others using you as a crutch for their own faults," the ghost said in a somewhat remorseful tone, perhaps dwelling on a tragedy in his long distant past.

There was a large pause before another voice tried to articulate its owner's thoughts, surprisingly the voice was Holly's.

"Do dryads have an afterlife?" asked the tree spirit in fearful tones, clearly voicing one of her darkest fears.

The ghost thought for a moment, unable to give an honest answer that would soothe the girl's troubled thoughts. Finally, he settled on a position he was happy with, "It depends on what you believe child, many religions believe in afterlives, and a number in reincarnation, and more in afterlives for all things. But no one can give an absolute answer, the only people who can have passed beyond the reaches of all, even necromancers. We call it stepping beyond the Veil, and so far, no one's ever stepped back. I wish I could offer you more in the way of reassurance."

"You're not the only one," Holly muttered.

"Back off Holly, he's done nothing wrong," her host warned as gently as he could. The Paladin Order may have had a lot to say on the evils of those who raised the dead. Still, there had been little on the dead themselves; beyond that they should be laid to rest and thus enjoy their eternal peace and thus, with no social stigma associated, Alec was rather warming to the wise ghost.

"Yeah sure, of course you'd side with the other human," Holly accused bitterly.

"That would be rather difficult young dryad considering in life I was an elf," Ente calmly deflected the verbal assault, though somehow, this failure to rise to the bait only served to annoy her more.

"Now you're just being picky," she muttered, folding her arms across her chest.

"I would hardly call being a different species being picky, given your argument," the ghost replied reasonably with the composure and pointedness of a seasoned debater.

"Whatever," Holly said under her breath, the young dryad feeling rather picked upon.

Alec rolled his eyes. It seemed Holly's issues weren't solvable by anything as simple as discussing them, though, hopefully, she at least had a better understanding of why she was angry; he certainly did, and it had allowed him a modicum of sympathy for the dryad.

He brought his gaze to bear on the gently glowing soul jar. "Who cares about the next life? It's what we do in this one that matters."

"You've a surprisingly… empathic view for one so young," Ente observed. "But, and I hope you'll excuse the accusation, those words sound as if you're repeating them rather than creating, not that I'm trying to imply that you don't understand what you're saying, clearly you do or your observations would not be so apt."

"You'd be right," the teen admitted, "I had a very good teacher."

"Clearly," the ghost replied. "If we weren't in paladin territory I'd say they were a necromancer."

"He's a monk of the paladin order actually," Alec informed the ghost.

"Ah, now that would explain it," Ente said thoughtfully. "The monks have always kept themselves apart from the petty conflicts and prejudices of their orders. Do you know which monastery?"

"I'm afraid not. And what do you mean prejudices? They just dislike necromancy," the teen pointed out.

"Have you ever been told why?"

"Because it's evil, the dead have earnt the right to rest, to force them to do our bidding is just cruel." Alec offering what was either an opinion or propaganda.

"Speaking as a member of the dead I'd rather have to disagree, I personally would be glad to be of some use or value to society after my death," Ente argued.

"Yeah but you're a necromancer, of course you'd say that, it's what you've been brainwashed to believe," Alec pointed out.

"A good point but you've been force-fed your beliefs as well," the ghost countered.

"No I haven't, I made my own mind up," Alec complained.

"And were you presented with a balanced argument which shows both sides of the debate? Were you presented with a clear cut choice without the threat of dire consequences?" Ente demanded firmly, seeming to actually take affront.

"Well no but-"

"Then you did not make your mind up, it was made up for you," the ghost stated.

"But-" Alec began again.

"There are no buts, if you were not given the opportunity of an informed choice then you did not choose."

Alec gave up, the ghost was clearly completely intractable on the matter, and Holly was looking far too amused at the argument for his liking, not to mention that he couldn't suppress a sneaking suspicion that the ancient necromancer was correct.

"So what do we do now?" he finally asked the ghost.

"My advice would be to get what rest you can, once Erebus wakes you'll be spending the day walking bar meals and even they will be eaten on the go if possible," the necromancer informed him. "As for you Holly, I'd suggest that you spend your time trying to come to terms with yourself, you made your choice now you must live with the consequences and it will be an unhappy life if you choose to spend it lashing out at all around you."

"Sounds reasonable," Alec agreed, removing his jacket to lay beneath his head.

Holly, however, paused from her moping to glare at the crystal, "Did I make an informed choice or did someone choose for me?"

Chapter 5

Alec didn't know how long he'd slept for, the thick forest canopy preventing him from tracking time by the position of the sun. He'd barely been awake for ten minutes before he'd found himself on his feet and trekking through the forest, teeth slowly grinding away, or perhaps grinding down, on hard biscuit from Erebus' pack. There was something of a change this time; rather than Erebus leading the way, Holly was in charge.

The scarlet haired dryad was quite enjoying her newfound authority as she led them both to the eastern edge of the forest. At least that was the theory, Holly had never been more than a few hundred metres from her tree before this, and thusly her directions were mildly dubious.

But Holly's actual navigation abilities were irrelevant as she wasn't actually navigating. The forest was, the young dryad merely asking for directions to a place the humans called Circulus Seruatis or at least that's what Erebus had told her as they set off that morn.

"What's she doing?" Alec asked after about the fifth time the girl told them to stop before hurrying out of sight amidst the trees.

"She's getting directions from the other dryads of the forest," Erebus explained.

"Couldn't you do that?" Alec enquired, wondering why they'd needed the dryad for something so simple, then wondering why he was thinking of their group in the collective sense as he was still being held against his will.

"Oh, anywhere else in the world certainly but this is the Forest Von Mori, the trees aren't so fond of humans but they wouldn't deny the request of a fellow dryad, Holly's presence means we shall pass through unmolested by anything of this forest. Well anything sapient or plant-born anyway," Erebus imparted with a slight smile. "Why? Are you regretting your decision already?"

"I don't think she likes me," the youngster admitted.

"Friendships take time to build, you can't expect everyone to like you instantly. After all, as the saying goes, the Necropolis wasn't built in a day," Erebus told him before continuing to muse. "In fact, a reasonable number of my friends started out trying to kill me..."

"Hang on, why would this predator thing still be after us if we now have Holly?" the boy demanded, thinking back to the mage's earlier comment.

"Because Lu- the predator is not of the forest, it followed us in."

"Why would it do that? I mean if it's a predator then surely there is easier prey than us," Alec enquired, the necromancer's story no longer making sense.

"It is not some mindless beast as you would understand it, this creature hunts us for the same reason it wiped out your village, it is a being of unparalled hate and lust for power," Erebus said, voice both solemn and sad.

"They're really dead then?" Alec asked, almost inaudible in acknowledging his fear. The necromancer's word was suspect, but Von Mori had confirmed the existence of this fell hunter, and if the legends he'd heard were true, then the soul of the forest was unable to lie.

"I'm afraid so," Erebus confessed, "there are worse things than necromancers in the world."

"Why didn't you stop it, you're a necromancer, you have all this power, why didn't you use it?" Alec demanded suddenly, a new anger in his voice.

Erebus placed his hands on the teen's shoulders, kneeling so they were level as he held eye contact. "Calm child, there are a multitude of reasons, but first you must trust what I say to you now." He took a deep breath. "You will never know what it cost me to watch people dying for me yet know I could not intervene. I would have forsaken this life in an instant to save them but I have been bound to other responsibilities."

Alec opened his mouth to shout about how the mage should have done it anyway, only to stop as he noticed the tears in the necromancer's eyes, not yet enough to fall but getting close. Instead, and showing great tact, the boy asked, "What responsibilities?"

"These things don't happen in a void, that this creature was bold enough to engage in such slaughter means bad things are happening elsewhere. The fact such a massacre can happen is something the Council of Mages need to hear about, monsters like this haven't existed since the time of the Last Necromancer-Paladin War."

"The what?" Alec asked, not a historian by any measure.

"Think of it as the last major punch up between paladin and magician, happened about five hundred years ago. Rather optimistically called the Last in the hope the peace would endure this time, presumably it will be renamed if it fails." Erebus explained patiently, unable to resist a slight, if weary, smile at the easy distraction of youth.

"What sort of monsters?" the boy asked, wondering what creatures could be that dangerous.

"Oh both sides had evils, we had the dread healers, the hungry mould and the flesh heaps. The paladins had the seraphim, the null cloud and, of course, the Mindbreaker." The necromancer almost whispered the last one, his tone one of reverent horror.

"Those are just names," Alec complained. "What were they like?"

"I wouldn't know. I wasn't there. But, going from some of the recounts I've heard…" Erebus paused, unsure where to begin. "The dread healers were an abomination, no, a perversion of that noble art. My order had wiped them out to a man in aeons past. But, when it looked like magic would pass from this world, we brought them back, a resurrection on an unprecedented scale."

"What made them so dangerous?" Alec pressed as the necromancer paused for breath.

"They could kill with healing, block arteries, stop the heart, cause a bleed into the brain, and all they needed was a touch, and not all needed even that. To use healing for murder, it's unthinkable."

"Then why did you do it?" Alec enquired fairly.

"We were desperate, we were the last stronghold of magic on the continent. And the paladins sunk far lower than us. Octavus the Mindbreaker was… I'm not sure how to explain it, he was a mentalmancer, or neuromancer as they call it in the modern parlance, basically a mind mage the paladin order had captured as a child. For two decades they tortured him, broke him, and empowered him. He was the most powerful telepath the world had ever seen, and all he could do was lash out, forcing his own pain into those around him, and around him could be anything up to ten miles depending on his mood. He had an escort of paladins in nullsteel plate. It was pure butchery, our side were too busy writhing in agony to fight back." Erebus finally stopped talking, looking mournful at such great loss of life.

"And this predator is one of those things you mentioned?" Alec asked, sounding not scared but more in awe at the thought of such beings.

"No, if only it were something as simple as that. Which brings me to the other reason I could not help, this being is almost immune to magic, against it I would be naught but an old man with a stick," Erebus lamented. "I'm sorry lad."

Alec didn't know what to say but was saved the trouble by Holly's triumphant return, the dryad wearing a broad grin. "Apparently, this town of yours is two days walk to the southeast."

"So you finally found a dryad who could do more than just point you vaguely in the right direction?" Erebus asked, back to his usual quiet and mildly more cheerful self from the moment the girl had emerged from the undergrowth.

"Yep, let's get going; it's this way." And with that, the dryad walked off in the direction she'd been pointing, the others having to break into a jog to catch up.

"You seem more cheerful," Alec remarked, slowing alongside her.

"Go away. I don't like you, I don't want to like you. Just go away," Holly snapped, only increasing her pace.

But Alec was undeterred; after all, if he was to be spending the rest of his life with her, then he'd best put the effort in now. Besides, both Erebus and his erstwhile mentor, the monk before him, had said, though, with rather different metaphors, friendships required work and effort, both to build and maintain.

"So what's it like being a dryad?" he asked, trying to draw her out of her rather spiky shell.

"That's a stupid question," Holly huffed. "It would be like me asking you what it's like being a human. You can't explain it, it just is."

There was a quiet chuckle from behind them as Erebus watched the young teen be rebuffed yet again, though it was good the boy was putting in the effort.

"Can you try and answer anyway?" Alec pressed, determined to develop a rapport with her.

"No."

Alec gave up, withdrawing back to walk alongside Erebus, who was already in conversation with Ente.

"I'm telling you dragon marrow isn't a good focus for wraith bonds. Too much power and too much residual life, any wraith worth binding will work the spell back on you, a focusing crystal on each point will allow you to rebound any assaults back on the wraith and you then do the bonds the slow way," Erebus explained patiently to the ghost, who vehemently disagreed.

"That's just for the minor stuff, for a malevolence class wraith you want dragon marrow," the ghost countered, the debate going completely over Alec's head.

"Why would you want to summon a malevolence class wraith? They're all locked away for a reason."

"Bah. In my day necromancers had a bit more spirit," Ente stated firmly.

"Yes, but in your day necromancers had little regard for the consequences of their actions, we're still tidying up after your 'bit more spirit' now," somehow Erebus managed to make it sound like an observation rather than a rebuke. "Now enough talk of work." He smiled at Alec, "Holly still giving you the cold shoulder I see."

"Yeah," the teen admitted weakly.

"Don't be discouraged, in time, once she's got used to being Sundered then she will think back to these early days and remember that you made an effort. Right now she's just looking for someone to blame, currently it's you for doing it to her, soon it will be me for making her do it, then Lady Von Mori for bringing her into this in the first place, then finally herself for agreeing to it. And then, once she has ran out of people to blame, will come acceptance," Erebus explained softly, careful to keep his voice too low for their young guide to hear.

"That makes no sense," Alec replied without as much tact in regards to his volume.

"It doesn't need to, it is simply the nature of people to hide their insecurities in others, and right now Holly has never felt so insecure in her life, and not without reason," the necromancer informed him.

"What were you arguing with Ente about?" the boy asked, the child's mind able to flit from subject to subject with ease.

"Just the trivial nonsense of academics," he assured the young teen with a slight smile.

"You sounded angry," Alec half-accused.

"Less angry, more passionate about my views," Erebus said after a moment's thought. "Not that I begrudge Ente his."

"That's code for 'you're still wrong.'" The ghost chimed in 'helpfully'.

"Why not? I mean if you disagree with his opinion then surely you must want to change it."

"Of course I do, but the only way to truly change

someone's views is through rational debate, not by anger or force, even if they seem to capitulate all you've done is demonstrate your own ignorance, for if you cannot make your point peacefully then clearly you can't have much in the way of fact to back up your point of view. Although with extremely recalcitrant listeners I have been known to lose my temper. But by doing so I have merely made myself look a fool to those around me, as a friend of mine would say 'If you've lost your temper, you've lost the argument"' Erebus smiled slightly, so far, from what Alec had seen, the necromancer was always at his most animated when discussing the more philosophical and metaphysical aspects of life.

Alec smiled as well; his own mentor, the monk, had been rather fond of the phrase as well.

Erebus sighed slightly, "Best we stop to eat," he murmured almost to himself before shouting for Holly to stop, the dryad not overly pleased due to not needing to eat herself, still she could see the sense in keeping her, for lack of a better word, host healthy.

The meal was a bleak affair, involving a bounteous feast of dry bread, hard cheese and almost gone-off salted meat from Erebus' own supplies. Regardless of that, it was still food, and the two ate it with the minimum of complaints. Hunger was always the best seasoning.

Unusually it was Holly who broke the silence, her tone timid and unsure. "What's it like? Eating I mean," the dryad asked uneasily. "I mean it looks disgusting, having to consume the flesh of animals and plants," she finished defensively.

Erebus laughed ever so slightly, allowing himself a moment of amusement before trying to think of an answer, but it was Alec who answered first.

"It's just something we have to do to survive. It's enjoyable most of the time but even when you don't like the food, you still have to do it," the boy explained as best he could.

"Yes but what's it like?" Holly demanded.

Alec floundered, trying to answer. "Well, uh… it's… I mean.. I-"

"It's a place called Up," Erebus interrupted; his answer met a blank stare from Holly. Even Alec looked momentarily puzzled before enlightenment dawned.

"A little less cryptic please?" Holly finally asked.

"I do suppose a little explanation is in order," Erebus admitted with a slight smile, "best make yourself comfortable, it's a bit of a tale."

The duo complied, crossing their legs after moving to slightly more comfortable sections of tree root, with Holly apologising profusely to the tree's dryad for such abuse.

"The world was flat, a boundless reality of lines and shapes. And one of these shapes was called Square, and Square was in a prison and had been for many years now. He hadn't seen another shape beyond the Triangle guarding his cell in all that time and was very lonely." Erebus paused for breath, amused to see that, despite the childishness of his metaphor, Holly was hanging on his every word.

"One day, out of nowhere, a Circle appeared in his cell, but like no other he'd met before, it was growing.

"How did you do that?' Square asked.

"Do what?" replied the somewhat confused circle.

"Appear like that,' Square clarified. 'Where did you come from?'

"Well, the circle took some time to think about this before finally replying, 'I came from Up.'

'Where's Up?' Asked Square.

"Again, there was a long pause as the circle tried to think of an answer. 'Up is Up.' The circle declared. 'I can't explain it… but maybe I can show you if you'll let me.'

"Well, the square was incredulous, 'How can you take me anywhere? I'm in a prison.'

"The circle was thoroughly amused, 'Let me show you.' And so the circle took Square up. And for the first time ever, the square looked down at the lines that held him captive all these years… and moved over them, gratitude almost overwhelming it. 'Welcome to Up,' said Circle, except it wasn't Circle anymore.

"What are you?' asked Square, yet to notice the changes to itself."

'I'm a sphere,' said Sphere, 'and you're now a cube.' Well, the square, now Cube, gave this due thought before saying simply, 'Thank you.'

"'Whatever for?' Sphere enquired curiously, clearly not seeing the sheer scale of its gift.

'I've been in prison for two years now; I think a little gratitude at my release should not be unexpected,' Cube said thoughtfully. 'So how do I get back…' The shape sought an appropriate word, not properly versed in the vocabulary needed when discussing dimensional transfer, 'there?' Cube finally settled on weakly."

Erebus paused as he took a moment to observe his enraptured audience of two; the dryad was leaning forwards in her improvised seat while Alec, who had heard the tale before, was paying rapt attention. The necromancer suppressed a smile, pleased to see he still had skills beyond mere magical pursuits, then, taking a deep but silent breath, he plunged back into the narrative.

"'I'll do it for you,' Sphere promised, 'but first, is there anywhere you'd like to go?' the shape asked.

'Just home,' Cube said gratefully, heading in vaguely the right direction, or so it hoped." Erebus paused for dramatic effect, "Surprisingly, it turned out that the shape's guesswork directions were right, so, home, at last, Cube prepared to say goodbye to his newfound friend and rescuer. 'Thank you for everything,' it said solemnly, 'my friends won't believe it when I tell them what happened.' And Cube was right, they didn't," Erebus concluded watching their reaction with an expert eye, two of them in fact. The duo were looking rather contemplative, Holly particularly.

Finally, after an age, Holly looked up and declared, "I don't get it."

Erebus smiled kindly, composing an answer, only for the boy to beat him to it. "Think of it this way; it's impossible to comprehend something you haven't experienced by being told it; you have to experience it," Alec hypothesised, glancing at the necromancer for approval; he may not entirely trust the magician's motives yet but had already learnt to trust his knowledge.

Erebus gave the subtlest of nods in response, not wanting to steal the audience.

"Why not just say that?" the young dryad demanded in the aggravating nasal tone she was rapidly perfecting.

Erebus took this as his cue to get back in on the conversation whilst his protégé floundered. "Most people find the extended metaphor more effective, not to mention you'd have questioned the outright answer; the metaphor allows you to work it through in your head while the narrative is unfolding."

"Oh," was the quiet response, the young dryad looking thoughtful.

The necromancer stood slowly, stretching as he removed the kinks from his spine as well as flexing his arms. "We've rested long enough now. Best foot forwards, both of you."

Obediently, the two youngsters got to their feet whilst the mage shouldered his pack, then, with a theatrical flair, he hooked a leather walking boot under his staff, flicking it up into a waiting palm. Less than a minute later, the clearing was empty as the trio tried to put further distance between themselves and their pursuers.

Chapter 6

Saiko sidestepped his opponent, almost lazily bisecting it with a flick of his wrist. The vine fell lifeless to the floor, the forest rapidly learning to leave him alone in favour of easier prey. Currently, easier prey was the Honourable Sir Olteph of Nydyll. The heavily armoured warrior was finding the forest to be slow going even without the aggressive agricultural assault; the thick plate mail so heavy that his feet sunk a few inches into the dirt rapidly turning into bog, the mud clinging to the nullsteel alloy of his boots, forcing the man to wrench his foot out of the ground with each step. But now, he wasn't moving at all as vines and roots had managed to ensnare all four limbs whilst a thick root from a stout oak was making a valiant effort to pull his head off whilst it sizzled and cooked where it touched the metal.

Out of the goodness of his heart, Saiko decided to intervene. Hacking through a bramble patch busily growing to block his path he made it to his comrade's side, noting Olteph's sword was at the man's feet, squeezed from the paladin's fingers; going from the blood dripping from the gauntlet, the roots had actually been successful in crushing his hand.

To the knight's credit, he was still fighting, his sheer physical strength managing to tear some of the vines apart, though the roots proved of sturdier stock, holding firm against Olteph's attempts at movement.

Firstly Saiko slipped a dagger from a wrist-sheathe,

forcing a small gap using the point as a lever to push the finely sharpened blade under the root wrapped around his colleague's throat, then he twisted the edge sideways, cutting through it with ease as he fought off another floral attack with the other hand, the slim falchion making short work of the varied tendrils trying to rip him apart as he laid about with it as though it were a forester's machete rather than an instrument of war, each root, vine and branch falling still at a touch from the enchanted blade.

Olteph choked out his thanks; the thick root had managed to crush the steel plate guarding his throat but not quite enough to crush tender flesh behind it. The dagger was resheathed in a gentle flourish as the falchion was brought down in a two-handed strike, freeing an arm, a series of hacking slices freed another arm, but then disaster as the forest lashed out, binding him in place. Defending the paladin had been enough of a distraction that the dryad legion had got past his guard.

Straining against the vines, Saiko quickly realised he was a dead man, the trees applying enough pressure that it was only a matter of time until his arms were wrenched from their sockets and then from his body entirely. He intensified his struggles, dropping his beloved blade as he grabbed the vines, his movements too restricted to reach the arming swords on his back or any of the smaller weapons upon his person, the human barely managing to avoid screaming as the vines grew thorns in retaliation. They wouldn't have done much good anyway; only his dagger and the falchion were nullblades.

Just as he was sure he could feel flesh beginning to tear the pressure on one arm stopped, the resulting imbalance wrenching him sideways where he fell in a heap, though rolling smoothly to his feet, the dagger being palmed from a wrist-sheathe and used to saw through the vines on the other arm. His rescuer pressed his main blade back into his hand.

"We even?" Sir Olteph asked in a voice reminiscent of gravel being milled.

"We're even," The Swordsman confirmed as the paladin stalked off to aid another of their beleaguered fellows, but it proved unnecessary, for, without warning, the attacks ceased, vines going limp and roots going still.

For a few moments, the only sounds were the irritated shouts of the squad hacking their way free of their entrapment.

As they grouped back together, Saiko took the time to take a headcount. Twelve out of a platoon of fifty. Alas, the rank and file were dead almost to a man, though only he seemed to view this as a great loss.

Sadly Lutan's personal retinue had mostly survived, a group of self-entitled toffs and sycophants with more titles than brain cells whose only collectively redeeming feature was the ability to wave a sword around in such a way as to prove dangerous; although Olteph, was, in Saiko's own words, decent enough when spoken to over a flagon of ale, hence why he'd focused on saving him over any of the others so ensnared. The good news about all this was that it made the former mercenary indispensable. Lutan needed at least one man by his side with an idea of how battles actually worked.

It was the two surviving soldiers that were currently causing trouble, at least for the retinue, having, upon the arrival of leafy vengeance, both stabbed the Honourable Lord Cisk, Commander of the Lord Protector's Guard, in the back of the neck, short swords driving smoothly through the weakness where helmet met breastplate. In Saiko's opinion, it had been neatly done; the snob probably wouldn't even have felt it.

Nullstone, that was the problem. The rare mineral was the only substance that naturally neutralised magic, and whilst every knight of the Paladin Order received a set of nullsteel armour, be it chain or plate, the footsoldiers did not. Even paladin coffers did not run that deep.

Needless to say, that faced with magical opposition, the two cut-throats had decided a touch of mutiny was very much in their best interests, stripping the lord of his armour with a speed and efficiency to leave squires in awe, splitting the pieces between them.

"The penalty for treason is death!" proclaimed Sir Bareth as if volume were a sufficient substitute for logic. Though, to be fair to the man, he was correct, a novelty that would probably have stunned a lesser constitution into silence.

"So, more often than not, is the penalty for gross stupidity. We are surrounded by enemies and you want to kill off a sixth of our number for keeping their heads in a crisis," Saiko snapped sharply, hoping that his rather generous interpretation of events would be an end to it.

"Why are you protecting a pair of common murderers?" Lord Owen, Keeper of the Lord Protector's Peace. "The law in these matters is quite clear."

Saiko's eyes flitted to Lutan; the paladin nodded ever so subtly.

"Well, far be it for me to interfere with the law. Particularly after what we've done, because massacres are so lawful, but I digress, what trial shall we give them?" the master swordsman's voice was sickly sweet, like a rare poison, cloying in the ears and mind. Most men would have taken note of such a tone, but not Andun Owen, the Keeper of the Peace was convinced he had right on his side, or at least the law, the man under the common misapprehension that the two were one and the same.

"Trial? This is war, we are fully within our rights to summarily execute them," Owen declared imperiously, drawing his sword.

Saiko was faster; by the time the broadsword was halfway from its scabbard, the tip of his falchion was making gentle orbits an inch from the odious paladin's Adam's apple. "I do believe the precedent is for officers to receive a trial." Around him, there was the silky screech of blades being drawn. "After all, justice doesn't just have to be done, it has to be seen to be done."

To Owen's credit, he seemed entirely unphased by the threat, though the broadsword didn't slide a millimetre further before, after much thought, sliding back into its scabbard, "These men aren't officers, sir, they aren't even corporals." Somehow Saiko suspected the sir wasn't for him. "Now Sir Bareth please arrest this man."

The knight took two steps towards the mercenary. There was a flourish of the wrist, and suddenly a knife was in Saiko's hand, eight inches of steel tapering to a point with violent intent written all over it. For example, said point was pressed ever so slightly into Sir Bareth's throat where he'd failed to stop his charge in time, a single droplet of crimson rolling down the blade's edge as the knight tried not to breathe. Throughout this, Saiko's other arm hadn't wavered in the slightest.

With consummate calm, he looked up at his allies, who were looking menacingly upon him, "Might I point out I only have two arms? If I am attacked again, then either Sir Bareth or Lord Owen is going to have to die for me to defend myself. Now while I don't personally view this as a loss, I feel you may view this differently. Just a thought."

"Swords down, Sai, swords down," a quiet voice ordered softly; that was always the first thing anyone noticed about Lord Protector Lutan. No one noticed him until he spoke, just a face in the background; his armour was grey and dull, the result of a high null alloy. It was battle armour pure and simple, unadorned and unapologetic, pitted, scratched, and in a couple of places partly slagged, it was armour with a single purpose: the hunting and killing of mages. Naturally, Lutan loved it more than he would his firstborn, should a woman ever turn his head.

Grudgingly the sellsword obeyed, the knife disappearing back into the mysterious recesses of his sleeve.

Triumphantly Owen rubbed his hands together, "As I was saying, execute the two privates Sir-"

"And as I was saying, and thank you for allowing me to interrupt you, your lordship, but I am technically a general in the glorious army of the paladin order. This does give me the right to give promotions in the field I do believe, so please tell me on what grounds you are refusing Acting-Captains Ghash and Molchester a trial?"

The Keeper of the Lord Protector's Peace ground his teeth in frustration, "This is an abuse of power, and you know it!"

"True, but I believe it to be a necessary one, can you say the same of your own?" General Saiko deflected calmly, watching the man almost explode with hypocritical indignation.

"How dare you?" came the affronted response of applied idiocy.

"I dare because I observe," Saiko stated in the same calculatingly infuriating tone of calm. "I could tell tales of your actions that would terrify generations to come so please don't try to get out of this by bluff and bluster. Accept my actions and my lips will remain sealed on yours."

Lord Owen glared venomously for a few moments before conceding his defeat. "Very well, it is your right to give battlefield promotions, we will have this trial you so dearly desire, here and now."

Saiko looked to Lutan, seeking help to end this lunacy. He got a wink instead; clearly, he would have to resolve this on his own. "May I point out that there aren't enough of us to properly conduct a trial, nor witnesses, character witnesses and evidence collected?"

"That won't prove necessary," the Keeper of the Peace said smugly, "I am qualified to both review the evidence and pass judgement."

"Why do you want these men dead so much?" the sellsword asked tiredly, gesturing to the two soldiers who had remained silent throughout this; after all, there was no point arguing; they were guilty. Still, now that Lutan was making sure it didn't come to blows, they had migrated to guarding what passed for the perimeter. "And if you have the gall to say justice, I will run you through here and now."

Once again, Saiko got to watch his lordship swallow his anger and pride as he took a deep breath. "They broke the law, isn't that enough?"

"Not for me, no. Please, Owen, see reason, as much as we will all miss Lord Cisk, now is not the time, nor is it the place."

For just a moment, it looked as if the paladin would argue but, albeit with poor grace. "Very well, my hanging can wait."

There was a laugh from Lutan. "Not for too long I hope. Now if you're done wasting our time I'd like to talk to my advisor."

Owen grinned, "You heard the Lord Protector, on your way sellsword."

"It was the sellsword's advice I was after," Lutan chastised mildly. "Perhaps you could assist us by lending your strength to the perimeter."

With the Keeper of the Lord Protector's Peace safely out of hearing, the two relaxed, Lutan going so far as to take out a small pouch of tobacco, tearing a small lump off and popping it into his mouth to chew. "Want some?" he proffered his companion.

"No thank you Lutan, can't stand the stuff I'm afraid."

"You're far too professional at times, Sai. You should find yourself some source of fun, every man should have a vice I always say."

"I already have a long list of vices, one more would be hazardous to my health I think."

"Very well, your opinion?"

"We should turn back now," Saiko said bluntly. "The trees here are young and weak but were still enough to reduce the soldiers we brought to fertiliser, if we go deeper then nullstone will mean little, particularly if they have forestguard; which they will."

"You sound like you've done this before," Lutan said expectantly, one hand going to the belt of equipment on his waist to play with a deep green gemstone about the size of a thumb, green sparks seeming to play across the surface in anger.

"Once, a long time ago," the killer lamented with a sigh, "it's not something I'm proud of, dryad killing is a dark art for any man."

"We have need of your dark art, old friend."

There was another sigh, "Why must we pursue? The forest wants to kill us and even if we survive the dryads, the trail is cold."

"Ah, but I know exactly where Erebus is heading."

"Erebus is it?" Saiko chuckled. "I never thought you'd be on first name terms with a necromancer."

"I was duped by him a long time ago, before I understood how evil they could be. Now please change the subject."

"Very well, why do you keep Owen around? The man is a liability."

Lutan laughed humourlessly, "You see this armour? It came from one of the best and largest smithies in all of Contemnere, his family own it, Lord Owen's rapid rise in the Paladin Order is the reason our weapon shipments always arrive on time."

"So much for a meritocracy," Saiko quipped shaking his head in a despairing understanding.

"I will admit the man has little merit in and of himself but have we ever had a late arms shipment? No, our armour and weapons are always on time and always of superior quality. And all because we put up with Andun Owen." Lutan smiled, "Not a bad trade-off all things considered."

"Not all of us have your patience," Saiko pointed out.

"True, Lord Owen for example. On the subject of Owen's patience, or lack thereof, your two new protégés, are they any good?"

"Well I certainly can't fault their initiative and their bladework was pretty handy under pressure, though

Ghash needs to guard his right side better. Other than that… not sure, they've got the raw talent but they've already picked up too many bad habits to be worth the extra time to break them."

Saiko finished his analysis, looking at his employer to see if he agreed.

Lutan stayed quiet for a long time, deep in thought. "Would they be worth keeping around as bodyguards?"

"You'd have to invest in training them, and find a way to secure their loyalty, but yes, I do believe so."

Lutan smiled, "I may know just such a way, once we've caught the necromancer-"

"Erebus," Saiko said mock helpfully.

"Yes, Erebus. Once we catch him here's what I want you to do…"

CHAPTER 7

As the sun rose to the point that light could viably navigate its way through the dense canopy, Alec awoke to the sound of feet sliding ever so slightly on grass, the dawn dew making the ground ever so slightly slippery. With great effort, the boy opened sleep crusted eyes and sat up. Beside him, Holly did the same. Yawning, the boy stretched and took a moment to take in his surroundings and the events unfolding before him.

Erebus stood poised, his quarterstaff held low before whipping it around, then transferring the stave to his right hand, his left thrusting forwards in an open fist. Then he ducked low, swinging the staff again before thrusting the gem capped tip forwards. For a minute or so, the man whirled, swung and stabbed before drawing to a breathless halt, sweat dripping off of his chin.

"Morning Alec, Holly." The necromancer panted, striding over to his pack to allow himself a couple of mouthfuls of water before carefully unwrapping the remnants of a dry loaf of bread, his knife too blunt to cut the granite loaf. So instead, he hit it hard with the hilt, causing the bread to crumble, then he divided it between himself and the child as Holly walked out into the trees, soon blocked from view.

They ate in silence, dry bread needed a lot of concentration to eat properly, and as this particular loaf was beginning to grow mould as of last night, it required additional concentration to ignore the taste. Nevertheless, the two were glad of it; both had known the stabs of unyielding hunger.

When at last every sizeable crumb worth the effort to consume it had been consumed, Alec grinned, "So what was that weird dance thing you were doing?"

"I was going through my battlemage drills," the necromancer confessed, "in case we're caught before we reach safety. I might be a bit rustier than I'm comfortable with when it comes to hand to hand."

"Shouldn't you have been doing some magic then?" the boy queried the obvious question.

"I told you earlier, this monster is all but immune to magic, I'd be reduced to throwing fireballs, no if we are stopped then we'll need to fight at close quarters, well I say we, if the worst does happen I want you to take Holly and Ente and run for the village, we can't be far now," Erebus ordered confidently as he shouldered his pack.

"What's bad about fireballs?" Alec asked whilst the necromancer retrieved his staff from the sodden ground.

"Just a single burst of heat, you'll get some nasty flash burns, tiny bit of kinetics from the air expansion but nothing lethal unless you're prepared to be ludicrously inefficient, you want a steady flame for fire magic," the mage began to explain, only to cut himself off as Holly reemerged from the forest, looking heartbroken.

Instinctively Alec moved to stand beside her, placing a hand comfortingly on her upper arm, "What's happened?" he asked the young dryad, only to receive distraught sobs in return.

Gently as he could, Erebus pulled Alec aside and knelt in front of the distressed girl, taking her hand as he met her gaze. "Let's find you somewhere to sit, and then you can tell us what's happened, okay?"

"…' kay", Holly mumbled. The dryad allowed herself to be led to a comparatively dry patch of fallen leaves; grass was unavailable because they'd been unable to find a decent clearing to settle in for what had remained of the night. Erebus also took the time to unshoulder his pack.

"Now, it may be none of my business, and should that become apparent I promise to drop the subject at once, but please tell us what's happened to get you in such a state," the necromancer said soothingly, sitting down in front of her.

Alec moved to sit beside the dryad but was waved silently away by the youthful necromancer, who didn't want to crowd the poor girl. For a fraction – of a fraction – of a second, the boy looked affronted, the emotion harsh and ugly on features more used to smiling, but then, as swiftly as it came, the look dissolved, replaced by concern for the quaking girl who had been made his responsibility.

"V-v-von Mori's dead," stammered the girl, staring intently at her knees whilst she hugged them to her chest, somehow appearing to shrink in even further upon herself.

Erebus froze, for the first time since Alec had met him, the venerable sage seemed unsure of himself, hesitant to respond to the news as horror, shock and disbelief flashed across his face, the three emotions vying for dominance, only to be forced back as the mage schooled his features back to calm. A thin mask of serenity.

Eventually, he found words. "Where did you hear this?" each syllable clipped with uncertainty.

"The forest, can't you hear it? the entire forest is screaming," Holly mumbled into her knees.

"I'm sorry Holly, we humans can't hear the pain of plants, do you think we would have invented the axe if we could?" Erebus only half-joked, still looking more pale and drawn than his usual pallor as he rubbed at the bridge of his nose. "Sorry, that was most insensitive of me, I just can't believe it. Have your fellow dryads provided any insights into how this happened?"

"Your paladin killed her," Holly said flatly, not looking up. "Why did you have to drag us into your stupid war?"

"All wars are stupid, my dear; it's just a question of which side is being the idiot," Erebus said calmly, "and somehow, I doubt Lutan has done this thing. He may be a bastard of the highest order, but he simply lacks the power that would be required. I'm as powerful as a necromancer can get without being a lich, and it was nearly the death of me to restrain her ladyship for more than a few moments."

"Lutan? As in Lord Protector Lutan?" Alec asked fearfully, suddenly full of his own concerns.

"Yes," Erebus admitted quietly, unable to meet Alec's gaze through guilt at his lie, a lie by exclusion perhaps but a lie all the same. "I'll explain later Alec, but please, one problem at a time. Let me deal with Holly first."

The teen glared slightly, finding the necromancer to be annoyingly reasonable. Erebus ignored it.

"Did your fellow tree spirits have anything to say about how Lutan supposedly performed such a feat?" he asked Holly, voice awash with scepticism.

"I didn't ask," the girl confessed, bursting into fresh tears, the viscous sap leaving thick trails on her faintly green cheeks.

"I will see if they will be willing to converse with the likes of me," Erebus informed them, not wanting to send the dryad for whom it would clearly be asking too much of. "Look after her Alec, I will return as soon as proves possible."

"Why do you have to go at all?" the boy demanded petulantly, not wanting to be left alone with the distraught dryad.

"Because there is a more than moderate chance, if Holly's reaction is anything to go by, that I will be attacked by the forest when I call upon it. I'd rather you weren't there for that, it gives me slightly more options for my defence," the necromancer explained, looking serious, and more than a touch tired.

"But surely if you're not here, then they'll attack me as well," the boy fretted, foreseeing an army of killer trees in his near future.

"No, Holly will protect you; assaulting you is the equivalent of assaulting her, and if they have any respect for the late Von Mori, then you are safer right now than you have ever been in your life," Erebus said with a wistful smile before returning to his calm façade, the transition so quick and well-practised that it was almost like throwing a switch for the mage. "Now, please excuse me."

The magician took a moment to retrieve his quarterstaff before disappearing into the gloom of the morning trees.

Once he was suitably far away not to be overheard, the necromancer sat down, his quarterstaff across his knees as he waited, rather than the eldritch ritual he'd suggested he would perform, Erebus merely waited for word of his presence, alone and vulnerable as he was, to pass through the forest, now it would all depend on which dryads had the courage to approach him.

As expected, it was just a couple of minutes before the first tree spirit made its presence known, the dryad rising quietly from the earth in front of Erebus.

Her skin the dark muddy brown of old tree bark, the surface of her face pitted and cracked. Her mere presence washed over the necromancer like a physical blow, a great weight on the fabric of reality, even more so than Von Mori.

"I am Yew," the ancient dryad proclaimed. "And you, mage-child, are in grave trouble."

Erebus swallowed nervously, the dryad near thrummed with necromantic energies, enhanced further by her age and presumably the great vitality of her tree. There were reasons yew trees were known as the tree of death. One was the poison they contained; the lethal taxin, which was also found in the dryad's touch — one of the reasons that Erebus had promptly separated further away from the tree spirit, nearly tripping in his perhaps indecent haste.

The other reason for the ghastly stigmata upon this particular variant of dryad was that they both possessed and amplified necromantic power, which had at one point millennia ago resulted in a paladin crusade against the genus. Needless to say, upon attempting to 'cleanse' Forest Von Mori of the tree, the paladins suffered one of the most humiliating defeats in the history of their order. In fact, rumours abounded that upon the crusade's defeat, the entire host, or at least those corpses still with limbs, had been resurrected as zombies by the forests of the world as an act of petty, if justified vengeance. Cursed to lay dormant but aware of their state of undeath as a guard against any further paladin incursions, though the tale was so old that few dryads, let alone flesh and blood beings, would be able to ascertain their veracity.

Struggling to ignore the sheer energy of her presence, her magic, so similar to his own, almost resonating in his blood, Erebus locked gaze with the dryad. “I am no stranger to danger,” he replies simply.

The dryad smiled darkly, “Perhaps. But right now an excess of half a million dryads wish to see you torn asunder. Do you still fancy your chances?”

Erebus met her dark smile and raised an inquisitive eyebrow, “Did I say I fancied my chances? Still if so many would see me dead, where are they?”

“Don’t play coy with me necromancer. You didn’t make your third century by means of ignorance, you know most can’t move from their trees,” Yew growled, patience wearing thin at his quietly confrontational attitude.

“Unless my eyes deceive me, and I won’t entirely dismiss the possibility, improbable as it may be, we are still surrounded by dense forest, and still my limbs remain rather firmly attached to my body,” the magician pointed out with the irritating reasonability which was either near-inhuman gift or carefully cultivated art, once more completely evading the real issue entirely. Despite the time pressure placed upon him by his pursuer, he seemed content to wait for Yew to reach her point in her own time.

“Only because I have ordered them not to,” Yew stated firmly, almost openly daring him to argue further. Fortunately, Erebus seemed to judge that her veneer of self-control was sufficiently cracked to gauge her motives.

“We can continue evading the issue, Lady Yew, but I assure you that moving directly to whatever it is you would ask of me is a far more efficient system.”

“Very well, I want the paladin, and all those foolish enough to travel with him, dead,” Yew snapped.

The necromancer merely laughed, "Your posturing was unnecessary, m'lady. Lutan's death has been on the cards ever since he instigated this sorry little affair. Though a touch of patience may be needed on both our parts."

Yew didn't seem to share his mirth; the tree spirit was shockingly impatient for one so old. In Erebus' experience, any magical being over the age of five hundred required more than a gentle nudge to bring their attention and efforts to the immediate situation. One of the drawbacks of immortality was that immortals tended to take the long view on everything.

"Why? The paladin is mere hours from you," Yew snapped informatively.

"If he's so close, then why haven't you killed him yourself?" Erebus asked, the twinkle of humour still alive in his tone after all the question was technically rhetorical, he merely wished to engage the grieving dryad's brain to see the present impossibility of this task as things stood; Lutan would die, he even hoped by his own hand, but there was no way that he could kill the man in his current situation, his magic was no match for the paladin's armour.

"Don't be a fool. That much nullstone in one place; its agony even from here," Yew growled, perhaps explaining her belligerence.

"My case in point, you - a magical creature - are sending me, also a magical being, to kill something you can't harm because you're magical, that's flawed at best," Erebus stated.

"But you're much weaker than me, you'll just feel a great discomfort whilst the stronger dryads like me are currently undergoing what should be classed as torture."

"Unfortunately, that gives the opposite problem.

Nullstone's proportionate weakening means those with enough power can't get near him, while the rest can't kill him." Erebus smiled weakly whilst shrugging ever so slightly, "You have to admit it's one hell of a catch."

The dryad looked thoughtful, "There is perhaps one thing I can do to swing things in your favour. Take a walk with me, I'll take you to my tree."

Understanding was instant for the old mage, his voice shocked and just a touch reverent, a massive change from the calculated calm of earlier as he replied, "Lady Yew, I'm honoured you would grant me a boon, but such a weapon would be of little use, it would only channel necromancy to any great degree, and such magic is not for the waging of war directly upon a foe. Necromancy facilitates violence by proxy, I can't attack with it."

"I believe you will find yourself mistaken on that account. Don't necromancers have a spell to rapidly decay the flesh from a corpse, for when you wish to expose the bones beneath?" the dryad said with surprising, or given her nature and age, unsurprising, knowledge of Erebus' own art.

"Well yes but-"

"And is there any technical reason it couldn't be used on living flesh?" Yew pressed further.

"Well it requires a lot of energy - I-I can't, it would be an abomination. An abuse. One does not use necromancy to kill, I'd be as bad as the dread healers, worse even," Erebus protested, his great veneer of calm shattering under the implications.

"You must make a choice necromancer, your morality or be responsible for the next great war. Both sides have had half of a millennium to rearm, do you really think anything will survive?" Yew proclaimed, a realist spouting the deepest darkest dreads of doomsayers throughout recorded history.

"There are other considerations to take into account." The necromancer sighed, looking wracked with pain from the decision before him.

"None come to mind," Yew harshly dictated, not a phlegmatic person by nature.

"That's because they are my considerations and not yours." His calm exterior once more, if rather shakily, in place, "I have my… apprentice to consider."

"You told Von Mori that the boy was not your apprentice," the old dryad pointed out coolly.

"How can you possibly know that?" Erebus replied reflexively.

"Young dryads are terrible gossips," Yew imparted with something approximating a smile, if not an excessively cheerful one. "Now let us walk."

Foreseeing a great need of the help on offer, the necromancer nodded his acquiescence, proffering an arm to the tree-spirit, who accepted graciously. "Lead the way then, but bear in mind that I make no promises as to what actions I take regarding Lutan; this is merely to increase the options available. "You have a lot of courage to admit that," Yew conceded with a slightly friendlier smile, "but when the opportunity presents itself, I expect you to strike, or you won't be leaving this forest."

"Threats ill become a great dryad such as yourself, Lady Yew," Erebus chastised gently; the necromancer somehow possessed of enough confidence of his own powers, or perhaps enough surety of his own morals, to rebuke a being who was currently throwing death threats.

"Don't be a fool child, threats are a means to an end, yours or Lutan's."

Erebus merely shook his head, allowing her to lead him to her tree, a yew tree of truly gargantuan proportions, nearly a canopy in its own right, its bark pitted and cracked. Its presence was ominous, a feeling backed up further by the lack of other trees; not a single seed had dared take root within fifty yards of Yew's wooden abode, the ground bare and dusty greyed mud beneath his feet.

"Shall we make this quick?" he requested, "Only Holly and Alec have been alone for fifteen minutes and I don't want to return to yet another argument."

"I find it most odd that such a weak-minded necromancer as yourself is viewed as a pinnacle of your order, have the dark arts truly grown so weak?" his lamentable companion enquired in sickly sweet tones, laced with more than a snakebite's worth of venom.

Erebus, however, did not seem to take offence at first, simply smiling at her with tranquil gaze, "No my lady, we have grown strong enough to no longer need power over others; instead, we merely seek power over ourselves. All that remains of our time of weakness are the worryingly unforgiving memories of the paladins and misguided relics such as yourself."

The dryad, and her tree, momentarily bristled with affront, "I think perhaps you don't need my help after all," she snapped, crossing her arms as she restrained herself from tearing the irritating human before her in twain.

"That would be unwise," Erebus said, a twinkle in his eye. "I remain your only realistic option for killing Lutan, so there is no point withholding aid from me, it would merely serve to your own detriment."

With a heaving sigh of annoyance, Yew unfolded her arms, visibly seeming to deflate as she released her indignation. The man was right; she could not harm him yet, but, she decided, there would be a reckoning later. For now the dryad simply extended a vine wrapped arm at her tree. Wood boiled beneath the surface for a few seconds before emerging out of the tree entirely. A quarterstaff, fully formed and measured perfectly for Erebus' height.

As though he was frightened it might shatter at the slightest touch, the magician reached for the dark wood, fingers tenderly wrapping around it, plucking the weapon from the air before giving it a brief flourish, testing the weight and balance, and finding it just a touch bottom-heavy — Yew had apparently taken the time to ensure that whatever focus the top took wouldn't upset the balance too much. The long cylinder of wood was perfectly smooth, better than a world-class sander could provide, and nearly thrummed with the magic of undeath, and that was ignoring the focus it provided for Erebus' own necromantic magic. All he needed for it now was a focusing crystal to place atop it in the small cradle the branches at the top had formed, which, he guessed, would likely open and clasp on to whatever he chose for the focus, the gem acting as a magical lense. It was a noble weapon, if unfinished and unrefined, and Erebus said as much, minus the criticism.

Yew smiled, pleased despite her dislike of the man, "Now all that remains is the paladin's death."

"A gross oversimplification… but certainly a possibility." He sighed, voice trailing off into nothingness as he wrestled with his ethics, "Please return me to my apprentice now."

"As you wish," Yew said before stalking off through the trees, forcing Erebus to jog after her.

Whilst all of this was taking place, Alec was being faced with his own crisis of confidence. Not only was he having to worry about what would happen when Lord Lutan caught up with them, but he was also having to calm and console the bereaved Holly, who was busy sobbing into her patch of leaves; the boy knelt beside her as he gently patted her on the back, wishing he had Erebus' skill with words. The necromancer, the boy, was sure, could have stopped Holly's pain with a mere sentence. It was a foolish thought, born of the mistaken observations of a child, the optimistic myopic view of one too young to see the flaws in others.

But while he may have lacked the aura of diplomacy that his new mentor seemed to exude, Alec still attempted to help Holly find peace with her loss.

"You should probably drink something," he suggested, idly wondering exactly how much crying it would take to get dehydrated; a question only further complicated by the dryad weeping sap instead of the typical salty tears.

Holly didn't reply, simply continuing to weep, her bark-hued cheeks now encrusted with hardened sap. She did, however, accept a mouthful of water from the canteen Alec offered her before breaking into a fresh bout of tears.

Finally, Alec had had enough; as gently as he could, he rolled her over, carefully manoeuvring the unresisting form into a sitting position before propping her up against a tree. "Talk to me Holly," he instructed, trying not to snap at her.

"She was just always there, you know." The girl sniffled, a hand wiping the sap from her cheeks, at least that which hadn't hardened into an amber shell. "We'd never spoken before the day I was Sundered but you always knew she was there, watching… caring…"

"I'm sorry," Alec said simply, no other words coming to mind.

"You don't know what it's like, having everything you've known just ripped away from you." She blubbed, not noticing how Alec's expression had just stiffened, a rictus snarl as he just managed to not shout at her, instead breathing deeply and slowly, a calming exercise courtesy of the monk.

Seconds trickled by like sand in an hourglass, punctuated only by the sniffling of Holly trying to regain control over her sobbing. Finally, and with great self-control, Alec said, "I do know what it's like, Holly, Erebus tore me from everything I knew as well, and, if he hasn't lied, our lord protector has butchered everyone I've ever met, including my parents. So I really do know how you feel."

The speech seemed to reach the young dryad, the girl turning to look sympathetically at the teen for a few moments, taking in the fact that not only was Alec suffering as she was but also holding it together a lot better.

"H-how are you so serene about all this then?" she nearly demanded, hoping for some sort of insight, some mystical cure for grief. A desperate naivety on her part, but purely understandable to any unbiased observer.

"I don't really know," Alec replied in the same slow, level and carefully emotionless tone of one masking their emotions and doing poorly at it to boot, the words gradually speeding up as his thoughts turned more personal. "I think it hasn't really sunk in yet. At first, I thought Erebus was lying on principle, and though I have come to trust the man somewhat, I'm still unsure. And we've been on the run from I didn't know what, and everything's been so confusing and mixed up, and I feel like I'm nearing a point where something is just going to snap, and I'll start blubbing my heart out." The boy paused for breath, eyes moist as he almost came apart at the seams, but he did hold it together, knowing innately that they couldn't both afford to be slaves to grief right now.

Holly smiled wryly, wiping more tears away, "Guess we're both a mess."

"Guess so," Alec agreed quietly, sitting down beside her. "I hope Erebus gets back soon."

The dryad blinked owlishly at him, though reopening her eyes was an effort as the sap almost sealed them beyond the reach of daylight permanently. "I thought you paladin types were meant to fear necromancers?"

"We are but Erebus is too… nice to be afraid of," Alec replied. "It's like every fibre in my body wants to hate him for taking me from home, getting my parents killed, even simply being a necromancer. Yet he's been nothing but considerate."

Holly shrugged, "Necromancers are like that, or so we're told. Some of the most selfless magicians ever to live, or unlive for that matter." She smiled weakly at her own pun. "So what's so special about this Lutan fella anyway?"

Alec frowned, fear etched on his young face as he began to explain what he knew in hushed tones of awe and dread.

"Before he became a lord protector, Lutan was a great warrior, they called him the Magebane because of how much he hated magic. Nothing was ever proven but if you believe the stories he would hunt down any magician with a fanatical zeal, killing anyone who offered them food or shelter, and executing their families as well," Alec finished, glancing around nervously.

Holly was far less reverent of the tale, "So what's he been doing since he became a lord protector? Whatever that is."

"Lord Protectors are in charge of defending vast stretches of land against any threats. It's the second-highest rank in the paladin order, they can requisition whatever they need and their actions are held accountable only to the Protector's Council and the High Paladin himself."

"Surely this council thingy isn't going to just let him get away with killing the people he's meant to protect?" the dryad demanded.

"No. They won't," Erebus stated firmly, emerging from behind a tree, though they couldn't be sure he'd been eavesdropping, and from what they knew of the man, such an action would have been out of character in the extreme. "But as we are currently the only ones who could tell them, I'm sure Lutan is feeling reasonably safe from accountability of any sort."

"Is that why he's after us then?" the boy enquired, "to escape justice?"

"Alas, nothing so simple and selfish. Lutan actually believes that there is nothing wrong with his actions, he genuinely sees magic as a blight upon mankind, given the chance he would destroy it all; mages, elves, dryads, vampires, the unquiet spirits and even the dragons," came the quiet and near-mournful explanation.

"Surely no vampires is a good thing?" Alec asked, clearly quite bemused at the idea that it might not be.

"Don't judge an entire species solely on their diet," Erebus chided gently, "they have a right to live just like anybody else."

"But they eat people," the boy protested vehemently.

"You eat meat don't you? Would you say that negates your right to live?" the necromancer asked, remaining quiet and softly spoken as he chipped away at one of the boy's core beliefs. Never a nice thing to do but necessary when the belief is harmful to others.

"It's not the same thing," Alec spluttered, clearly not seeing the comparison.

"Isn't it? Animals must die for you to live, just as for vampires to live animals must die."

"But people are different from animals," the boy pointed out.

"Are they really?" Erebus asked. "What's the difference? As I've had a large number of biomancers tell me the only provable difference is merely a matter of species."

"But people are different, we can think, we have feelings, we can love!" Alec insisted with emphatic romance of the soul, if not understanding of it. The necromancer merely smiled, the boy having fallen into the trap laid by him for such an unwary gesture of eloquence.

"Alec, if you place a chimpanzee, and a series of crates in a room, without reach of food it will stack the crates to reach the food. Clearly a sign of intelligent thought. Whilst on one of the southern continents there is a spider with intellect so formidable that it can learn to mimic the signals of other spiders and strategise how to catch them, sometimes taking half an hour to reach its chosen location of attack. Birds such as rooks and crows will make tools from twigs to get at food otherwise unavailable. So please don't be of such great hubris to think that the qualifications for thinking merely involve being able to stand up on two legs," Erebus explained patiently, setting out his argument by heavy use of example, evidence being by far the superior of rhetoric and volume. "And as for love and emotion, a cat will cry if in great pain, purr when happy or wag its tail if angry or annoyed. Dolphins and lion cubs will play amongst themselves, though not with each other - just to be clear. A swan will sometimes commit suicide if its mate dies. What more proof of love or loss can you need than that? Just because we can't understand what they say doesn't mean they are in any way inferior to us."

"I-I'd never thought about it like that," Alec admitted, looking slightly ill. "But doesn't that mean that every time I've eaten meat that I've essentially partaken in a murder?"

"Perhaps," the mage conceded. "But death is the facilitator of life, for any living thing to survive, other than plants, though even there there are exceptions, one must kill to survive. Be it an animal, plant or mere cell. All you can do is try not to cause unnecessary pain through your actions."

Holly was notably smug at this, at least until she remembered that she was, by nature, or more accurately by intricate spell work, no longer a plant and thus just as murderous as her host. Her two companions tried not to be too amused, instead focusing on their debate, the conversation proving a great diversion from the troubles plaguing them.

"Now, let us return to the original point of disagreement, do you believe vampires do not have the right to live?" Erebus said with great solemnity.

"No, they do have the right," Alec conceded with a weighty sigh. "But so does their food, so where do you draw the line?"

"Fortunately we seldom have to deal with such anymore. The vampires themselves dealt with that," the necromancer said with a warm smile. "Now we need to get back on the move but if you're still interested in a few minutes I'll give you something of a vampire history lesson as we walk."

"I'll still be interested," his young charge assured, getting to his feet and then offering Holly a hand up. An act of chivalry which the girl for once accepted with good grace.

It took the disparate trio two minutes to get back on the road. Though more technically, it was a forest trail upon which Holly's advice had proved the catalyst, the grieving girl assuring them that they were mere hours away from Erebus' mysterious destination.

Once they had successfully settled into a sustainable pace, Erebus began his history lesson.

"One of the first things you need to understand is that vampires have always had a humanist element, I use humanist because in this case humanitarian would have a new meaning entirely. Go back a few thousand years and it was considered fashionable for the more wealthy vampires to leave the families of their victims a large stipend to ensure that they could at least live their lives in relative comfort, a process now viewed as quite barbaric by vampires in general, however, this progressed to kidnapping, again leaving a fee for the families, the victims kept alive for years by careful siphoning of the blood." Erebus paused, awaiting an input from one of his two students.

Surprisingly neither spoke for some time, choosing

to think about their question rather than ask out of reflex. The master necromancer smiled to himself, stepping ahead of them to hide his happiness; the boy was learning fast, as was the dryad, no matter how unintended an addition she had been. He could only hope that she would be strong enough to protect the boy until he accepted his own power.

"This isn't a history of vampires," Alec said with great certainty, the question implicit in the statement, "just a history of their feeding habits."

"I know, but I thought this the best point to start at considering your concerns, particularly as a complete history of vampirism is entirely impossible."

"If there isn't time until we get to this town of yours, I wouldn't mind picking it up later," Alec assured him, interested beyond words by his first hint of supernatural education, a syllabus that in the world he'd been brought up in was only permitted to paladins.

"Alas time constraints aren't the issue, much of vampire history has been lost, too many purges I'm afraid, it's notoriously difficult to maintain a library when the primary weapons against your species includes fire."

"Surely some of the older vampires themselves-"

"Again; purges," Erebus cut off before continuing the lesson. "The next stage after that was to siphon blood off of willing volunteers, either from a single donor if the vampire liked travelling, or from a group, though the single donors seldom lasted long unless the vampire showed great restraint. Around the same time, small groups of vampires began to subside on animal blood. The important part to remember is that these were never mainstream groups. The majority of the vampires up until around four hundred years ago considered such practises as disgusting and subversive. It was only the paladins that changed that, after a hundred years of peace with magician-kind, and no signs of a break in the truce the Paladin Order could finally turn its full attention to vampirism, and for the first time, we made no attempts to defend our undead brethren. Magic users had also decided enough was enough, though I'd like to think with a heavy heart for they had been one of the Necropolis' most stalwart allies in our hours of need. The result was that the vampires sued for peace in less than a month and a compromise was reached: vampires who ate in a non-fatal manner would have all the same rights as any other citizen of the area they resided in whilst any vampires who kept killing would find themselves facing a dedicated task force of paladin, magician and vampire. Naturally, predatory vampirism all but vanished over a mere few years." Erebus smiled wistfully, "It was the first time that paladin and necromancer realised what they were capable of when they worked together."

Holly stopped, turning to face them, "Why would necromancers help fight their own allies?"

"Everyone is familiar with the concept of 'the enemy of my enemy is my friend' but no one questions what this means when the enemy ceases to exist. Necromancers have been desiring to be a pacifist people for millennia, vampires may have been allies of necessity for time immemorial but once we had peace we no longer were so desperate as to tolerate the wholesale slaughter of people."

This seemed to be met with acceptance from the contrary girl who carried on guiding them, the forest finally beginning to thin, the trees reducing in size as well as number. For the first time in days, they could see through the canopy to gaze upon open sky.

Alas, the moment of joyful realisation was shattered as Erebus held up a hand for them to stop, appearing to listen intently for mere seconds before his eyes widened with realisation, grabbing both Holly and her host by their collars and shoving them roughly forwards.

"Run, and don't stop until you're inside the circle!" he ordered with great urgency, fear flickering deep within granite grey eyes for a scant moment, too fast for either of them to catch before it was buried behind the wall of calm that Erebus wore on his face.

His two young charges obliged him, taking off at a veritable sprint. Alec, proving faster, instinctively grabbed Holly's hand, dragging her along despite the nails digging into his palm, reciprocating a pained gasp from both parties though it did nothing to decrease their pace. Alec's fear echoed through the bond they shared, not bothering with a mental smokescreen like his necromantic mentor.

As the duo disappeared out of sight, Erebus removed his new stave from his pack coiling an arm around each of them, the two staves, ebony and Yew, of reasonably similar hue, but that was where the similarities ended. The ebony had had its shaft almost worn through by time and use, the runes having been carved and recarved many times over the many decades Erebus had possessed it, the obsidian skull that capped it had been custom made with a threefold purpose, the first was that it was a perfect copy of the necromancer's own cranium; complete with lower jaw, this provided a significant enhancement for any mental magics he might employ, be it mind reading, telekinesis or the protection of his own thoughts. The second was the material itself. Obsidian was a good channeler of necromantic energies as well as certain envenomed spells along with other members of the darker healing arts - though Erebus would sooner boil himself in hydrochloric acid than use them, ironically a spell to do this would be assisted by the skull. The third and final reason was not quite as eloquent, though there was a simple beauty to it; such a large amount of obsidian weighed several kilos making it a veritable bludgeon when magic was impossible or undesirable.

Yew's staff had no such refinement; unadorned and unenhanced, it was still many times the superior of Erebus' beloved travel companion in terms of the raw power residing within it, not even accounting for the lensing effect it provided to necromancy. In time, if its owner survived the coming years, it would likely become an object of legend as runes and further lensing mechanisms such as crystals were added; there was a reason dryads of such strength rarely directly aided mortal affairs, such weapons could prove game-changers. In the case of this particular weapon though, it would take years at the minimum to become the purposeful tool of its counterpart; for now, it was a thing of primal energies and of great moral difficulty for Erebus.

"I know you're there," he stated firmly to the forest in general, retreating after the two teens. Unsurprisingly there was no response.

Anticipating the sudden appearance of a knight in dented armour at any moment — shining armour typically being a sign that the knight in question didn't actually do any fighting or travelling — he moved slowly, constantly turning to scan his surroundings for movements of violent intent, and disconcertingly finding none.

"This a waste of both our times," Erebus loudly declared, once more trying to draw out his foe. "Your ruse has failed, just face me. Show a shred of courage for once."

Again there was no response.

Erebus discovered why when the trees thinned to nothingness, revealing Circulus Seruatis in its late morning glory.

It was a large village, the population too low to truly qualify as a town though architecturally it more than qualified. The buildings both large and spread apart with each a wonder of aesthetically applied wood and stone in its own right, with several towering above the trees that surrounded the defining feature of Circulus, its boundary, a circular wall of almost terminally-boring grey rock, no more than a foot high, too low to act as a defence against even an army of gnomes. Erebus took in none of this, eyes focused instead on the armoured men standing on the edge of the boundary, one of whom, clad in thick, heavily dented nullsteel plate, currently had a crushing grip on his protege's shoulder. Alec's expression pained and horrified. Horrified because as painful as his restraint was, it was nothing next to Holly's, the dryad a weeping, writhing ball of pain, a nullstone collar about her neck.

The sight made the necromancer's blood boil, for once his emotions written plainly across his face for the world to see. With great wrath, he directed both staves at the man, advancing towards the clustered knights like a dark avatar of unbridled fury.

"Lutan!" he bellowed. "Release them both and you can still come out of this alive."

The paladin holding Alec merely smiled beneath his helmet, "Now why would I do that, *old friend*. You are powerless so close to the circle, let alone so close to our armour," he sneered. "Give me a reason why I should unhand your apprentice when he provides such brilliant leverage over you."

"-He's not my apprentice you idiot: he's just a child who your petty vendetta has left orphaned and alone. Have mercy Lutan, for the sake of the laughing child I once knew, show a shred of human decency and let them both go," Erebus pleaded, an impassioned appeal to any morality still residing in the withered husk of his adversary's poisonous heart.

For a moment, it looked like the plea would work as some of Lutan's companions, only five in number now, appeared uncertain, unabsorbed from the cult of personality that was the lord protector. Only one betrayed no remorse as uncertainty danced behind Lutan's helm, perhaps the tattered remnants of old friendships and memories attaining a tentative grip on the paladin, but to Saiko, it mattered not what order he gave, or decision was made, his own conscience far too stained with blood for one more death, or score of deaths to matter now. Unlike his comrades, he lacked the great shield of self-righteous piety that made murder easy; instead, he'd learned to think in terms of survival, kill or be killed, albeit clad in a cheap coat of honour. He knew the darkness of hate and revenge, had spent years around those consumed by them, yet apart from such motives by way of employment. His was not the mind behind murder, merely the sword it reached for. Whether that made him better or worse than those who purchased his services was an argument as old as war itself.

Perhaps this was why Saiko alone was entirely unsurprised when Lutan threw the boy to the ground, the paladin's sword rising from its scabbard as an answer, and so with two-handed grip plunging it downwards towards defenceless flesh and cold soil beneath it.

Even Saiko was surprised by the speed of Erebus' reaction. The bolt of lightning struck the armoured paladin full in the chest, a seething ribbon of white-hot energy stretching from the obsidian skull to Lutan's breastplate as it threw the man backwards as though he were no more than a ragdoll.

Lutan bounced twice upon his journey, each leaving furrows in the earth as he came to a stop just short of the boundary. Shockingly he got to his feet, breastplate glowing a cherry red at the point of impact, the metal so thick that as the heat diffused through it, it became merely uncomfortably hot rather than the intended lethally, whilst a layer of carbonised rubber — a treasured secret in the production of mageproof armour — stopped the electrical component from killing him by stopping his heart in an instant.

The toll on Erebus was far more telling, the old man on his knees, for once using the staves for balance. "Perhaps I am not as powerless as you thought." He gasped as Alec used the concern of Lutan's retinue for their master to his advantage, freeing the now near-catatonic Holly and dragging her over to the necromancer, moving behind him for relative safety. The only eyes on him those of Saiko, the mercenary making no attempt to intervene, content to observe the conflict unless ordered to participate directly.

Again Lutan smiled beneath his helm, a skilled observer able to see the amusement through the thin eyeslit, "How many years did you burn on that spell alone?" he asked.

"Thirty at least," Erebus confessed, "but I think the next shot will be the death of you."

Lutan merely smirked, "Bareth, Ghash. Kill him."

One of the knights was all too eager to oblige, charging forwards with a roaring, if wordless battle cry in an attempt to sever the necromancer down the middle with an overzealous overhead swing.

Erebus sidestepped, Yew's staff swinging from low to high, just like in his drills earlier, to impact hard on the knight's helm, the ringing in Bareth's ears enough to stun and daze the overconfident thug.

Dropping his other staff, he swung back around, almost wrapping it around his body as he took one of Bareth's legs out from under him.

To the knight's credit he didn't fall, instead stumbling backwards as he tried to regain his balance: he never got the chance. Erebus drove the middle of his staff up through his jaw, the helm unable to protect him from the sharp blow as Bareth's head snapped back, a brutal crunch indicating the necromancer had successfully snapped his neck.

The knight slumped in an untidy sprawl.

It had all been so fast and fluid that Ghash hadn't even closed the distance yet. Perhaps if they'd both rushed the necromancer, then they'd have overwhelmed him, but the soldier doubted it. His opponent was too calm and prepared to be rushed. He decided to respond in kind, stalking and circling slowly, sword held guardedly in front of him, waiting on his foe to make the first move as the remaining three paladins — Owen, Lutan and Saiko — watched, each drawing their own analysis of what was happening.

Erebus also circled, though the centre of his orbit was not his opponent, instead making certain that his body remained carefully interposed between the soldier and Alec.

The tension was palpable under the watchful gazes, Erebus and Ghash waiting upon a single decisive act of foolishness.

Ironically it was neither of them who made the error, "Just bloody kill him," shouted Lord Andun Owen.

For a fraction of a fraction of a second Ghash's attention was diverted; on pure instinct and skill, he managed to raise his sword up to stop the overhead strike only to find it a feint, Erebus reversing the quarterstaff so it swung up through the swordsman's now open guard to strike him square between the legs. There was a collective wince from the males involved as Ghash dropped his sword to clutch at his wounded testicles, his scream silent as he sought the air to give voice to the localised agony. He didn't have time to find it as Erebus stepped into his space to drive the shaft of his staff into the unfortunate soldier's nose, driving the bone-deep into the brain. It was unlikely the fact his death was nearly instantaneous was a consolation to him.

Calm and cold as death, Erebus picked up his own stave. "And then there were three…"

Lutan merely smirked, though none could see it. "Did you get all that Sai?"

"Indeed," The master swordsman assured, finally drawing his blade against the necromancer. "Shall we dance sir?"

"My fight is not with you," Erebus said calmly before throwing the young man backwards with a wave of air, again channelled through his own staff.

Before Saiko could rejoin the fight, Erebus levelled Yew's stave at Lutan, a necrotic green energy gathering around the tip where a focus of some kind would one day be placed, the deathly essence of decay more an impression than a sight in the later morn sunlight, translucent yet nauseating.

In a show of great willpower by both parties, neither Erebus nor Lutan looked away, and thus as Erebus unleashed his blast of pure rot, Lutan stepped aside laughing as the effort brought his nemesis back down to his knees in the dewy grass, staining his shins with chlorophyll and mud.

"I didn't think you'd be this obliging," the Lord Protector sneered, marching slowly towards his fallen foe, savouring victory after nearly three decades of waiting.

Erebus watched Lutan's approach with trepidation, a mask of fear painted blatantly across his face, until the paladin got too close and, striking like a snake, he swept Lutan's feet out from under him.

The knight fell heavily though he managed to roll away from the kicks the necromancer was attempting to rain down on him, the magician's state of weakness partially feigned, but even at his best mere flesh would always come off worse than steel plate.

As Lutan regained his feet, he saw Erebus smiling broadly. "I told you that shot would be the death of you."

Lutan frowned. "You missed," he tried to sound smug, but there was uncertainty now.

"Always so egotistical, even as a young boy," Erebus reminisced, "I wasn't aiming for you."

The mortal risked a look behind him to find that even so near to midday, the boundary had lit up like a beacon. An ethereal and ephemeral dome of spiderwebbing energy playing across its surface from the point of Erebus' strike.

The necromancer sighed, "If you surrender now I promise you won't be unduly harmed. However, I'm afraid you'll be stuck here for the rest of your life."

"You think to incarcerate me? The Paladin Order will have me out within a month." Lutan actually laughed before pulling out a knife, "And he's not here yet; I can still kill you."

"When will you learn to accept your mistakes? Your strike force is demolished and the forest despises you. The only recourse left is for you to seek asylum in Circulus," Erebus stated with reasoned certainty.

"The forest won't be a problem," the paladin assured, fingering the gem at his throat.

"I suspected killing her was beyond you," Erebus said with a morose smile, once more interposing himself between teen and paladin, this time all three of the survivors converging upon him. He chuckled dryly, "If I had a hat I'd take it off to you. Dare I ask how long you've been planning this, or does the magician never reveal his secrets?"

"You're stalling," Lutan observed coolly, closing the gap enough that he was in striking distance, waiting on his cohorts to do the same.

Again Erebus merely chuckled, directing a knowing smile at his erstwhile friend. "Distracting actually." From behind Lutan came the distinct sound of metal impacting metal. The necromancer's grin was almost malicious in its vindication. "I think you'll find that that is checkmate old friend. Now hand over the good lady and I'll make sure you live to see trial."

Lutan risked a glance behind him.

Owen was on the floor, and Saiko was locked in a heated exchange with another fighter, the newcomer a startling tableau of symbols, writings, runes, glyphs and simple geometrical shapes adorning his deeply tanned skin in an intricate and complex arrangement which drew the eye even more with the variety of starkly contrasting colours therein. In fact, if one were to stare at them long enough, they would seem to move of their own accord, though it was probably, but only probably, the viewer's imagination.

They were certainly moving now as muscles bulged and flexed beneath them as their owner parried, blocked and countered in an entrancing dance of blade on blade. The newcomer's sword whistling through the air at such speeds that Saiko was having to give ground to avoid giving his life.

Lutan turned back to his own foe. "He still has to win."

"True. Shall we await an outcome, or do you want to fight me yourself?" Erebus advanced, weapons ready.

As predicted, Lutan backed down, having long known the necromancer was the superior in skill at arms, "We'll await an outcome."

"You must have great confidence in this one," the robed mage observed quietly as the pair clashed, again and again, dripping sweat already, and in the case of Saiko, breathing raggedly as he fought not to give ground, convinced that if he could just hold it here he might get an opening. "Ah, and I see you've given him a spellbreaker blade. You really have been preparing for a very long time."

"You mock me even now?" the paladin growled, sheathing his knife and drawing his sword in a single smooth movement, only to have it knocked from his hands by a firm tap of the staff by Erebus upon the flat of the blade.

"Always so quick to anger," he chided as, behind Lutan, Saiko finally gave ground after several light cuts to his forearms which, whilst minor, would have been fatal from many an enchanted blade, his opponent just too fast for him to keep up with.

At first, the master swordsman had been exhilarated; it had been many years since he had found a fellow student of the blade capable of matching him; in fact, he was widely regarded as amongst the top ten on the continent, yet somehow, despite knowing every other member of that exclusive list by name, sight and style, he was finding himself utterly outclassed by this newcomer.

Now a hint of fear was creeping in as every feint was met by an unyielding guard, every cut deflected and the mere act of parrying sent shudders down his arm, jarring it enough that he didn't dare try to outright block, and his foe kept coming, not slowing, weakening or making sound beyond when their blades collided, to add insult to his several injuries the tattooed man wasn't even breathing heavily.

Saiko pulled back, reduced to just giving ground in the hope to catch his breath. It worked partially, he was no longer having to strain himself just to keep up, and as long as he made sure to avoid going straight backwards, then he wouldn't be running out of space any time soon, buying him time to think at least.

The words of his employer, soon to be erstwhile employer, were less than white noise to him, Saiko's world now little more than himself and his opponent.

In a flash of inspiration, he changed styles, dropping

into a long fencer's stance. The falchion was unsuited for it, but a sudden change of technique could easily throw even the most veteran of opponents; however, as he adjusted his grip on the hilt the blade was snatched away by a vicious blow, his foe having adopted a different grip himself, using two hands on the bastard sword, and swinging it as one would a club to bat the sword across the clearing.

Chapter 8

Alec had watched amazed as the fight had happened, first Erebus' electrifying battle against the Lord Protector himself, though he'd been a touch distracted getting Holly and himself out of harm's way; after that, it had been almost like watching some kind of performance, with the necromancer as the star, if not necessarily the winner, for as the heavily armoured knight had charged forwards, broadsword raised, Alec could see no way the magician could triumph wielding no more than a pair of sticks, yet the necromancer not only defeated the knight but humiliated him with his comprehensive staff work and superior speed.

After defeating the knight, his killing of the mere soldier was almost inevitable.

The boy could not help but feel useless, he couldn't do magic or fight, yet people were dying around him, and he was helpless to intervene. However, it certainly appeared that Erebus had the situation well in hand as he successfully bluffed Lutan twice within a single minute, once with the blast to the barrier and the second when he'd lured him within range of his staff. But Erebus and Lutan's conflict had proven an abysmal appetiser compared to the swordfight that followed, the two moving too fast for the eye to follow. In fact, the first Alec had seen of the tattooed newcomer was when he slid the dagger up through the gap in Owen's armour, where helm met breastplate, the stiletto cleanly traversing through the spinal nerve and into the brain.

The remaining member of Lutan's entourage had responded almost as fast, his sword seeming to leap into his hand as he charged. Before Lutan could turn, the two had met in the middle in a lightning flash of blades.

Then, all too quickly, it was over, Lutan's stooge disarmed and helpless.

To Erebus' eternal credit, he didn't gloat, electing to take a deep calming breath before tapping Lutan on the shoulder, "I am afraid you will need to hand over your sword old friend."

"This isn't over," the paladin growled. "Not while I have Von Mori."

"Yes, about that, I will be wanting that gem as well. You can expect the kidnapping of an elder dryad to be amongst the charges brought against you when this makes trial," the necromancer warned.

Lutan ignored him, focusing on The Swordsman who had so brilliantly duelled Saiko into submission, "It's not over," he muttered as in one smooth movement he redrew his dagger and threw it.

The blade pinwheeled end over end, unerringly towards The Swordsman's heart, to be smoothly batted back to whence it came, only for him to gasp as Saiko drove two knives of his own into the poor man's chest.

Simultaneously Lutan sidestepped the oncoming projectile, the tables turning in a single moment of distraction, then turning again just as rapidly for an awed Saiko who barely saw the cross to the jaw his nemesis bestowed upon him with great generosity if not gentleness. The blade master slumping like a dropped sack of potatoes albeit with less grace and a weightier smack upon hitting the ground.

As the world seemed to settle back to peace it was torn by Alec's shout; the boy knelt beside the fallen figure in black robes, the staves next to an outstretched hand as Lutan fled for the encroaching concealment of the trees. For a split second the tattooed fighter made to pursue the fleeing figure but instead dashed over to the fallen sorcerer, rolling him over to reveal the dagger Lutan had evaded firmly entrenched in his chest, Erebus' mouth was already leaking blood from internal haemorrhaging but still, he managed three words.

"Go after him."

"No child, why would I take a life when I could just as easily save one." After pulling the dagger out, the man removed a pair of gloves to place his hands directly on the wound. There was a brief flash of green light, which for reasons he couldn't begin to comprehend, put Alec in mind of the first shoots of Spring. "There, that will suffice for now," the man mumbled to himself.

Erebus made no answer, having lapsed into blissful unconsciousness though whether from his wounds or the spell Alec could not discern.

With a slight shrug, the man hoisted Erebus over one shoulder, then the unfortunate Saiko over the other, apparently with no discomfort at supporting the weight of both men. "Bring the dryad, apprentice, and your master's staves," he snapped before heading back towards the boundary. "I will await you in the town square."

There was little Alec could say to that, particularly as his erstwhile captor, now companion and perhaps mentor's fate may hang in the balance. With a tired groan of exertion, the teen hoisted the catatonic dryad over his shoulder, the brash and aggressively independent tree spirit too out of it to consider complaining, though she let out a weak whimper of pain as Alec crossed over the low wall.

The dryad was surprisingly light even for so slight a figure; Alec would have been surprised by this if he'd been aware of the exhaustion of Erebus when he'd been forced to carry them both. It was a slight magic from the bond the two now shared, an act of latent intuitive magic derived from the young dryad and further enhanced by Alec himself, if unwittingly.

As he stepped into Circulus Seruatis, it seemed to Alec as if the sky had darkened, as if the world had lost its colour somewhat, vibrant green dimmed to drab hues, and somehow life was no longer worth living.

Despite this overbearing, near all-consuming depression, Alec kept going; he didn't really know why. He just knew it concerned Erebus and some order he'd been given.

If the aura of depression had been weaker, he might have laid down there to sleep or die, but as it was, he couldn't even summon up the will to question the orders he'd been given.

As he moved away from the barrier, the feeling began to fade, some of the boy's old vitality returning with each careful step; the bizarre magic would have to remain a question for another time, one where Erebus was fully recovered from his injuries.

As Alec passed the buildings, he noted the people watching him go by, only mild curiosity in their eyes. These people were clearly used to dryads, though a moment of clarity pointed out to Alec that they would have to be this deep within Forest Von Mori. For a moment, he had a vision of Von Mori herself wandering down these same streets, the path he was walking having suddenly transitioned from foot-worn earth to actual cobblestones, the surprisingly urban buildings just didn't compute with the force of pure unrestrained nature that had been the elder dryad he concluded with a bemused shake of the head.

The town square was reasonably obvious when he got to it, a large square of even cobbles, dominated in the centre by a large well, currently covered by a thin bronze cap to prevent anyone falling in. And as promised, The Swordsman was standing by it, sans Erebus.

"Apprentice," he said calmly, the unfortunate Saiko propped up against the well wall. "You'll be pleased to hear your master is recovering well." The words were surprisingly formal, but there was a wealth of emotion behind them, both great relief and regret in the words.

"I'm not his apprentice," Alec replied, though he was no longer offended by the idea; after meeting a 'benevolent' paladin in the flesh, he'd had to seriously reconsider a lot of his previous opinions, the incident shaking his beliefs even more than Erebus' gentle yet pointed questioning.

And finally, he had accepted that his village was destroyed, and any hope of returning to that life had burned with it; the realisation left him feeling untethered; he had no expectations in the short term or long term.

"My apologies, clearly your place with the Grey Mage is a touch more complicated than I assumed. How did you come to travel with Erebus?"

"He… saved my life," Alec said slowly, feeling as if he were being tested in some way.

"Erebus has saved many lives, few of them travel with him," the man observed coolly, seemingly seeking something more in the answer.

"I wasn't given much of a choice," the boy said waspishly, not liking the attitude of the man.

"Sounds like a fascinating tale. But perhaps it would be received better in the warmth of a house." Almost tenderly, he picked up Saiko, carrying him into a house in the expectation that the boy would follow, which he did.

The man's house turned out to be a rather spartan affair, wood furnishings and cutlery, the bare minimum of drawers, the only true extravagances were a bookcase and a simple writing desk in what was probably a study, both stacked to the brim with their relative paper paraphernalia.

As the man settled into his chair, the straight-backed kind that leaves the user massaging the base of their spine and desperately trying to regain feeling in their buttocks for up to an hour later, Alec took the opportunity to read some titles from the bookcase. They had rather specific fields of interest such as 'Overcoming the Difficulties of True Immortality', 'The Breath of Cold Fire' and 'The Posthumous Autobiography of Nex the Dread'.

"Sorry for the lack of chairs; I rarely see anyone outside of town council meetings," the house's apparent owner apologised. "But I can assure you that that bit of floor is the most comfortable; it's where I do my meditation."

The patch of stone indicated was surprisingly worn, visible knee imprints in the floor which Alec did his best to match up to after he'd led Holly down flat on the cold floor, finding the position surprisingly comfortable, though he found his legs mildly dwarfed by the imprint; clearly made by an adult. "So, is Erebus going to be okay?" he asked, terrified in a way that something might happen to the necromancer, the man the closest platonic bond in his life whether he liked it or not.

The man smiled slightly, "It is my full expectation that he will make a complete recovery over the next month." There was a mild sigh, "Though it would be so much easier for all involved if he could just avoid mortal peril for a couple of years. But what really concerns me right now is your dryad."

"Do you know what's wrong with her?"

"In technical terms, no, but I understand the broader concepts behind her condition, though I'm struggling to believe there is anyone cruel enough to bind a purely magical creature with nullstone; even the paladins have banned it for being too cruel. The legal limit on null in magical restraints on anything that is intrinsically reliant on magic is five per cent; whatever Lutan used was likely in the low nineties. Any higher, and I'd imagine the metal would have been too soft to be used as a restraint of any kind." To his conscious audience's shock, he produced the collar in question, though at what point he'd obtained it, Alec couldn't remember.

"But what's wrong with her?" Alec asked timidly, looking both worried and scared, feeling a sense of responsibility for the small dryad, especially after having been overpowered by the paladin and forced to watch as they'd placed the collar on the flailing girl.

"You have to understand just how inimical null, refined or otherwise, is to magic. Were she conscious right now having it this close would result in screaming, to actually place it directly on the skin..." There was a momentary shudder, "That takes a special level of schadenfreude to consider outside of a nightmare."

"Schade-what?" the boy enquired with his childish

curiosity, a wondrous, beautiful thing after the events of the last hour.

"Schadenfreude, it's a word from a very old language, and the best I can find for what it covers, somehow sadism just lacks the panache needed to convey the malignance behind it. Where sadism is an enjoyment of causing pain to others, schadenfreude is joy at all pain a person experiences, whether you are the cause or not; it is bitter and irredeemable, the darkest of the four empathic emotions." There was a weariness to the words as well as the faint suggestion the mere subject may cause the speaker to burst into tears at a moment's notice, empathy's knife twisting deep in the man's chest as it threatened to tear out his heart.

For a short while Alec was stunned into a grimly thoughtful silence, trying to comprehend a mind with such malevolence; and, for the fortune of his sanity, failing. "But she's going to be okay, right?" he finally asked.

"I don't know, child," the man said with forlorn finality, "her mind has withdrawn into itself. If she successfully faces down whatever inner demons are currently confronting her, then yes, she will."

"Good," the boy said simply, visibly searching for something else to talk about.

"You were going to explain how you met Erebus?" The Swordsman prompted as subtly as was possible in the circumstances.

"Oh yeah, sorry. Where do you want me to start?" Alec enquired back, unsure how to begin such a narrative, the experience not one he'd previously undergone. There had been regular storytelling competitions in the winter, courtesy of the old monk;

the exercise in his words 'To expand the horizons and minds of all involved, and to allow impossible dreams to be expressed freely without fear of mockery or reprisal.' But Alec had never dared do more than listen for fear his youth would lead to the ridicule the monk insisted would not be permitted.

A sadness entered Alec's eyes, a deep pain as he realised his mentor must also have perished by Lutan's hand or order, for though both belonged to the Paladin Order, the Lord Protector would have been forced to put all to the sword to prevent reprisals from his few superiors. The thought of such a gentle soul, a man of peace, dying for a man's madness bit deep at Alec's own moral code.

"You don't have to if you don't want to," The Swordsman assured the young teen, interpreting the boy's obvious sadness as a response to his history with the necromancer rather than the tangential subject of the mentor whom he'd replaced; though, there was not even the possibility that the man could have figured out the true source of the boy's mourning short of omniscience or telepathy.

Alec settled upon a morose smile, "I don't mind," he assured the man. "But you need to bear in mind that only Erebus, Lutan and the soldier you knocked out know any of the details of what happened to my…" He paused for half a second, about to say parents before swiftly, almost imperceptibly, changing it to "village."

The eyes glinted for a moment, but not a word was said upon the matter. The Swordsman resorting to a tactful, "I see." The man bestowed a look of pure empathy upon the boy, "Then just tell me what you know, I'll receive two of the points of view in the coming weeks."

"Well, the first I knew of any of this, I'd woken alone in a cave…" Alec began hesitantly.

Over the next few hours, The Swordsman slowly teased the information out of the teen, listening with benevolent intent and Erebuseque patience and insight, encouraging when he faltered and expanding on every detail so nothing was glossed over in youthful haste.

Finally, he led back in his chair, with fingers steepled thoughtfully and mental exhaustion in his eyes. "How unfortunate," the man said simply as the light played across his tattoos, intricate spectra of red and blue dancing over his skin like children in a game of tag. "It would seem that war shall descend upon Contenmere once more… this continent has already seen so much bloodshed. Does it really need more?"

"Lutan might not survive to the edge of the forest," Alec suggested without much hope.

"Lord Protector Lutan, alas, has a pernicious habit of surviving. There's a greater chance of his succumbing to a conscience than the forest."

"Well, surely that's a possibility?" the young teen asked, though with even less hope than the last suggestion.

"He's a zealot boy. There is next to nothing he can't rationalise if it serves his purposes. Your village is proof of that," as he said those words, he looked regretful. "Sorry. That was thoughtless of me. Sometimes I forget not everyone is numb to death."

"It's okay," Alec whispered sadly, "it's his fault… I'm going to kill him."

"Don't be a fool boy, Lutan would crush you and not even have to break stride, if you got to him," the voice was firm, buoyed by authority and certainty modulated by a grim chuckle. "Worry not. By this time next year there will be a plethora of people, far more qualified, seeking his head. Even the nexomancers may get involved over a massacre of civilians."

"Nexomancers?" Alec pondered aloud, unfamiliar terminology proving an intellectual kryptonite for his curiosity, jolting him from his fugue in capricious fashion.

"Murder mages, quite literally the practitioners of the killing magics. Naturally, they have less social kudos than even necromancers. Not even other magicians like them as a rule of thumb, which is a bit harsh; some of their collaborative work has been truly groundbreaking." By the fond inflexion and positive accolade he afforded them, it was clear The Swordsman was quite prepared to wade against the current of popular opinion on this matter.

"Why would you want to study that sort of magic?" his young audience demanded, abject horror in his words and morbid fascination in his wide eyes.

"Well, the original idea for founding that particular school of study was as a preventative measure. At the time the Council of Mages, well a Council of Mages, nothing like the current one in structure or practise, had only just discovered there was an entire branch of magic whose sole purpose was the act of killing, and able to bypass or simply overwhelm the defensive countermeasures of the time. Obviously they only had two choices: To ban it or to embrace it in the hopes of finding ways to stop it. Naturally-"

"Surely it would have been simpler, safer and easier to just ban it?" Alec interjected, abruptly expressing his opinion in the thin guise of a question.

"In the short term certainly," The Swordsman continued smoothly, not showing his irritation at the interruption, "but the Council knew that it was inevitable that someone would rediscover it in time, regardless of how deeply they buried the discovery, or even if they burnt all the project's notes, materials and mages. And when the knowledge inevitably resurfaced it might not be in the hands of a small cadre of healers trying to find a permanent cure for the common cold, but a true madman, sociopathic and power-hungry… there was no way they could take that risk. And thus nexomancy was added to the growing list of schools of magical study."

"How did they know that the people they made study it wouldn't be power mad?" Alec asked, believing himself to have spotted a gaping hole in the decision.

"They didn't but they took all possible precautions: No one with a lifespan over two hundred - removing the possibility of a rogue immortal. Weekly sessions with a psychologist trained in telepathy. And if they really went rogue there was always me." The man smiled as the lecture diverted to a trip down memory lane. "It made a welcome change from exile, though how they thought they'd have enforced that without my agreement I'll never know."

"You were there?" the boy spluttered in shock, "the way you were describing it I'd thought this was ancient history."

"It was, about a thousand years by my reckoning," The Swordsman said blithely. "One doesn't have eldritch runes placed on their body for the visual appeal."

Comprehension dawned in the boy's eyes, "So those tattoos..?"

"Render me effectively immortal, yes," the man finished the thought for him with an expectant smile, easily foreseeing the next question to pass the boy's lips.

"So how old are you?"

"Technically that's a rude question," he deflected, feigning reproach at the breach in etiquette.

"Sorry," Alec apologised, looking ashamed at the immortal's reproach.

"It's alright lad, everyone does it. And between you and me," he leaned in over the time-weathered oak desk, voice lowered conspiratorially, "old enough to know Von Mori lies about her age." There was a mirth filled wink as he sat back into his chair. "Now, I'm afraid the conversation must take a turn for the serious. We need to find you a place to stay the night. Normally I'd place you in the guesthouse, but for the moment, that would be most unwise, and alas, our infirmary is going to be full with the blademaster, Erebus and the young dryad. Yes, quite the conundrum. Still, for every problem, there is a solution, except for paradoxes of course, but I digress, you'll simply have to take my spare room."

"Thank you," Alec replied politely, surprised by the generous offer. "But where will Holly stay when she recovers?"

The Swordsman laughed slightly, "I'm sure we can find more appropriate accommodation when the time comes, though your answer does you credit."

"And when Erebus recovers?"

"Then he will likely leave," the man said flatly. "Young Erebus lives for his job, if I know him at all then it will take great persuasion just to keep him here long enough for his wounds to heal properly. His obsession with duty really can be quite tiresome at times."

"Can't you just heal them with magic?" the boy asked logically.

"I'm no healer Alec," he answered with a mournful

shake of his head. "If it weren't that the knife had pierced his heart it would have been infinitely safer to leave him to bleed than have me help."

"Why is it so risky?" a confused Alec asked, unable to see how healing a wound could pose a greater danger than the wound itself.

"I don't know enough to differentiate tissue types. As it is it's a miracle I didn't accidentally grow cartilage, skin or bone over the wound, even now I don't know if I got the right muscle type, though whatever I grew it's clearly got the elasticity of muscle or it wouldn't have held… I think. To take a further risk at this point would be stupid to the point of homicide," the swordmaster explained. "He'd need a highly trained healer to properly deal with damaged heart tissue, and alas the only one in a three hundred mile radius is currently led down unconscious in the infirmary after having a dagger in his heart."

"Is there anything Erebus can't do?" the teenager asked incredulously. The necromancer a closed book to many a bibliophile of people, some of whom had been trying to access that particular volume for many years — so far, only a few had even been allowed entrance to the library, let alone located the shelf.

"Avoid daggers apparently," the immortal stated with blithe panache modulated by a guilty note.

"That's not funny."

"It wasn't meant to be. Now let me show you to your room, and then the rest of the day is yours to do with as you will," he stated with calm efficiency, getting out from behind the overloaded desk. "Follow me."

And that was that, there was no point arguing with logic and calm certainty, and no inclination on Alec's part to do so.

By some miracle of spartan decoration, the room was somehow more sparse than the rest of the house — sans study. It was devoid of windows, despite being by an outer wall, and lacked any of the other traditional methods of illumination, the chosen light source being microscopic gaps between the planks making up the outer wall, a wooden mock-up of an experiment on the nature of light, rending the entire room in a state of gloomy twilight at best, whilst the bed was actually just a sheepskin blanket, no mattress or pillow and the configuration of planks on the floor somehow elected to prove more uncomfortable than sleeping on a rock.

To further compound the misery of a hapless sleeper, as well as letting in light, the outer wall also allowed in the wind whenever it blew from the east, not in itself an exceptional occurrence despite its irksomeness if it weren't for the fact that this was the west wall.

With unusual insight, Alec compared the room to the rest of the house and reached an unusual and accurate conclusion, "This is your bedroom."

"I lied about the spare room, there isn't one," The Swordsman confessed flatly.

"Where will you sleep?"

"I won't. The perks of immortality, sleep is merely a luxury, not a necessity. Sorry for how grim the room is."

"I've slept in worse," Alec lied smoothly.

"I doubt it. Still, now you know where your room is, your time is once more your own. I'll have a proper bed brought in before evening."

The teenager frowned slightly, looking distinctly unsure of himself, "What should I do?"

"That is entirely your prerogative," the swordmaster assured, not realising that the boy's uncertainty came from a remarkable absence of hobbies on his part; Alec's free time mostly used to help on the family farm, or, in the winter, talking at length with the monk about whichever philosophical miscellanea was currently on the old man's mind.

"What can I do?" Alec rephrased, seemingly looking for some kind of catch for such a freedom.

"Whatever you want."

There was a long pause as the boy put this statement under great consideration, tasting the implications. "I enjoy reading," he concluded finally as if putting forwards a theory for peer review.

"We have a library," The Swordsman informed him, leaving the room and so not noting how Alec's eyes had lit up with childish glee as he followed behind him.

"Where?" Alec asked simply, face filled with earnest joy.

"It's the five-storey building in the centre of the village, by the tower," he directed, intending to add more, but the boy had already run past him, thundering down the stairs and out into the village.

"Youth," the immortal mused dryly with an amused shake of his head, not just pondering the teen in that statement but also the necromancer who'd brought him. Something told him the fallout from this morning was only just beginning, a flap of the proverbial butterfly's wings. He could only hope the world was prepared for the hurricane to follow.

Chapter 9

There was an exasperated growl as The Swordsman sat on the edge of Erebus' bed, having just placed the insensate Holly in the infirmary's only other permanent bed. It was a simply equipped station, about three hundred years behind modern magical healthcare; it tended to take a long time for new discoveries to make it this deep into paladin territory, let alone into the cold, dark heart of the Forest Von Mori within it. A forest one lich had foolishly remarked as being 'a minor challenge for the journeyman magician' within Von Mori's hearing, only to go missing a week later. The case had never been definitively resolved.

"You didn't half pick your times badly," The Swordsman told the unconscious form, reflexively checking the necromancer's pulse and breathing. "At the risk of being inconsiderate, couldn't you have waited two weeks to shake the foundations of society as we know it?"

"Hardly his fault," stated a voice from within the confines of Erebus' backpack.

The man looked at the bag appraisingly, a raised eyebrow sending an apparent tremor through the tattoos on his forehead. "You would be Ente; the ghost?"

"I see you took the time to interrogate the child," the ghost snapped coldly. "Well at least you're still the same; a coward through and through."

The Swordsman paused for a moment, pursing his

lips in annoyance. "I don't believe we've ever had the pleasure of being introduced," he said flatly, though he couldn't quite eliminate the growling undertones in the sentence.

"I'm Ente the Illuminator," the ghost declared. "And we have met."

With some effort, the immortal cast his mind back through the centuries, eventually narrowing the possibilities down to one. "You were the elf," he began slowly, as if waiting for confirmation, though none proved forthcoming before he ploughed onwards, "the one that insisted on sleeping outside so you could see the stars."

"I didn't expect you to remember," the ghost confessed.

"I remember a lot of things. I even remember what you said when I asked you why."

The ghost was annoyed; it was hard to loathe and despise someone who was being friendly. "I said because theirs is an eternal beauty. And you told me I was wrong." As he relived the memory Ente managed to reclaim some of his bitterness towards the immortal.

"Sorry but it's the truth. Stars die, galaxies burn, and life shall end, the cold hand of entropy will take everything and everyone given time, not out of malice, hatred or scorn but merely because that is the nature of the universe. We are but a brief flicker of a guttering candle, a moment of light in the darkness and all we can hope is to shine as brightly as possible in the time we have. All things end, live long enough and you'll see that," The Swordsman said with utter solemnity, his expression grave.

"That could prove problematic," Ente growled, and though The Swordsman could not see the glare being directed at him, he could certainly feel it.

"Only if you continue to be excessively literal," the man told him before his words took a turn to the chilly. "Now I believe you were going to tell me under what definition I am a coward."

"You could have stopped the fighting. One word and there would have been no wars."

"Yes. I could have intervened, sworn death and destruction on all who fought, and then what would you have had me do? Kill the Paladin Council of War? Destroy every lich that declared its defiance?" he asked wearily. "Diplomacy at swordpoint isn't diplomacy. People will rebel as soon as the threat is no longer present. The hardest lesson I've had to learn is that you have to let people, as a group, solve their own problems or they repeat them time and again."

"And all the people who died in the meantime?" the ghost demanded angrily.

"Would have died anyway. Death is the only inevitability, it's what you do before it that matters, present company excepted. You can't force peace and freedom on people, they have to have chosen it for themselves, made a choice to unite and rise against their oppressors. When people have bled and died for peace; then they will have an understanding of its worth."

The ghost went silent, deep in thought. The Swordsman didn't interrupt, instead seeing to his patients as best he could, cleaning out Erebus' wounds with a flannel soaked in a mixture of iodine and alcohol, the substance provoking a pained hiss even in unconsciousness. Then he turned his attention to the dryad, only to turn away when his medical repertoire fell short of the task before it.

"But you could do it. You could force a peace," the ghost stated stubbornly.

"There is a peace now. And not because one despot says so, but because it's what people wanted. You have to have patience, when the majority have had enough of something you'll be surprised how fast it ends."

"That's heartless," Ente retorted, "to let people suffer when you could change it.

The Swordsman had finally had enough. "Are you really that dense? All that would happen is they'd unite against me, then as soon as I'm out of the picture they'd return to fighting the same stupid war they'd been fighting before I turned up. You cannot force people to change, persuade perhaps but never force. To quote the young necromancer here, 'Anyone hoping to lead the revolution is clearly on the wrong side."

"But-"

The Swordsman slammed the door as he left.

As all this had been happening, Alec had found, with little difficulty, the library, its sheer scale making it obvious as it towered above all but a few buildings and then been promptly overwhelmed by it.

In his whole life he'd only ever seen eleven books, three of them philosophical discourses and a manual on the differential hardening of iron; the latter had been a gift from the old monk to the village's blacksmith, though the former had been a gift to the whole village.

There had been other books from the old man, a small book of hymns and poetry — which from the state of the spine and the ease with which the words rolled from the monk's lips Alec had always privately suspected had been his own copy — written in a delicate flowing script bordering on the calligraphic. This had been accompanied by a surprisingly matter-of-fact history of the Paladin Order; most of the spoken history was rather self-praising with heavy use of words such as noble and glorious. Alec had actually asked the monk once why there was such a disparity between the two histories.

The old man had looked up at him with benign amusement and said without trace of irony, "Because stories that simply tell people what happened are nowhere near as interesting as ones where great heroes triumph against foul creatures and cruel villains. True isn't necessarily interesting."

Of course, now he was beginning to doubt elements of even the matter of fact paladin version of history.

The other two volumes the monk had donated could only be described as odd. One had been a two thousand page manual on how to fold paper into the shapes of animals, whilst the remaining volume had been about a magical creature that looked like a humanoid fox known as a kitsune, rarely found outside of the eastern continent of Belsinan, many thousands of miles from Contenmere. The creatures were apparently masters of trickery and illusion who delighted in one-upmanship upon the other races, sometimes fatally so.

Of the three books not provided by the benevolent sage, two had been simple and outdated by several decades, farmers' almanacs, but the final tome had been a marvel. A crumbling dictionary, inks fading in places and some pages missing entirely, a lack of paper, papyrus or vellum in the village had prevented the attempts of repair upon it, but nonetheless, it had been an invaluable tool for both Adis and the monk which had led to unusual levels of literacy amongst the people of the village.

Thus the library was a small Renaissance in itself to

young Alec, his eyes wide with glorious wonder at the seemingly endless array of shelves, each shelf nearing three metres in height and a third that in width, every single one filled with compendiums, tomes and volumes, some barely thicker than a child's smallest finger whilst the largest almost required two men to carry.

Unbeknownst to Alec, the Seruatis library was amongst the largest available to man, rivalled only by the Citadel's collection, some of the magical institutions, two private collections and most of the elven libraries — by simple virtue of being older.

To the people of Seruatis there was a certain level of ambivalence to the library. Though from a rational perspective, it was inevitable; it was a tool, a useful tool but a tool nonetheless. The mystique of boundless knowledge loses its appeal to most people when they live with it every single day of their lives.

To Alec, there was no such apathy or complacence. To him, the library was beauty itself and yet posed a great question; where to start?

"Can I help?" enquired the sharp voice of the librarian from beside him, the woman moving soundlessly on the auburn carpet, her choice of garb an overcoat topped with a large hood.

The teen turned quickly, startled, and stopped still as a statue as he beheld his first gorgon; unlike the majority of people to find themselves doing so, Alec actually would have the opportunity to do so more than once. This was not due to any special quality bestowed upon him, nor the incredible foresight and protection provided by Erebus, but great caution on the part of the gorgon in question.

"Why are you wearing a mask?" Alec addressed the

obvious question, ignorance of the most innocent kind allowing him to address boldly a topic that the more well informed would treat with utmost delicacy if they dared broach it at all.

The gorgon smiled behind the eyeless iron mask, finding the forthright approach rather refreshing. "It's so I don't accidentally hurt people."

Most people would have been tempted to ask why, Alec, channelling Erebusesque perception, did not, opting for the more useful "How?", picking up on the subtle tones of remorse in the gorgon's voice.

"You've never heard of a gorgon have you?" the gorgon stated, a whole conversation taking place in the subtext.

"No," Alec professed, looking down, embarrassed at his own ignorance.

Another smirk from the woman, unseen by the world in general from behind the iron facsimile of her own visage. "We're a rather tragic species I'm afraid, evolution's little joke, or the victims of a mad goddess if you believe the legends," she declared in a tone that clearly showed that such beliefs were purest poppycock in her opinion. Despite the self-pitying nature of the words, there was nothing but confidence and surety of self in her stance.

"Why tragic? I mean how can being a gorgon be so bad?"

"Anyone who looks directly upon my face turns into stone," she said morosely, not excessively enthusiastic in her ability to turn a flesh and blood being into a marmoreal statue.

The teenager looked conflicted for a moment, now aware that he had, metaphorically, been tap-dancing on a minefield in terms of the delicacy of the subject matter. To his credit, he did not once seem afraid of her, perhaps believing in the natural altruism of all people, though having met Lutan, this was unlikely. Thus an observer would simply conclude that he had a sufficiently deft mind to realise the mask was a deliberate attempt to shield the likes of him from harm, at great personal expense, and at a speed faster than his instincts of self-preservation. All this resolved into a single sentence, apologetic to the point of confession, "Sorry if I was insensitive."

There was a hissed bark of laughter from the gorgon. "Don't apologise for something you couldn't have known."

"Um…" Alec began hesitantly, treading with far greater care now, "How do you know where you're going with that mask on?"

"Years of practise and I've got an exceptional sense of hearing, so I don't bump into anyone."

"Oh. Do you miss being able to see?"

"I can still see, I just can't remove the mask while the library has people in it. Late at night, I like to read some of the more fragile texts and copy them out so age doesn't cause a permanent end to them."

"You work here?" the boy asked, intrigued about the library's day-to-day runnings.

"Live here in fact. I've a room on the top floor. Now, what can I do for you?" the masked gorgon rephrased her initial question.

"Well, there's just so many books…" Alec began, only to be met by the harsh, sibilant chuckle from earlier.

"That you can't fathom where to begin," she finished for him, the sheer rapidity of the intervention indicating the frequency of the problem. "Well considering your apparent interest in my people… I can recommend some of the more accurate and impartial texts on gorgons, as well as a number on cockatrice and the exceedingly rare catoblepas." The librarian began to walk away with surprising speed, clearly not bluffing on her awareness of her surroundings, and upon reaching the shelves, began to pluck books from them seemingly at random.

"What's a catoblepas?" her young companion asked, whilst attempting, without success, minimal or otherwise, to sneak a glance at the titles.

In response she handed him a book, rather helpfully named Catoblepas. It was a surprisingly slim volume, soon accompanied, without prompting or enquiry, by a rather larger one about cockatrice. Then, after a considerable walk down the aisles to a section marked with a reasonably obtrusive gilded G. That the librarian knew this spoke volumes on her memory, though not as much as on her ability to unerringly remove the correct tome on the first attempt.

On the subject of gorgons, five volumes were plucked out in quick succession before just as quickly being offloaded into Alec's arms.

"Find yourself a desk and get reading," the gorgon ordered, preparing to disappear back into whatever shadowy recesses librarians inhabit when people aren't being either louder than a whisper, seeking advice or wishing to take a book out of the library. "Come find me when you've finished them all."

And with that parting instruction, she vanished amongst the aisles, leaving Alec in a pile of books large enough to obscure most of his vision and utterly lost amongst the shelves, though, by the time tested technique of wandering until finding one's goal, he did eventually find a desk and so settled down to read.

Back in the infirmary, The Swordsman was watching the unconscious Saiko with an expression that was part respect for a fellow master of their craft, part amusement, a slight dab of surprise and the merest hint of awe.

Piled up in the chair beside him was Saiko's personal armoury, the collection worryingly large and the source of the man's amusement, which while on the machinations of his patient's mind was not at his expense.

Despite an excessive number of centuries to his names, The Swordsman had never met anyone quite so well-armed.

He'd tried to be as unintrusive as possible in the circumstances, a matter only assisted by the four layers of clothing — technically, at least two could be counted as armour — each with their own caveat of violent intent. Despite the indignity of being stripped of weapons and clothing, though once it proved harmless, the latter had been reapplied, it was merely something that had to be done. Allowing a man with a violent potential greater than some assassins he'd known, to walk around armed would be foolish to the extreme.

First, he'd removed the swords, two slim arming swords strapped across Saiko's back, then the falchion's empty scabbard, idly noting the length of garrotte wire threaded into the belt it was attached to as well as resolving to pick the sword back up as soon as he had a moment's peace; he had a hunch about that sword.

Then there had been the cloak, weighted in just the right places to make it throwable as an impromptu net or surprise flail.

The cloak had actually been a pleasant surprise. The

many-hued dark grey cloth — no one who actually understood stealth would use black — spoke of both a certain fastidiousness to detail and a cunning originality, a rare combination in The Swordsman's experience. It also helped that the weave of cloth in question had been known to, if not stop arrows, then certainly slow them significantly, presumably reducing anything short of the chainmail punching bodkin, or a crossbow quarrel, to a manageable trifle for the armour two layers further in. Of course, with the advent of the needle bodkin, even plate steel was no longer entirely safe. However, the traditional broadhead arrow was still the archer's favourite, for, despite its parlous lack of armour penetration, it still had the pertinent perquisite of inflicting wounds that were significantly more likely to prove fatal.

The first layer of death, and prevention thereof, removed had revealed two bandoleers of throwing knives, overlapping across Saiko's chest; he hadn't even needed to remove them to know each would be balanced to perfection. Two knives in each bandoleer had proven worth a closer inspection, one — from the distinctive black tarnishing — was a silver alloy or at least silver-coated yet, by some miracle of the smith's art, actually managed to keep an edge. A werewolf killer's weapon.

It had not been quite as easy to identify the knife's nature as he was used to; the steel blades had all the gleam of granite on a dark night. The weapons of a true assassin rather than someone who merely wished to look the part. An affectation of machismo that proved all too common and oft all too fatal for the braggart involved.

The other knife of note was made of wood, presumably because the throwing stake had proven a complete failure when subjected to such peevish and petty concepts as aerodynamics, and so vampire hunters, wise enough to realise that what you wanted most of all when dealing with something strong enough to pull off your limbs was distance and thus had, unless of exceptional aim, been forced to make do with wooden-headed arrows and quarrels, as well as throwing knives that would go *thwack!* rather than *clang!* if they missed.

The robes the bandoleers were fastened around belayed the stealthy themes indicated thus far. The fabric was dyed — well likely dyed — the familiar reddish-brown of dried blood, presumably to conceal stains of such a nature. It was a lighter fabric than the cloak, perhaps a particularly dense wool or similar. Whatever it was it proved to have a worrying selection of objects, from a set of lockpicks to smoke bombs to actual bombs to a pair of stilettos sown into the lining with painstaking care. Each joined the growing pile alongside the robe itself, revealing the armour it was intended to hide.

The Swordsman's opinion of the man rose slightly further again as yet another facet of subterfuge was revealed; the thick cloak and wool robe hiding the armour quite masterfully, such that the first a prospective killer might know of it would be when their blade was turned aside, likely bringing them within reach of Saiko's own exceptional sword-arm and whatever weapon currently attached to the end of it. Lies within lies within clothing… he couldn't help but wonder how such a man had come to be in the service of Lutan.

The armour was quite interesting and, if his deductions were correct, of his patient's own design. A series of interlocking titanium plates suspended and woven into a spider silk mesh.

The existence of spider silk mesh was a subject of much contention among soldiers, mages and scholars alike.

For a considerable amount of time magicians had been aware that spider silk was, ounce for ounce, significantly stronger than the finest steel. So when asked, as a sign of increasing paladin/magician cooperation, to find a way to cheaply improve the quality of basic armour — which from a paladin point of view was anything not containing nullstone — one particularly ingenious specimen had suggested they try to mass-produce the stuff.

They had first tried doing it safely by using magic to modify goats in such a way as to produce it in their milk, but when the volume had proved insufficient, corners had been cut. Another team working on the project had simply made the spiders grow to excessive size, finally settling on an arachnid whose average dimensions and mass was somewhere between a rhinoceros and a small elephant.

Predictably it had collapsed under its own weight and suffocated. Alas, the team had proven to possess a dangerous combination of determination and poor foresight. So with predictable foolhardiness, instead of abandoning the venture as a doomed experiment, they began again, using magic where biology rebelled.

Miraculously this approach not only worked but proved to have its own failsafe as the spells supporting the arachnids, both figuratively and literally — had to be renewed every three days. Despite some accidents, though rarely fatal as antivenom was usually on hand, the yield of spider silk was quite high, and after the use of said silk to create some very thick protective gloves, so was the yield of venom.

There is an old expression 'from the ridiculous to the sublime' used as an attempt to convey that the sheer level of unthinking, brazenly stupid decision making is not describable by mortal man, rendering the observer into a state of near awe at the failure to foresee the consequences.

In this case, with demand increasing exponentially, one biomancer, a Professor Munsento, decided to remove the failsafe by making the arachnids intrinsically magical and thus sustaining the spells themselves. The one trace of intelligence in this decision was that he didn't release the genetically modified creature into the ecosystem on the basis that a good lawyer could deal with any problems this might cause…

Naturally, the spiders escaped and, without the failsafe, prospered, another ever-present danger in a world already full of them. By now, the arach had infested forest, jungle, desert and plain, with only the frozen south and tundra of the north being spared. And there were rumours that Munsento had survived, desperately devoting his life to fixing his mistakes; one particularly prolific rumour said that he'd travelled the world in search of natural predators of web-building spiders and enlarged them similarly, though the rumour was typically dismissed on the basis that no one could be that stupid.

Fast forward three hundred years and the project, consequences aside, had been highly successful in its initial aims and thus increasing amounts of armour were, instead of leather and iron, made of spider silk, light as a feather and harder than steel and thus in the case of Saiko's armour raised mild questions as to why he'd even bothered with titanium plates. In fact, to a suspicious kind of mind, one might speculate that the underside of such plates might have protective runes carved into them whilst carefully concealing the presence of such from his magic-hating employer.

The Swordsman elected not to check on the basis that it would be like smashing a fine statue to examine the stone's composition.

Another thing revealed by the removal of the bloody robe were the knives, one strapped parallel to the bottom of each leg and forearm. The latter of which had proved decisive in its nullification of the late Sir Bareth the previous day.

The fourth layer contained no armour at all, a mere silk body sleeve with some runes of cooling sewn into the fabric. The Swordsman could sympathise, without a light soft layer beneath it, such armour could chafe awfully and that many layers would be unpleasantly warm in the heart of winter let alone on the cusp as they were now.

After a cursory patdown to ensure that no weapons were left that were larger than a fingernail, The Swordsman left it at that, at least allowing the man his modesty, before he sat down in his chair to muse quietly on the sheer number of weapons. Each one purposeful and logically placed and yet on consideration with all the other weapons; excessive.

He'd have to think about this, but something told him that the potential before him was worth nurturing. Saiko was an exceptional fighter, for an amateur.

As he carefully retraced his steps, Lutan could not help but smile, almost whistling as he walked, nearly half a decade of careful, meticulous planning finally at fruition. There were loose ends to tie up and lies to tell, but for now, he just basked in the glow of success. It had taken nearly half his life, but the traitor Erebus was dead at long last. It was joyous to finally be able to take the first step towards letting go of his hate.

He'd imagined killing the necromancer a thousand thousand times, watching the life drain from that cold, heartless gaze.

There was a slight crunch as the heavily armoured paladin proved too great a weight for one dryad's skull, her body several yards away, Lutan walked on unperturbed; it merely served the foolish creatures right for interfering with his holy mission.

They'd hidden that from him. The very reason the Paladin Order had been founded. But he'd found it; when the betrayal grew too much to bear, he'd thrown himself into his training, and, recognising another who saw necromancers for the spawn of darkness they truly were, the Keepers of the Divine had accepted him into their ranks.

Even they had betrayed him in the end; when he'd suggested they step out of the shadows, they'd died like traitors too… pleading. A small part of him felt disgust at that; Erebus would never have begged for his life.

It would take him five days to escape the forest, including a day for him to tend to his wounds. It didn't matter; he had food and water enough for the journey, more than enough if he scavenged off the corpses of his erstwhile servants, and, providing he followed the carnage, not a dryad alive to try and stop him.

He'd have to organise a party of lumberjacks when he got home, a lesson to dryadkind on what happened when you crossed the Paladin Order. Without Von Mori, any defence would be hopelessly haphazard.

Of course, explaining what he'd done to Von Mori would be difficult, but already an excuse was forming, one that would be more palatable to the council than 'She got in my way.'

Lutan smiled darkly. Von Mori had been a thorn in the side of the Paladin Order for time immemorial, resisting all attempts to colonise within her borders; this wasn't strictly true, but to Lutan, it was true enough, and without the forest dryad's meddling, things would be changing shortly. The council might be hard to convince, but the paladin knew several business interests who would be extremely grateful.

Ahead of him a dryad waited, visibly trembling in fear as she stood amongst the corpses of her neighbours.

The Lord Protector was not a fool; no matter how distorted his worldview, stupidity was not an accolade that could be fairly lain at his feet.

Despite disagreements, in later years, he'd had a good teacher in the deductive process. Thus rather than casually beheading the creature as he walked past, he stopped, curious what message the forest considered important enough to sacrifice another dryad.

"Speak creature," Lutan commanded, causing the dryad to jump, raw terror plain in her hazel eyes, her gaze remaining fixated upon the sword at his hip.

"L-L-Lady Yew s-sends a message," the tree spirit stammered, "the-the necromancer still lives."

Lutan froze in midstep before drawing his sword upon the wretched creature, the poor girl falling over in her desperate haste to get away, scrabbling backwards in the blood-soaked dirt. She stopped as the tip of Lutan's broadsword came to rest casually beneath her chin, the dryad wincing where the nullstone alloy left burns from the contact with the bark hued flesh. "Now, let's have a little detail, shall we?"

"I-I don't know," she almost begged, "Lady Yew saw. That's all I know, I swear."

Lutan believed her, and so he slowly removed the sword from beneath her chin.

The dryad seemed to collapse with relief, and then Lutan's sword took her head off.

Dispassionately Lutan watched the light fade from her hazel eyes before wiping the blade clean on the corpse's clothes and resheathing it. It hadn't been anything personal; she'd merely ceased to be useful.

For scant seconds he considered storming or sneaking into Circulus Seruatis on his own to finish what he'd started. But a moment of thought was all he needed to rule out that idea; there were too many variables, too many unknown quantities and worst of all, too many unpleasant known quantities. After all, to put things in perspective, a plan years in the making, where nearly everything had been accounted for, had all but failed in the face of a few unknown details. A plan which had accounted for the village, for Erebus, for The Swordsman, even for Von Mori herself — ironically, what had seemed the most dangerous part was the only one piece of the plan to go off without a hitch.

And there was always the, rather likely, chance that this 'Lady Yew' was lying.

Having made up his mind, Lutan continued his route back to what he considered civilisation.

He would rest, rearm, and then, and only then, he would return.

Chapter 10

Twenty-six years ago…

The fires of the village illuminated the rising magician, a lone figure in crimson arrayed against a vast army. In the pale light of morning, the true scale of a single night of madness would become clear: This was not the only place to burn tonight.

Yet the army did not move as soulless eyes watched and waited for the order which would see them reduced to ash, and they did nothing. They didn't even breathe.

In the heart of the village, one building withstood the onslaught of the flames, as if by some miracle mere straw, thatch and wood were withstanding a heat which had reduced stone and metal to a flowing glowing liquid, a phenomenon which proved only mildly commentable to the six people sheltered within.

"Looking good Dalash," commented a figure in a black robe and hood, looking up at the woman in red who was sat crosslegged on a bale of slowly smoking hay at the very top of the hayloft. The woman did not respond, too deep in the threads of magic to hear the man, who shrugged amiably, returning to his conversation with his companions. "So has your son decided which branch of magic he wishes to pursue, Anton?"

Of the other four, two were also dressed in the traditional mage's garb, each denoting a different order by colour. One, the speaker, the eternal black of a necromancer. The second, young Dalash, the scorching red of a fire mage, a pyromancer. A third in the humble, drab white of a healer. And the fourth was shrouded in shadow, literally clothed in her own power.

Shadowmancers had had to claw their names way out of the dirt, perhaps harder than necromancers and, even necromancers would admit, less deservedly so.

Now they wore their power blatantly, a small shield of bravado, as if daring the world to take offence; usually, it didn't.

There was nothing extraordinary about this in itself; mages travelling together was a tradition almost as old as magic itself. Travelling with paladins, on the other hand, was, even now, exceptional.

The two paladin-knights were resplendent in finest steel, foregoing nullstone so their colleagues could work safely. In place of the trusted null, an intricate filigree of runes were carved into the metal, harkening back to an era where the precious rock had not been refined properly and even through the soot and ash coating it, the magic shone like an aquamarine candle, seemingly hovering on the surface rather than in the runes themselves.

From within his helmet Anton smiled, "The boy wants to follow in your footsteps old friend."

The man in the black robes chuckled lightly, "How's the rest of the family taking it?"

"Oh they've threatened to disown him; and me. Bollocks to the lot of them I say, it's his life, his choice."

"And your opinion old friend?" came the quiet prompt.

"I can't say I'm entirely pleased…" the paladin

confessed, "I was hoping he'd pick something safer, like healing or geomancy, I know you do your best, but you still have a three per cent attrition rate in the first year alone."

"I'll make sure he's got a tutor of some sort. Something powerful," the necromancer assured his ancient enemy; and close friend.

"Thank you. Now I assume you've some sort of plan to deal with our fiery friend outside?" Anton said, with complete certainty, this was the case.

"Dalash is dealing with it now," the necromancer said with a smile. "Though if this takes much longer I'll have the troops lend a hand so she can rest for a few minutes."

"You've an army of a thousand undead warriors, surely you can do better than a few minutes?" the paladin declared incredulously.

"Not really. The temperature outside is sufficient to melt steel, bone would be little deterrent I'm afraid," the robed figure explained.

"So again; what's the plan?" he demanded.

"To be patient."

"Do you have to be this cryptic all the time? Susan, what is he talking about?" the paladin snapped though there was no longer any malice in it after all these years.

The shadowmancer smiled, lowering her hood. "It's a battle of attrition. Standard duel tactic amongst the more powerful magicians, not that anyone would know these days with the bans on duelling. To maintain these sorts of temperatures and nullify them over a long period of time is beyond the capacity of any human mage. And so any magical artefacts in their possession are currently being drained of their reserves."

"Sounds risky, what if his reserves are greater than

Dalash's?" this from Karatas, the other paladin in their small group, the man barely out of his teens.

"Unlikely," the necromancer interjected, "Dalash is one of the most powerful pyromancers produced by the Academy Vulcanus in the last four decades, and the reserves she carries are significant, and should her reserves be insufficient I will lend my own strength to hers, I know enough of pyromancy to be of assistance."

"Surely this would be safer if Susan got the rest of us out of here?" this from the healer.

"No! So much magic in one place, They will be swarming all over it. We would be offering ourselves on a platter to Them," Susan's voice quivered with dread, the capital T in 'They' and 'Them' quite audible for those with the ears for it.

"Who are 'They'?" demanded Karatas suspiciously.

"We don't- " Susan began, hurt in her voice over this apparent distrust.

"You are asking for one of shadowmancy's greatest secrets," the necromancer said quietly, with dark solemnity. "It would be like me asking you about the seraphim population for example."

The horrified gasp was highly informative. He'd struck a nerve.

"Then how do you know of it?" Anton asked, apparently entirely unphased by this casual dropping of a paladin secret; in fact, there was almost a hint of resignation to the voice, as if such blatant disregard for secrecy was commonplace.

"I saved a man's life. He repaid the life debt with knowledge. And I studied under a shadowmancer for ten years, or umbramancer as it called it," the black-robed man said matter-of-factly.

"So what should we do in the meantime?" the healer asked, trying to defuse the situation.

There was a mutual glance up to the top of the hayloft where Dalash was sweating profusely. The occasional wisp of smoke rising from the hay.

"Is she as good as old Tyrone?" Susan asked quietly, nerves showing.

"Tyrone?" this from Karatas.

It was Anton who answered, the rest looking a tad too lost in miserable reminiscence to reply, "He was the pyromancer with us before Dalash. A good man."

There was a great finality to the words as if they had closed the matter of the mage's character in its entirety.

"What happened to him?" Karatas pressed, not seeming to be able to take a hint.

"He was overpowered using his own element. A rogue elemental," the other paladin replied mournfully. "The poor fool… the poor brave fool."

"Brave? More like stupid," Karatas exclaimed.

The necromancer caught Anton's punch deftly and calmly before it could connect with the younger paladin's face. "It's not his fault old friend. Envy the child his naivety," he said, old eyes gazing imploringly at his friend even as he caught Karatas' own strike, hand closing a vice-grip around the man's fist.

"How dare you mock me, magician?" Karatas spat, imbuing 'magician' with all the properties of an expletive as he swung with the other hand.

Blood arced out in a spray of crimson droplets from beneath the necromancer's hood as the mailed fist split his nose. With an expression of shock he released Anton's fist, squeezing hard on Karatas' hand with the intent of crushing the bones within it. For a moment it looked like he'd succeed as the metal visibly deformed in the uncompromising vice of the necromancer's grip, perfect impressions of his fingerprints stamped into the metal, almost a quarter of an inch deep, the steel conforming to the inexorable pressure. Against mere metal he would likely have succeeded, but before he could inflict a maiming injury upon his errant ally the armour's enchantments kicked in, a sheen of magical energy forming on the surface, the insubstantial substance proving utterly incompressible to the magically enhanced strength of the mage.

A wiser man might realise the point being made, but Karatas was young and quick of temper, a combination of factors to which escalation was a natural consequence.

As his dagger left the sheathe on his belt, the younger paladin felt a gentle prick under his left armpit as a white-robed arm pulled him into a vicious headlock. "I wouldn't try it if I were you," assured a low voice just behind his ear. "My blade is maybe half a centimetre from the artery supplying blood to your left arm. No, don't move, my hand might slip and then you'd bleed out in just over a minute. We wouldn't want that."

The paladin froze, hardly daring to breathe. His eyes glanced at his comrades-in-arms. None of them seemed inclined to help; in fact, amusement would best describe what little expression was visible beneath hoods and helm. Gathering his courage he spoke quietly to his captor, his voice little more than a croak, "You can't kill me, you're a healer. It's against your oath."

"That could be the case, yes, but are you willing to stake your life that I'm a man of my word. Afterall I distinctly recall you saying… now what was it? Ah I remember…" The voice was purest poison, sweet and lethal, dripping slowly as it suffused towards the small set of synapses marked 'Primal Terror'.

"I'm sorry, I didn't mean-" he half-pleaded only to be cut off as the healer continued in a perfect imitation of Karatas' hateful baritone growl. "Mages, what do they know about oaths? How can you trust a man who can weave lies into reality itself?"

Karatas swallowed nervously, trying not to struggle as fear, cold as ice, seemed to wrap around his spine. Wide-eyed gaze noting the way his other companions were studiously ignoring the confrontation. The necromancer having gone so far as to ascend to the top of the hayloft to assist the struggling Dalash; a hurried, whispered conversation taking place in the rafters as the two mages shared the mental strain of neutralising the flames cascading down upon their oh so very flammable shelter as their comrades squabbled below.

Back at ground level, Anton was watching what was, at this point, essentially a much-needed lesson in humility and understanding.

The tension had been slowly building since the young Karatas had been foisted upon the squad after his predecessor had been the unfortunate recipient of a lifetime's supply of chimaera venom, though, in this instance, the lifetime in question was a scant fifteen seconds.

Apparently, some administrative bigwig had decided to assign the rookie, fresh out of training, to a squad of professional killers on the basis it would 'smooth the rough edges' which everyone — bar the almost as recent if nowhere near as inexperienced Dalash — had instantly rewritten those four words into 'hopefully he'll get killed' within the comfort of their own heads.

Somehow the young knight had annoyed someone

in authority within the Paladin Order. This was the only reason they had tolerated his nonsense for so long, though now, after three months of clashing and no sign of the maverick spirit they'd envisaged, it appeared one of them had finally run out of patience.

Despite this apparent abandonment, each member of the group, beneath their façade of nonchalance, was, in fact, preparing to leap to the defence of the indoctrinated fool should Dwight take things too far. Even to the death of their friend if necessary for each knew the healer's past and, though they entrusted him daily with their lives, each had sworn an oath upon something held dear, that should the former Dread Healer ever fall from the path of redemption then his death would be the result. Killing paladins for being an annoyance would be a significant step off of that path, no matter that each had at some point daydreamed of gently sliding a long dagger up between his ribs.

Yes, they would defend him, and then when whatever bloodshed had run its course, they would cut him off as if they had never known him, except perhaps to poison his career. Dwight, for his many faults and irredeemable past, was their friend and brother in hardship, and they did not kill friends lightly.

And so guarded expressions watched as the lives of two men hung in the balance. Fates to be decided by the words and deeds of the next few minutes while above them three minds duelled at the speed of thought, foregoing the drama of the wizard's duels of legend, just action and reaction as magic twisted and warped under implacable wills and immense powers.

Dalash was a master pyromancer despite the doubts of her comrades. She had been handpicked from the Academy Vulcanus, and even the much-missed Tyrone had lacked her raw power and potential. The grizzled veteran had been a master of all the forms of fire and heat, a technician not a powerhouse but despite her strength, and even with the necromancer's willpower alongside her, Dalash was losing as the improbable happened, for as her power waned, her resources drained; rubies of unnaturally fiery lustre dimmed, lesser gemstones shattered and runes warped and yet the pyromancer outside did not weaken, his magic only waxing, stronger, more uncontrolled.

The young woman sent a panicked glance towards her black-robed colleague as realisation dawned only to see calm determination in his passive gaze.

"I feel it too. Go tell Susan it is time to leave. I will hold it for now," the voice was so terribly calm.

"But-"

"No buts child, the Vulcanus has rather failed in its duties here. We must simply limit the damage until the ascension is complete." There was a mirthless chuckle. "Duty unto death. Now go tell them to stop bickering and pack their things back up. I have years enough to spend to buy the time needed."

Slowly Dalash stood up, the young woman stretching stiff muscles before hopping down to ground level.

While this had been occurring, the situation with Karatas had failed to resolve, the healer still holding the paladin at knifepoint. The rookie wasn't helping his case either as he attempted to struggle free, though, despite his threats, Dwight had not driven home the knife. He had wanted the man frightened and repentant rather than dead, and thus, as soon as Dalash's feet had hit the floor, he pushed the paladin away, the blade disappearing back into the recesses of his robe.

"Trouble Dalash?" the tone was sincere, if perhaps a touch hopeful that trouble would indeed be the case.

"Too much trouble," she admitted, slightly unsteady on her feet. "Our out-of-control- magician is half an hour away from being a full-blown elemental."

Dwight winced, "Heads are going to roll for this one."

Susan nodded in agreement, "Over three hundred dead because some desk-jockey lost track of the paperwork."

Anton shook his head, "A touch harsh, you try tracking a single tick in a ledger, especially when some mages can take centuries to achieve that level of understanding of their element."

"Susan's right," this from Dalash, the young woman making no attempt to defend her order. "There are two ways to ascend to embodying an element; by understanding it utterly or by raw power. We don't bother tracking understanding, no point; they tend to ascend peacefully, and there's no practical way to track it. Power on the hand tends to be highly volatile, in fire mages particularly, mirroring the nature of fire, and with no idea of how to control what's happening to them. Those people we do keep a studious track of. If one wasn't recalled to the Vulcanus in time then Susan's right, heads will roll. Though there's another worry, this would make two elemental ascendances missed in under a year, I know two's just a coincidence, but that's a hell of a coincidence."

"So what did the cantankerous old git have to say?" Anton asked fondly, tone belaying the viciousness of the words themselves.

"He wants us to evacuate-"

"No way! No way at all!" Susan declared angrily. "You're asking me to commit suicide."

Dalash folded her arms, "Let me phrase this another way, you can stay here and definitely die, or try and leave and only probably die."

The shadow mage frowned thoughtfully, genuinely mulling over her options. "You're sure there's no way we can fight our way out?"

"None that involves any of us still breathing at the end of it and while I'll admit maybe two of us would consider that a mere inconvenience neither of them are us, so it's up to you to decide," the pyromancer said flatly before frowning. "The fire's stopped."

"Merely redirected I'm afraid," the necromancer informed them, smiling as they all went for their weapons. Not one of them had seen or heard him move. "My army is engaging him, I predict we have maybe five minutes until they have been reduced to ash unless one of the archers gets very, very lucky."

"We could always join them, take advantage of the distraction to strike." Surprisingly Karatas' suggestion was met with nods of approval.

"There's no point," the man in black said flatly. "He's holding a flare sphere hot enough to vaporise steel from a foot away and there's some sort of spell deflection as an outer shield. I've been throwing air blades at him for over a minute, nothing's so much as scratched it. On a really good day we might be able to punch through together, but frankly we backed the wrong strategy by trying to tire him and now two of us are exhausted," the necromancer stated calmly. "Now Susan, it's now or never."

All eyes went to the trembling woman as she stood tall, clenching her fists so tight her skin turned white as fresh snow as she tried to suppress the tremors of fear trying to course through her frail form.

"Safe journey my friend," the necromancer said solemnly yet warmly. "One way or another we'll be seeing each other soon." Similar comments were expressed by the rest of the team, even Karatas managing a convincing goodbye.

Susan smiled morosely, "See you all soon." And then she stepped into one of the deeper shadows, somehow stepping in a direction not normally available to mortal man, disappearing as she passed across the threshold of darkness.

Moments later she emerged, screaming soundlessly as she collapsed to her knees; her entire form – clothes, skin and even eyes – seemed to be coated in tar, yet not the meagrest glimmer of light escaped the surface while the flesh seemed to dissolve before their eyes, exposing muscle and then the bone beneath. Three recoiled in primal terror, the necromancer, however, drew a knife from within the recesses of his sleeve yet was too slow as in a single smooth motion Karatas stepped forwards, drawing his sword to cleave Susan's head from her shoulders, the skull rolling into a corner to dissolve quietly.

Silence reigned as they watched their erstwhile comrade dissipate into nothingness.

Karatas started as a hand was placed gently on his arm, nearly spitting the necromancer upon his blade out of sheer nerves.

"That was a brave thing you did," he said simply, stepping back away with a respectful nod. "Now it would seem our options are but one. With escape denied us there is nought we can do but fight unto our last." Calmly he shook each of them by the hand, "My friends, it has been a pleasure."

"Likewise," Anton enthused warmly. "And that applies to the rest of you as well."

Similar comments abounded until silence descended; there wasn't time to say all they would wish, so each restrained themselves to quiet farewells.

"Shall we?" the necromancer enquired, unbarring the wooden double doors and pushing them open, proceeding calmly outside. Already the fighting was beginning to conclude as the last of the skeletal horde met a final fiery death.

The others followed, weapons held ready. Anton moved carefully in front of his colleague, slightly to the right of the necromancer so he could shield the man without blocking his shot. The movement was utterly subconscious, born of years of working together.

The sun may have set hours before but the sky seemed as bright as a clear summer noon, the pyromancer making a passable alternative to the great celestial orb.

"We haven't got long until the ascension peaks," Anton observed calmly as the mage returned his deranged attention back upon them, fire quite literally in his eyes as his own inferno began to consume the man as the final stages of his ascension unfolded.

The paladin was right, his black-robed friend concluded, in minutes they would be dealing not with a man but an elemental. Magic given physical form.

And then they would die.

Chapter 11

It had been two days since Alec had arrived in Circulus Seruatis, and he'd spent nearly all of it in the library devouring text after text under Dus' watchful eye.

To the teen it had been an enlightening experience. The reading had been tough going at first, to the point the gorgon had quickly grown tired of having to explain any words the boy had never come across before. Not that she would change it for the world.

The boy was a reminder of kinder times, times when she'd been able to walk free and safe. When her children had been alive.

Alec, for his part, had been fascinated by what he'd learnt of the histories and abilities of the three species of 'stone gazer'.

The catoblepas, for example, were, many, many generations ago, the most common of the stone gazers, the almost cattle-like reptile a common sight in rocky areas, as were the statues of people who saw them.

There had been attempts to domesticate and farm the deadly creatures, blindfolding them so they couldn't turn people into nothing more than a decorative lawn feature.

Predictably it had gone terribly wrong, catoblepas going berserk when deprived of the sense of sight.

Eventually, humanity had, according to the surviving memoirs, got tired of its irksome neighbours and started possibly the most cautious and well-planned cull in history requiring years of training on how to fight blindfolded culminating in thousands of deaths, both in training and on the field of battle itself.

Ultimately this crusade was successful, driving the catoblepas extinct in many regions. The bizarre reptiles had, however, undergone something of a resurgence in recent years, finally domesticated under the watchful, and no less dangerous, gaze of the gorgons. Whole herds now existing in their colonies in the Kholteph mountains — a mountain range the paladin-born Alec had never heard of before.

Gorgons were a much more interesting topic. Many books unable to agree on a cohesive history for the species, all agreed they were far more recent to Contenmere than either of the other two and, that whilst there were no recorded earlier sightings on the other continents, the author in question had had the honesty to point out the problems inherent to gorgon sightings, as well as, that both of the adjacent continents Byzale and Belsinan, were more than sufficiently large to lose an entire civilisation without any real effort at all.

Thus the search for a two-hundred-thousand-year-old statue of truly exceptional quality continued, albeit with ever decreasing quantities of hope.

Other theories were both more fantastical yet more likely. Some claimed they were the shock result of an early paladin experiment with nullstone, others that it was a necromancer attempt to bypass the same.

The one theory universally decried as lunacy, yet included by Dus all the same, was that, way back in the mists of time, a savage goddess, mad with power, did curse one of her own priestesses over a perceived slight, making it so that for all eternity the young woman would never again be able to gaze upon the face of another living being.

For an encore, and perhaps to set the grounds for an insanity plea, for surely there could be no other reason for the goddess to then go and curse the priestess' two sisters to the same fate.

According to the book, such was the goddess' power that despite five decades of toil, the mages of the time were unable to break the curse, many being struck down for their perceived hubris.

Whatever the gorgons knew as the truth of their true origins, they appeared to be keeping it to themselves.

Dus herself had been equally unforthcoming when Alec had asked her which theory was true. The gorgon had merely laughed, "All guesswork and children's fairytales," she'd remarked dryly. "Historians need to find better things to do than speculate and promote allegory."

"So none of them are right?" Alec persevered.

Dus had refused to comment further.

Now, after two days of reading the boy was beginning to grow, not quite bored but drained somehow, as if there were only a certain amount of dry, humourless text a person could consume in a given length of time; it wasn't that the information within wasn't interesting, it really was, but the people who wrote it down appeared to be actively working to make it about as dreary as a conference on the analysis of the minutiae of the minutes of a meeting about a conference.

The complete lack of emotive language was thoroughly depressing, and as Alec stepped out into the daylight, it was as if a great weight had been lifted from his mind and spirit.

The world was vibrant and full of life. The air awash with sounds and smells.

With a spring in his step, Alec resumed his exploration of Circulus Seruatis.

Meanwhile, in the infirmary, Saiko awoke for his second day of captivity. He'd spent a day shackled to the bed with only the dying necromancer and the tattooed soldier for company. Neither of whom had been particularly talkative.

Not that he was complaining; compared to some of the captivities he'd been forced to endure, this was the gilded cage with all the trimmings and an en-suite. Actually, the lack of a real en-suite was his one complaint; the needs of his bladder had been growing increasingly pressing. As if in answer to his thought, the tattooed soldier walked in, apparently unarmed, and walked over to the bed, not looking up as he calmly undid the restraints.

Once both legs and an arm were free, the mercenary tensed, preparing to wrap his legs about the man's throat; a sufficiently tight sleeper hold would put nearly anyone out within five seconds. It was one of the few certainties in life, like the sun setting in the west or the tides.

"Don't," the man said calmly, unlocking the final manacle.

Saiko didn't. Something about the tone told him he wouldn't enjoy the result. Instead, he opted for a question, one that had been nagging insistently at him since he'd first woken — which had been a surprise in itself. "How are you still alive?"

"Would you believe really good luck?" The Swordsman asked, watching the man massage his chafed wrists, taking his answer from the venomous glare this earned him. "Very well. I am, for the lack of a better word, immortal."

"No such thing," Saiko said with reflexive dismissal.

The Swordsman laughed darkly, "You're probably right. Let us say immortal until proven otherwise."

The merc seemed unconvinced, perhaps desiring to test this theory. "So why have you released me. Am I free to go, or are you throwing me to the dryads?"

"I'm afraid those options are rather synonymous at the moment. Your employer has managed to turn the entire forest against him and those like him; which in the case of the less distinguishing dryads counts as all humans, or in a few cases bipeds in general. Not that it matters in your case: they all hate you."

Saiko sighed deeply, "I knew it was a mistake as soon as he did it." He snarled, clearly annoyed though whether at the act itself or the consequences thereof, The Swordsman couldn't tell.

"You were present when Lutan slew Lady Von Mori?"

"He didn't kill her," Saiko replied quickly, finally moving from his wrists to begin massaging some circulation back into his ankles.

"The forest would disagree with you."

"That's because the forest wasn't there! Urgh, you know what I mean." It was an unusual outburst from the typically reserved mercenary, but being blamed for a crime he hadn't committed rankled. Especially when he considered the long list of crimes he *had* committed.

"So want to tell me what did happen?" The Swordsman enquired personally, leaning casually against a wall.

"What's in it for me?" his captive demanded with the bluntness of a sledgehammer and basic self-interest of a veteran politician.

"Parole. For now."

Saiko gave this due consideration, "What's the catch?"

"Why does there have to be a catch?" The Swordsman asked, feigning intrigue at the swordsman's suspicion even as amusement glittered in his eyes.

"Why would you allow a professional killer to freely roam the streets? I might do anything; kill someone for example."

The Swordsman merely smiled, "Because I want to."

"Besides, parole is for officers only. Everyone knows that," Saiko complained.

"Which, according to the insignia about your person, you certainly qualify as an officer," the tattooed man said, moving over to Saiko's possessions, all neatly piled in the corner. He began rifling through the mercenary's stuff, removing various badges of office, items of heraldry and similar from the pockets. They'd been idly noted with curiosity while he'd been disarming the man, and since then, he'd taken the liberty of looking up the insignias he'd failed to recognise. Selecting one, he showed it briefly to his captive, presenting each in turn, "Let's see… General in the Noble and Glorious Army of the Paladin Order, Lieutenant in the Drachmat Light Cavalry – Third Regiment and ah yes… Captain in the Hyperias Wyvern Rangers, an interesting title considering the last known wyvern, Diamede the Sarcastic, died seventy years ago. I'm reliably informed his last words were: 'Of course I'm not ill, I'm coughing up blood for fun.'"

Saiko smirked slightly, "An honorary title pending the rediscovery of wyverns."

"Fair enough, but is my point made?"

"Very well, parole," Saiko acquiesced. "Conditions?"

"No murder and no attempts to escape," his captor said calmly.

"Very generous," the mercenary mused aloud. "Any chance of you telling me what you really have planned for me?"

"It's not much of a secret plan if I tell you, anyway I haven't finalised anything yet." The Swordsman couldn't help a smirk, the tattoos dancing across his face so as to avoid getting scrunched in the lines this created at the corners of his mouth. "Do you accept these conditions?"

"Of course I do. I've hardly a choice have I?"

"There's always a choice," The Swordsman declared coldly, arms crossed. "Now grab your stuff, and I'll take you to the dining hall."

"I'm going to need to use a latrine first," the merc said emphatically.

"Very well. Go outside, there's a public outhouse, fourth building on your left. Good news is we have indoor plumbing."

Half an hour later, Saiko was ready to go to the dining hall, an impressive feat considering he'd returned after barely two minutes. It turned out that Saiko's armour and weapons took a long time to properly equip, the man choosing for that reason to sleep in the armour where possible — the camo-cloak doubling as blanket and pillow — well that and the generally pervading paranoia of those who survived long in the paid murder business. The dining hall was an exceptionally large stone oblong with merely a single floor visible. There was nothing grandiose about its exterior, where great monuments loomed, it lurked. The stone was an unremarkable grey and thus was only remarkable for being stone in a town built, with very few exceptions, from wood, though Saiko could guess why.

The building had clearly been built to be defensible, should the town ever be overrun for whatever reason. The roof had small crenelations for archers as well as several cauldrons above the door that Saiko would have bet his life's savings could be easily tipped to pour hot pitch, oil or molten metal down upon any foe who thought a battering ram was a good idea.

As The Swordsman threw open the massive doors, the room below went deathly still as those partaking of their midday meal stopped to stare for just a moment, then quickly went back to eating.

In that time, Saiko had got a good look at the expressions, a mix of fear and hate which the mercenary found most worrying; it had all the hallmarks of a mob in the making.

"They're just scared," The Swordsman assured, answering the question hanging in the air. "Your patron is a threat to everything we are and everything we represent. It's only to be expected that they're nervous of you."

"Nervous enough to act upon it?" he enquired whilst surveying the room and its varied inhabitants.

It was a lot larger than he'd expected, with the floor almost thirty feet down from the doors with stairs, built to a scale far greater than for human use, leading down to it. Should an enemy ever breach the doors, the inhabitants below would be reasonably easy pickings for a disciplined squad of archers or crossbowmen, though something told him they wouldn't have it all their own way.

Possibly it was the massive ballista pointed at the doors which gave this impression, the siege engine elevated on an oak platform across the hall so it was level with the door, several scorpioballista around it like baby dragons next to their mother. He also noted the ballistae were manned as if fearing an attack even now.

The people currently in the room were perhaps even more formidable; Saiko counted four dragons, all quite young, two giants, at least thirty other various sentient creatures of myth and legend and a near score of humans, all armed to the teeth.

"No, they would never lay a hand upon you without violent provocation or permission," The Swordsman declared with utter certainty. "Did Lutan not tell you what this place is?"

"I presumed an academy for mages or a magicians outpost."

"What in the name of Mortis the Ascended gave you that idea?" the immortal being laughed.

"Lutan usually restricts words like heresy, blasphemy and blight for magician business," Saiko said with a shrug.

"This is a sanctuary. A place of peace," he noticed his new charge's incredulous look at the siege engines and assorted personal armaments. "Sometimes peace needs defending. It is one of life's great dichotomies. I'm pleased to say that since its founding, no hostile force has ever breached these walls."

"Then why are they so jumpy?" the man asked as they began the low and slightly difficult process of descending the stairs.

"There's always a first time for everything, and with Von Mori absent, this place has never been more vulnerable. Not to mention there are a few who, should their presence here ever become common knowledge, would bring the legions of the world down on us. And no, I won't point them out."

"If they're such a threat why let them stay here?"

"Because that is the promise of this place. Sanctuary for all who seek it. Even Lutan could seek safety here if he chose, and I would be oathbound to give him shelter. You ask why they're jumpy, they're fleeing war and persecution, deserved in some cases, undeserved in others, but all are equal in this place. As long as no resident antagonises another they may stay here until old age takes them."

"If they aren't allowed to fight, then why let them keep their weapons?" Saiko asked whilst carefully weighing up the drop-down to the next step; it was just large enough to make a step uncomfortable but not quite enough to warrant a jump

"How would you feel if I took your weapons from you?" The Swordsman admonished calmly.

"Nude I suppose, just sort of… incomplete," Saiko admitted, realisation dawning.

"Exactly. The only trade some of them have ever known is war. And besides, they still hone their skills daily; in fact, practise begins in two hours for those so inclined. You can join us if you so wish. You might learn something," The Swordsman jested as they reached the ground before leading him straight into a side door actually built into the staircase. "Kitchen's this way."

"So what do I actually call you?" the merc asked, trying to force conversation now that the current topic seemed to have run dry.

"Well, my actual name is almost unpronounceable since the language it originated from died, and I've never cared for any of the bloody titles they've given me so many just call me, Swordsman. Or The Swordsman if they're writing a book or feeling pretentious," The Swordsman shrugged, opening the door to the kitchen.

The smell hit Saiko like a rapturous hammer blow as heavenly scents suffused the air. The kitchen was boiling with frenzied but purposeful activity. At the centre of it all, an orc bellowed orders at the top of his lungs yet still only barely audible in the hubbub.

At just shy of seven-foot he was an impressive specimen, daubed in woad warpaint in the markings of his tribe. A casual read of the markings, a useful skill provided you didn't stop to read them mid-fight, told him he was dealing with a war chief, master of his tribe. A count of his ritual scars proved beyond his mathematical abilities, each one indicating a kill on the battlefield, whilst some of the scars were unfamiliar to him. Barechested, the orc would have been a terrifying figure on any battlefield if it weren't for the jaunty look his chef's hat gave him.

Upon noticing them, the orc ceased its shouting, walking slowly over to the two interlopers in his domain, "Well? Wha' ya wan' wiv me?" the orc demanded, "Can'cha see oi'm busy?"

Saiko frowned at this, thinking quickly as a hypothesis formed. "No need to put on an accent for the newcomer."

"Can't blame me for trying," the orc said fluently. "I've managed to string some newcomers along for years with the 'all orc tork loik dis' spiel. It's one of my few pleasures in life." He offered Saiko his hand, which the mercenary shook firmly and was pleasantly surprised to find his fingers intact at the end. Even when being gentle orc handshakes were known to break bones. "My name is Agh'zak Skullcrusher, and I'm pleased to say that I'm the finest gourmet chef this side of the afterlife."

"Certainly an impressive claim," Saiko said with a

smile. "So what exactly makes a master of armies give it all up for mastery of a kitchen?"

Agh'zak laughed, a roaring guffaw that seemed to turn the room into an echo chamber, the steam hanging in the air unable to dampen the orc's mirth as it bounced from wall to wall. "Delicately put human. Let it suffice to say that the long term survival prospects in the culinary arts are significantly better than in the fighting arts. Now, I believe it is considered polite in most human cultures for both of the people conversing to introduce themselves."

"So it is," Saiko admitted, already warming to the good-natured orc. "Saiko. Master swordsman."

This earnt a quizzical look from the chef, "You have met the person stood next to you right?"

"Yes. And I lost," Saiko conceded. "But the fight had been reasonably well matched up to that point."

"How hard did you hit this guy?" Agh'zak asked with amusement painted plainly upon his face.

"Nowhere near as hard as you seem to believe, the boy has a natural talent. Given a few decades to whip him into shape I could probably make him an exceptional fighter."

The chef appeared to consider this, "High praise indeed. Now, what brings you to my humble kitchen? I hate to cut the small talk short like this but I can only leave these louts unattended for so long before they burn something, or use the wrong ingredients or if the idiots are really out in force someone will mistake fricassee for fry." He gave the traditional sigh of the much put upon but was smiling as he did so.

"Two bowls of whatever today's stew is," The Swordsman said amiably.

"You know there's food out in the dining hall." It

wasn't quite a rebuke but was all the more forceful for it.

"I always bring newcomers to see you. Helps them understand what we're about and annihilate their preconceptions."

"I wish you wouldn't," he grouched, looking around the kitchen. "I'm sure it's a useful method of induction, but every time someone manages to- Perkins! You idiot, I said ground ginger, not diced! Ground! You'll ruin the texture!" With that, the orc was gone, back to micromanaging over twenty people whilst doing as many tasks as personally possible. Somehow able to know almost instinctively how long each dish still needed and what it needed.

"He's certainly… passionate about his art," Saiko remarked, observing from a safe distance.

The Swordsman smiled, "Aren't all who seek true mastery of any skill? Alas like all the greats throughout time it has left him rather lacking in social graces. There are dictators who've ruled with less of an iron fist than he rules his kitchen." He shrugged non-judgmentally as one of Agh'zak's many assistants appeared, proffering a bowl to each of them.

Saiko took the bowl and, with great self-control, managed to put it down on an available counter before it burned through his fingers, "You could have bloody warned me!"

"Warned you about what?" the immortal replied blankly even as his own bowl billowed steam.

"That the bowl is hot enough to melt steel!" the mercenary snapped.

"It is?" the man frowned, "…sorry. He means well, my fault entirely." His hand darted out, grabbing Saiko by the fist with such alacrity that Saiko didn't have time to react before the almost forgotten flare of healing magic filled the mercenary's hand to heal the minor burns inflicted. "Probably best you don't try eating that. Agh'zak's right. Mistakes happen when he doesn't directly supervise, there's probably enough poison in that bowl to kill a score of dragons."

"Why-?" The question hung in the air, incomplete yet understood.

"My fault. It's the tattoos. I got some to detect and counteract poisons put on my tongue, but it's left me with damn near no sense of taste. Same problem with temperature. The literal effect is that I shall not be affected by temperature changes caused by external influences, so Agh'zak makes the food piping hot so that, for just a moment, I can feel it before the magic takes effect."

"Sounds like a real pain," Saiko said, trying to empathise. However, it was difficult, like blindness, it was something easier to show sympathy for than empathy, for only a rare mind had the imagination to truly envision life in the absence of a sense."

"It is, though Agh'zak's rare culinary flair has made it far less so. It will be a tragedy when old age takes him."

"So is there any chance of food I can actually eat?" the former mercenary griped, his stomach choosing that moment to rumble in accordance to its owner's complaint.

"Certainly," Seruatis' protector assured him before promptly disappearing into the miasma of steam which pervaded the kitchen, carrying upon it the spectral scents of herbs and spices, the dominating smell of roast meats and the olfactory allure of good gravy.

Just being in the room had increased his hunger tenfold.

It was fortunate then that The Swordsman returned promptly, carrying with him a bowl of stew presumably lacking the toxicant tastes of its predecessor.

Apprehensively he took the offered bowl, pleased to find that while the bowl was hot, it no longer represented an imminent threat to his fingers.

"Best we trespass upon Agh'zak's domain no longer than necessary," his guide suggested, leading them both back to the massive dining hall where he promptly sat down at one of the many tables, blending seamlessly into whatever discussion was animatedly taking place.

Tentatively Saiko took a seat at one of the few empty tables, imagining his presence would not be entirely appreciated by the other patrons.

To his surprise, before he'd managed to take so much as a single spoonful of stew to his lips, he'd found his attempted isolation disturbed, a woman in hood and mask taking the seat opposite him, curiously the mask didn't extend past her nose and was entirely lacking in holes for the eyes.

"Can I help you?" he asked politely, spoon hovering in midair.

"Harm the boy and I will end you," she said simply before leaving the dining hall entirely.

Saiko looked around cautiously, trying to see who may have overheard the brief, ominous exchange by intentional eavesdropping or supernatural hearing, but no one appeared to be paying him any attention, nor was anyone deliberately doing so as far as he could tell.

Finally, he got around to trying the stew. It was cold, not an unexpected result when the mouthful in question had been on the spoon for almost a minute, the lone lump of meat and two chunks of barely identifiable vegetation initially upon the wooden spoon had been forced to vacate after his quick check for observers tilted the utensil.

Still, what broth was left proved flavoursome, rich and filling, which was all one could ask of a good stew.

It wasn't the best meal he'd ever eaten; there was, after all, only so much that could be done with a stew for by its very nature, after hours on the boil, every ingredient tasted the same as all the flavours diffused into the broth.

Despite these fundamental limitations, it was delicious but, given the large size of the bowl, also mildly boring by the last few mouthfuls. However, if that was what the orc could achieve with a simple stew, for Saiko had been unable to find any ingredient more exotic than a carrot, then he was more than keen to try Agh'zak's other endeavours in the chef's craft.

For a long time, he'd been focused upon his meal, far more so than he'd normally allow, and thus when he looked up, the masked woman was sat across from him once more, albeit in a different mask, though surely only arcane transport could have allowed her to get so close without him noticing even accounting for his distraction.

"I believe I may have made a poor first impression," she said with false regret.

"I've had worse," he replied in cautious tones, his actions belaying his words as he watched her warily.

"I just get overprotective sometimes," she explained.

"Hurt what boy?" the mercenary asked, feeling he'd rather missed the context behind the original threat.

"The one your employer was going to kill just to make a point," the masked woman growled accusingly, even if it came across as more of a hiss.

"Perhaps you could take that up with him?" Saiko suggested tentatively, not enjoying his role of proxy.

"You stood by and watched. In my books, that makes you an accomplice," she informed him calmly. "If I had my way… well…" the woman leaned in to whisper quietly in his ear.

Slowly the colour drained from his face until most vampires would seem tanned by comparison, and for a moment, it seemed that Saiko's stew would be making a reappearance.

Finally, she leaned back in her chair with every sign of nonchalance, "I hope we're clear."

"As a glacial lake," the survivor of over a hundred battles assured her timidly.

"Wonderful," she said cheerfully. "You can call me Dus, and I'm sure we'll be very good friends."

"Yeah, great friends," Saiko mumbled, making an in-depth study of the bottom of his empty bowl. "I want you to know I wasn't going to hurt him; I mean, why would I? I'm on parole."

"Good then, we won't have any… misunderstandings," she all but purred.

"Why do you care?" he asked abruptly. "It's not like he's your child."

"No, my children are all dead, murdered in their sleep by 'brave men' like you," Dus spat her anguish, the only thing greater than her rage. "All for the great and despicable crime of being alive. Tell me sellsword, have you ever watched your children's heads be paraded through the streets?"

"No ma'am," Saiko said slowly, "I've never had a child."

"Don't try patronising me sellsword," Dus snapped. "Just remember what will happen if you hurt the boy."

With that, she stormed out, though the size of the dining hall rather reduced the gesture to amusing as opposed to its dramatic intent.

Saiko watched her go with something of a sigh, "And to think I was beginning to like it here," he lamented idly, more for the benefit of supernatural eavesdroppers than himself.

Slowly he rose to his feet, bowl in hand, and walked over to The Swordsman's table, "Where do I need to go to wash this up?" he asked politely, not allowing his current vexation to pierce through the façade of his demeanour.

"Just put it down anywhere. They're all enchanted to return to the kitchen after going untouched for more than ten minutes," the master of swordsmanship answered with gentle amusement.

"Neat system," Saiko observed.

"Most of the time, though it's not unknown for the overly talkative to have their meal vanish before their eyes." Clearly, the concept amused him.

The mercenary rolled his eyes, placing his bowl back down, "So my parole, where will I be staying?"

"That would be your choice, up to a point," The Swordsman explained cautiously.

"The choices being?"

"Well you can continue to stay in the infirmary or move into one of the guest rooms."

"What's the catch with the guest room?" Saiko demanded, mind working quickly.

"Why must there be a catch?"

"Because it's an obvious choice. There is no reason not to pick the guest room unless there's a catch."

The Swordsman smiled, gaze inquisitive as he asked, "And is that all you figured out?"

"No. This is a test of some kind, though why I'm being tested remains unclear." He smirked, "So did I pass?"

"You had until you asked if you'd passed," The Swordsman replied evenly, "now where do you want to stay?"

"You still haven't told me the catch," Saiko observed calmly, suspecting this too was a test.

"True, true. Well the problem with the guesthouse, as it stands, is the other guest."

"This guest being?" Saiko prompted, mildly bored of the melodrama which seemed to almost emanate from the immortal being, as if, after thousands of years of life, he were under constant threat from terminal boredom.

"A vampire by the name of Brachus."

The mercenary allowed himself a snort of amusement, "Ah. Don't worry, unlike my erstwhile employer I know how to play nice with those of the undead persuasion. Underworld above, my third girlfriend was a vampire."

"Alas that's not the problem. He's currently blood-crazy after his supply of synthaglobin ran out."

Saiko winced, "I think I'll stick to the infirmary… can't someone just donate a pint or two to soothe the cravings?"

"I wish. Half of this bunch of crazies have qualities in their blood which are poisonous, some of them placed there intentionally. The other half for reasons of their own simply refuse. We have some blood donors but they're all fully tapped out sustaining our permanent vampire population, taking on another would likely result in someone dying."

"Ouch," he said sympathetically. "Can't you donate some blood?"

The Swordsman laughed darkly, "I wish. There's a moratorium on my blood being used for sustenance or magical experiment."

"Why…?"

"The latent magic level in it's too high. The last vampire to drink some spontaneously combusted, then the remains flash froze everything within fifty metres."

"I'm willing to spare a pint," Saiko offered magnanimously. "Though I hope no one objects if I stay in the infirmary for the time being."

"I thought you didn't have a problem with vampires?" The Swordsman enquired sweetly.

"I don't, but it will take weeks to slake his bloodlust if I'm the only donor, and if I'm light-headed with blood loss, then sleeping under the same roof as a vampire made mad with hunger, borders on a suicide attempt," Saiko explained patiently.

The explanation was met with an approving nod, "Full marks."

"So my parole… do I need a chaperone?" the parolee enquired.

"Only if you think you do."

"See you around then," Saiko said nonchalantly, walking to, and with difficulty up, the stairs.

Being back in the fresh air and sunlight was a minor relief, and he took a few moments to enjoy it before beginning to wander aimlessly along the dirt roads, past rows of houses, a small farm and what was he was reasonably sure from the noise was a tavern doing surprisingly good business for early afternoon.

It was at the outskirts of the city, with little but farmsteads between him and the wall, a construct whose magical nature the master swordsman was more than a little bit interested in, that something caught his eye, a single glint of metal near the wall itself.

Curiosity piqued, he ceased his aimless wandering and broke into a jog towards the glimmer of mirrored sunlight.

As he got closer, the small star of reflected glare revealed its secrets, a lone woman, a long blade in each hand, moving through katas with such speed and grace that it seemed more a dance than the studious application of a martial discipline, though not a discipline he was familiar with.

Not wanting to disturb another's practise, he elected to stay at a respectable distance until she'd finished.

As she stopped her training, the woman turned to glare at him, piercing green eyes filled with a burning hostility, "What is it going to take for you guys to get the message? I'm not some blasted lucky charm so leave me alone."

"Calm down ma'am, please. Two points. One, and I can't stress this enough, I have absolutely no idea who you are, and two, this is my first day here."

She blushed slightly at her mistake. "Oh… sorry." Her gaze descended to his hip, "Do you know how to use that pigsticker?"

"I'm one of the best I know," he replied honestly.

"A glowing assessment I'm sure," she drawled, "if I knew who you were."

"If you've some training blades, maybe we can find out how glowing," the mercenary suggested.

"No training blades, we'll just have to make do with what we have," the woman said simply redrawing her swords, both long, curved and single-edged, putting Saiko in mind of a scimitar though the blades appeared to lack the necessary heft.

"Steel blades? We'll kill each other," he spluttered, his own sword kept to a razor's edge — one which never needed sharpening or care. He knew he was good and suspected she was as well, but accidents did happen.

"That's dealt with easily enough," she declared simply, running a finger along the edge of each of her blades. Saiko could only watch in astonishment as the metal dulled then browned, finest steel transmuting to polished oak before his eyes. "Now your blade please."

"You can definitely reverse this?" he enquired, not ready to forsake a prized possession to her without assurances.

"Naturally. It's a simple trick when you know how."

"Isn't everything?"

This earnt a gentle smile, "Perhaps."

He smiled back, recognising a kindred spirit. With a mildly excessive flourish, he relinquished his favourite sword to her, a slim falchion Lutan had given him as a token of gratitude the third time he'd save the man's life, the very same blade The Swordsman had struck a good twenty metres across the clearing outside the wall. "What's your name?"

"Alisha," the word kept to a crisp three syllables, some of the coldness creeping back into her demeanour at the mild personal enquiry. "Yourself?"

"Saiko," he replied, watching her expression in the now faint hope of a glimmer of recognition; as well known as he was in Paladin territory, he might as well have been from another world for all the recognition that earned him here. That and the fact master swordsmen appeared to be a penny a dozen in this place, a fact which should have annoyed him far more than it did.

Alisha ran her index finger along the blade to blunt it before she began to transmute the metal, frowning deeply as it resisted her efforts. "Where did you get this blade?" she demanded with shocking ferocity, brandishing it at him threateningly enough for the mercenary to take a solid step back, knives appearing in his hands as if by magic, though reality was much more mundane; the mercenary had spent several months learning how to make use of spring-loaded wrist sheathes and, in his opinion, it had been time well spent.

"Whoa there, Al, watch where you you're swinging it will you? I'd rather not end an illustrious career in a freak sparring accident if you don't mind," he pleaded, showing his hands in a universal gesture of peace and goodwill, a gesture rather ruined by the vicious knives he was holding.

"Where did you get this?" the svelte woman demanded, voice low and soft but so very dangerous.

Saiko recognised the tone; it often preceded a killing. "It was a gift from a friend. Why does it matter?"

"Because this is a pure nullstone blade," she stated with something approaching reverence. "This *gift,*" — she all but spat the word — "is worth more than entire kingdoms, people have sold their souls for less. And yet someone gave it to you?"

Saiko laughed nervously, "You're crazy, everyone knows nullstone's too soft in its pure form to make a weapon, let alone hold an edge, and besides, Lutan's not that generous."

"You really have no idea what this is do you?" she asked cryptically, apparently shocked at the existence of such ignorance.

"Enlighten me," Saiko requested dryly, knives disappearing back into the recesses of his sleeves, a gentle click signifying the mechanism returning to its armed position.

"This is a spell breaker blade, only eight of them were ever made," she said, practically caressing the falchion as she spoke. "Enchanted to be practically indestructible, to always maintain its edge and to destroy any form of enchantment or other magic with which the edge comes into direct contact."

"That's impossible," he said in disbelief. "You can't enchant null."

"You can. It's just very difficult. It takes four things to make null take an enchantment. Indomitable will, exceptional magical ability, a truly masterful grasp of runes and the various skills of a master blacksmith," Alisha explained to him. "There have been twenty recorded artificers with the requisite skills and each has made unique and irreplaceable contributions in the realm of magical artifacts which repel magic. But only one had the audacity to take it a step further; Diregnan Strausst managed to weaponise the magic negating powers of nullstone."

This earnt a snort of laughter from the mercenary, "I think the Paladin Order's already pioneered that particular method."

"It's almost cute how naïve you are. Comparing nullsteel to this is like comparing the sound of someone hitting a piano with a hammer to the majestic cascade of a full orchestra at work."

"What's the difference?" replied the world's most disinterested music critic.

"I sincerely hope you're talking about the swords," Alisha declared.

"Probably. So you were about to explain what's so special about spellbreaker blades that nullsteel doesn't do just as well?" Saiko prompted.

"He focused the null field to extend no further than the edge of the blade… at least that's the theory, but the effect is that should the blade come in contact with a magical object, it ceases to have any magical ability, which was fine until a smartarse in the Paladin Order figured out magicians are technically magical objects," she elaborated with the erudition of a born academic.

"You're joking right? There's no way that the magical community would tolerate the existence of such a weapon," her audience declared, spotting an obvious flaw in the history being presented to him.

"They didn't, but considering a single nick from a spell breaker could render even the mightiest and most learned mage to a mere babe in arms, it was not until the twenty-third Paladin-Necromancer war that they actually managed to get their hands on one." She paused for breath, voice bizarrely choked with emotion as if remembering an anguish of ages past. As improbable as it was, the twenty-third war was eight centuries in the past and she fit none of the usual criteria of the long-lived — unless exceptional beauty counted. No pointy ears, out in sunlight, no obvious magical tattoos or talismans, and even the best healers struggled to maintain the façade of youthfulness for more than a couple of centuries. Yet, somehow he could tell that this woman had been there, fought there and suffered there.

"How did you dispose of it?" he enquired curiously, slowly piecing together the reality of things.

Alisha's sea-green eyes widened for just a moment, "Well deduced."

"Thank you. I'm not normally this observant," Saiko remarked with genuine surprise.

The woman smirked knowingly before returning to the deathly seriousness that seemed to form one half of the stark duality her personality seemed to take. Both, as best the mercenary could tell, carefully catered façades for someone who had known too much pain in their life to let others close. He wasn't sure how he knew it, but he did.

"In answer to your question, we flung it into the heart of a dormant volcano in the hope that if it survived, we would never see it again, only to have it return to us in an eruption fifty years later. The worst part was that it wasn't even the same volcano. The fires of the world's core could not destroy one of these swords, and now, after all these long years, another has found its way into my hand." She stopped for a moment, letting that sink in whilst regarding the man opposite her with an intensely studious gaze. "The Swordsman must trust you greatly indeed to let a blade so inimical to both our way of life and himself remain in your care." With a deft swing she flipped the sword in question to offer it back to him hilt first.

Saiko took it back with rather more deference than when he'd given it, "You said they were only nearly indestructible, how would you go about destroying one?"

"In theory? Just clash two spellbreakers against each other edge to edge, each would destroy the magical properties of the other. Unfortunately the energies released would be so great that the conservative estimate for the resulting crater is half a mile deep Now I believe we were going to spar?"

The mercenary chuckled depreciatingly, "With what? I just found out my sword is a priceless, indestructible, immutable artefact with the potential to shatter the world like a dropped wine glass."

"You've got knives haven't you?" Alisha rhetoriced dryly.

"Against a master swordswoman?" he asked with similar rhetorical intent.

"Don't tell me it's because mine's bigger… I might start to wonder if you're compensating for something," she goaded with a wink.

It was but the work of a moment for two daggers to be placed in her hands, sometimes male pride was amusingly easy to manipulate, though part of her suspected Saiko wasn't quite as egotestical as he seemed, simply playing the role for her benefit.

A quick splash of minor spellwork and the blunted wooden knives were deftly thrown back to their original owner, who was already beginning to regret his ego and would no doubt be given further cause to regret it in the very near future. While it would be pure hubris for him to declare he was without peer with a sword, up until three days ago, he'd been able to count aforesaid peers on his fingers. Alas he was under no such illusions about his knifework; he was skilled, but his knives had always been for throwing, and as a distraction at that, or the first of a number of last-ditch defences.

Saiko shook his head, trying to clear the doubts from his mind, indecision and fear as much his foe as the woman before him and in many ways more deadly.

At an unspoken signal, both stepped adroitly back to a safe distance, flowing smoothly into their stance of choice as they began to circle each other, unblinking, poised, two apex predators waiting for the perfect moment with which to strike.

One of them found their moment.

With a valiant warcry Alisha span through the air,

swords seeming to orbit her as they moved to bisect him.

On his best day, with his preferred weapon, Saiko would have struggled to block even the first strike.

He'd blocked six before he'd realised what was going on and a further twelve before he recovered from his surprise.

He fought as a man inspired, with a speed born of superlative and superior instinct, faster than he'd ever fought before and yet lacking the franticness this implied, each movement a perfect economy of motion. Each knife met a sword, yet even with whatever profound influence had overcome him, it was a trial not to have the short blades ripped from his hands by the sheer force of each blow. Clearly, the lithe form was the disguise for some spectacularly compact muscles.

By some miracle both of them maintained this furious pace, neither landing so much as a glancing blow nor slight nick. And then he blocked a blow that never made contact.

Alisha's open hand struck his throat where she'd simply let go of her sword in the moment of contact, rendering him off-balance as he overextended.

Saiko collapsed to the floor, gasping and choking as his daggers fell limply from his hands. His sparring partner proved unsympathetic, arms folded with amused dispassion as she waited for him to recover from his coughing fit.

"Well fought," The Swordsman said from beside them, startling the pair, drawing a sharp jerk and gasp from Alisha and an aborted wheeze from poor Saiko.

"I really wish you wouldn't sneak up on me like that," Alisha snapped waspishly, proving that time did not heal all wounds, clearly here annoyance had festered.

"Or you could learn to listen more carefully," he chastised whilst offering her sparring partner a hand up, which he gratefully accepted, slowly rising to his feet, most of his focus still on breathing. "So what do you think of him?" the immortal enquired, indicating Saiko with a thumb.

"Potential," Alisha replied cautiously. "Why?"

"I was hoping you might be willing to train him," he elaborated, "the boy might benefit from your inspiring influence."

The response was as vicious as it was quick; a sharp slap rang out over the field, "How dare you! I came here to avoid people who wanted to use me, and now you, the very man I fled to for sanctuary, is now seeking to exploit me in the same way."

"It would just take a month of your time I promise, just until the Confluence is over," he promised her, looking utterly wretched and guiltridden as he did so.

"What changes after a month?" she demanded, less than mollified.

"I will be able to devote my own time to his training," The Swordsman explained patiently.

Alisha gasped, wooden blades falling from her hands as her right moved to cover her mouth.

"You do both realise that I get a say in this right?" Saiko interjected with only mild annoyance and more than a touch of amusement.

"Nominally," the de facto if reluctant ruler of Circulus Seruatis agreed noncommittally. "But considering the path you've chosen for yourself, I can't see a refusal in your future for any reason but wounded pride, and in that case you simply wouldn't be worth our time."

The mercenary fumed, but silently, pride wounded.

"I still haven't agreed," Alisha snapped, still thoroughly annoyed.

"Come on Al, I know for a fact that you've missed having someone to spar with," he wheedled. "Consider it him doing you a favour."

"I will consider it," she snapped, stalking off, practise aborted.

Saiko frowned, as confused as he was amused, "Well I know it wasn't me who annoyed her."

"Smug doesn't suit you." The immortal laughed and was gone, not even a blur.

"I can see why she hates that," Saiko said to himself before looking down at his still wooden knives. "…Damn it."

Chapter 12

When Erebus awoke, it was a physical strain to simply open his eyes, a great weakness upon him the kind brought on only by a botched accelerated healing. His own body's energy reserves were pillaged to fuel the spell, breaking down muscle and fat to do so.

In many ways, he supposed he should feel fortunate to have woken at all, but all he felt was guilt at the lives that would be lost due to the events now set so very inevitably into motion. When news of his survival finally reached Lutan, and it would, be it a week or a year from now, this vicious cycle would begin anew.

With an iron will he crushed his self-pity; it was beneath him and beneath the memories of the victims that had been consumed already by this idiotic feud. Slowly he sat up, opening his eyes by determination alone as he began the slow process of funnelling magic into his now feeble muscles. A week's disuse was bad enough, but magical consumption had reduced the hardened traveller's physique to little more than that of soft cheese.

The room was at least familiar, the Circulus Seruatis infirmary, had once been almost a second home for him for over a year. In the dusk of night, the room was lit by only a single beeswax candle which cast a warm, comfortable gloom over everything, including the occupants of the other two beds.

It was with a saddened heart he observed Holly in the bed next to him, the blackened, burnt flesh of her neck rendered all the more ghastly by candlelight. That was another mistake he'd struggle to atone for. For a child to be tortured in his care… once again, the iron will was brought to bear, this time upon his self-doubt. Short of prescience, there was nothing he could have done and thus no blame he could lay at his own feet for this crime.

Those thoughts turned his gaze to the other occupant, Lutan's stooge, beaten black and blue, although, with the limited light, it was more black and really dark grey for alas in darkness, all hues were rendered equal. Erebus frowned darkly; whilst he had no love for the mercenary or his trade, he'd always believed The Swordsman to be above torture.

Somehow simply staring at the man was enough to wake him — a useful skill for those few with the capacity to learn it. There were few visible signs: a slight deepening in breath, the barest change in body tilt — just enough to obscure one arm from view.

"That won't be necessary," Erebus assured him from across the room, mildly wounded as the man laid his sword across his lap regardless.

"Considering I helped pioneer a murder plot against you, you'll have to understand if I don't take you at your word," Saiko informed him smoothly, eyes focused upon his face. Erebus knew the look, he'd seen it in the mirror sometimes, constant calculation behind the eyes.

"An understandable caution," Erebus admitted evenly. "Now why are you carrying a sword?"

"I was granted parole," the mercenary replied briefly, not liking the necromancer's tone.

"Curious. And why would he give parole to a known torturer?" he enquired sweetly, though with a dash of venom in it.

"I'm not going to even speculate on his motives,"

Saiko responded honestly enough, a hand still on the spellbreaker's hilt.

"Where is The Swordsman right now?" Erebus demanded, getting out of bed with great difficulty.

"Asleep most likely."

"He doesn't sleep."

"Then I've not the faintest idea," the merc snapping, laying back down to try to sleep, sword still across his lap.

Erebus staggered over to a half-full water jug, "I'm going to need some assistance with this."

A single eye cracked open, "You want me to pour you a glass of water?" he asked in disbelief.

"No," the magician replied as if it were the most foolish question he'd ever heard. "I need you to hold it still."

"Why?" Saiko obliged by asking the obvious question.

"Because I rather suspect my hand will catch fire when I trigger his wards," the necromancer said flatly. "Or rather all of me will, I can just limit it to the hand."

Erebus flourished a hand, which true to his word caught aflame, a brilliant blue flame which, fortunately for his continued health, extinguished when plunged into the jug of water; with exceptional reflexes, Saiko managed to get to the jug before the sudden movement could tip it.

"You called?" The Swordsman asked quietly from the corner of the room.

The jug smashed as Saiko practically leapt from his skin, though Erebus merely turned to glare at the man, "I told you not to save me."

"This coming from the man who considers orders as simply a form of formal advice?" The Swordsman cajoled. "I had a choice; save a friend or kill an enemy.

And I've lost too many friends and killed far too many enemies."

"And thanks to your blind altruism thousands may die!" Erebus half-shouted.

"And I will have to live with that," the tattooed man replied with utmost solemnity. "But given the choice again I would change nothing."

"You aren't the only one who'll have to live with it," the necromancer declared bitterly.

"If your burden is too great you know all you have to do is ask," the victim of his ire replied calmly.

"And do what? Spend the rest of my life here reminiscing about 'the good ol' days'?" Erebus snapped, clearly feeling less than generous towards his host.

"You don't really think that," The Swordsman states with irritating serenity.

The necromancer seemed to collapse in on himself, "You're right, I don't."

"You do know there are less risky ways to contact me I hope?" The Swordsman asked as he began to help his friend back to the sickbed.

"Less risky perhaps, but a summoning spell was the quickest available and I was prepared for the backlash."

"So I saw." The ancient creature chuckled to himself, "What do you intend to do now?"

"Whatever I need to," Erebus informed him, "this has to end."

"So what's your next move? And if it involves leaving before you've recovered then forget about it."

"My continued presence here endangers everything you've built. What sort of creature would I be to allow this sanctuary to come to harm?"

"One in need of said sanctuary," The Swordsman

declared from the heart. "Situations like yours are why I founded this place, and I won't abandon my principles at the first signs of danger."

"And if he brings an army?" Erebus tested, going straight for the worst-case scenario as if in the vague hope that his benefactor might decide to withdraw his protection.

He appeared to give the question due consideration, "I fully expect him to bring a full legion of men. As do half of the other residents." He gave a minimalist half-shrug, "If it's any help most of them are fine with standing and fighting, though there's the usual minority who just want to hand you over as soon as the enemy is at the gates… not that we technically have gates, but there's nothing to worry about on that front. The last person to suggest it, Dus told in no uncertain terms, if they tried anything she'd personally shove their gladius where the sun shineth not, handle first so they have to cut their hands getting it out." The immortal laughed darkly, the threat clearly appealing to his sense of humour.

"She always did have a fiery temper," Erebus agreed with just a touch of ambivalence.

"Not to mention a soft spot for you and yours," The Swordsman added, pleased he seemed to be getting through to the old necromancer.

"How long was I unconscious?"

"Just over a week."

"Ouch…" The necromancer winced, "Combine that with a double dose of magic-induced fatigue, we're looking at a rehabilitation period of months."

"That's fine. We'll simply have to put together some semi-permanent accommodation for yourself and Alec." Once again, there was the half-shrug, somehow failing to indicate any single emotion.

"How is the boy settling in?" Erebus enquired, concern creeping into his voice.

"Quite well, quite well," he was assured, "though he may be slowly driving Dus insane, she's been serving as a living dictionary and encyclopaedia as he tries to read the entire library. She says she's never met such a prolific devourer of literature before."

"What's he been reading?"

"I'm told he's already gone through half our texts on stonegazers, oh and he's also started swordplay lessons."

"I was rather hoping to keep his exposure to violence at a minimum," Erebus admitted, massaging his forehead as if trying to stave off a headache. "Who's the teacher?"

"You've said it yourself, Lutan will, eventually, discover you're still alive, and, unless you plan to leave the boy with us for the rest of his natural life, you'll have to take him with you, and we both know he deserves better than what a life here can offer him. All I can ever hope to do is to give him a small chance at survival should Lutan catch up to you before you reach the safety of the Necropolis."

"You forgot to answer my question," the necromancer pointed out, making no further protest against the training itself.

"True enough. Let us just say that I've given the job to one of my most promising students." He answered with an enigmatic smile.

"That isn't an answer," Erebus complained, not overly fond of receiving cryptic answers even if he enjoyed giving them, a mild hypocrisy that was hopefully forgiven when compared to all the other vices available.

"No, it's just not an answer you like," The Swordsman pointed out. "Why does it matter?"

"It didn't," he replied. "I was just curious if it was anyone I knew, but now you aren't telling me and that means I want to know."

"You truly are more stubborn than is good for you," his ancient friend observed calmly before relenting. "Very well, the child's tutor is young Saiko here, he's got a surprisingly skilled teaching technique for a former hired killer."

"Him?" Erebus exclaimed incredulously, barely able to believe his ears, the necromancer's shout sufficiently violent to make the observing mercenary loosen his sword from its sheath, Saiko having listened to the conversation unfold with fascination. He'd always wondered what was meant by the term 'verbal sparring match' and had been pleasantly enlightened by the answer; he'd never expected it would have the potential to be as vicious as the regular variety.

Fortunately, from Saiko's point of view, Erebus did not annihilate him with a blast of necrotic energy, instead launching into a furious, if somewhat justified, tirade at the immortal.

"Have you lost all sense of humanity? You've assigned as the teacher of a traumatised child, one of the men responsible for the murder of his parents, the destruction of his home and the deaths of every man, woman and child he has ever known and you can't see how this might be cruel?"

"Well, I've received no complaints from either of them," The Swordsman replied mildly. "And Alec's progressing well."

"Have we become nothing more than a game to you?" he asked gravely. "After millennia of protecting people have we finally become nothing more than toys or pieces on a board?"

"Of course not," the venerable warrior protested, deeply offended at the implications, "but the boy is too young to let hate fester upon the tongue. Best to kill it now before it has time to grow. Besides Dus has made it quite clear what the consequences of upsetting the boy will be."

"You knew?" Saiko exploded, not excessively impressed at this revelation, "Why didn't you intervene?"

"As your teacher, I felt it to your benefit if you were forced to fight your own battles," his tutor replied sagely, as eyes that had watched the rise and fall of civilisations regarded the, by his reckoning young, with an almost parental warmth.

"How can I possibly fight a battle when murder is forbidden here?" the irate student demanded.

"In your question lies your answer," The Swordsman replied, practically riddling poor Saiko by this point. "Now I suggest rest whilst the necromancer and I move our conversation elsewhere."

Something in the tone told Saiko that the suggestion would only remain so if he complied.

The very idea of being sent to bed like a disobedient child was insulting and, in any other circumstances, would have qualified as an incitement to violence for the mercenary. Still, the chance he'd been offered here was too great to be squandered. Clamping firmly down on his pride, Saiko resigned himself to going back to sleep whilst his mentor and the necromancer departed for regions unknown.

Erebus remained silent for the duration of the journey, bearing with good grace the indignity of having to be supported on the way there; the necromancer wise enough not to overexert himself magically or physically in his weakened state. He'd simply have to learn to rely on other people for things physically beyond him; as a healer himself, he'd advised the same to many patients over the years and was surprised to find himself treating his own advice with the same resentment as his former charges.

The library was dark as they both stopped outside it, the only sign of life the faint glimmer of a single candle in a single window of the top floor.

"Interesting place to hold a meeting," the necromancer remarked. "Public buildings aren't exactly renowned for their privacy."

"Perhaps they should be," The Swordsman suggested, "but this particular example is an exception regardless, especially at night." He smiled with a tender warmth reserved only for his long term charges, "Besides the pool of eavesdroppers here is limited to just Dus unless someone's suicidal enough to risk listening in while she roams the shelves unmasked."

"She still wanders at night?" Erebus asked, a touch amused at hearing his friend remained predictable in her habits.

"Not so often these days," the immortal admitted, "ever since someone had the gall to write her biography for the most part she's spent her nights writing her own version."

"Sixty years is a long time to be writing a book," Erebus observed. "Particularly for so prolific an author as Dus."

"She's led a very long life," the immortal said diplomatically, not specifying whose lifespan he was using for comparison. "I even found her reading books on how to retrieve old memories and improve long term recollection."

"Has she looked into oneiromancy or hiring a psychomancer?" the necromancer asked, professional interest piqued.

"Problems with both I'm afraid, deep memory retrieval requires eye contact and learning dream magic has far too many risks without a mentor to perform a shared dreaming," The Swordsman explained, clearly having pursued these lines of enquiry himself.

"If it's a lack of a dream mentor, I'm able to set up a shared dream," Erebus offered. "I spent a couple of years with the astral projectors of Velag'daum."

"A kind offer, though alas that is not the issue. A dream sharing is a more intimate experience than Dus is willing to undergo, still, I suggest you offer regardless, the gesture will certainly be appreciated and there's always the chance she would make an exception for you."

"Hmm… certainly a conundrum," the mortal mage mused, dredging the depths of his knowledge for a solution. "What about using polarised or reflective lenses to mitigate the risk of transmutation?"

"Doesn't work, both parties need to be able to make eye contact."

"Damn… what about using an immortal?"

"Most of us lack any intrinsic magic," The Swordsman answered, calmly shooting down just another suggestion.

"Some of you do," Erebus objected. "The Artist, The Enigma… at the risk of going off-topic, I've always wondered, why do immortals take titles rather than just keep their names?"

The Swordsman chuckled morosely, his own name long lost to the annals of history. Deep down, he was surprised it had taken his friend this long to ask, "At first, it was for our own protection." He laughed at the quizzical glance this earnt him, fully aware of the dichotomy inherent in that answer, "Not physical protection, emotional. Back before my time, a particularly fiendish man discovered an easy way to leverage an apparent immortal. Our families."

The ancient creature sighed deeply at the existence of such calculated evil before resuming his narrative, "Back in those days, or so I'm reliably informed, a lot of immortals spent a lot of time with their descendants, it was their way of not distancing themselves from their humanity, or goblinity etc. After a couple of particularly world-shaking blackmail schemes, the man responsible was killed and his army butchered to a man. Cruel perhaps but the example was enough to buy time to call a Confluence of Immortals where the decision was made to write our mortal identities out of history. It was felt at the time that titles would be sufficiently impersonal to prevent us forging close personal ties in the future."

"Well, that certainly failed," Erebus remarked, committing the pertinent details to his borderline encyclopaedic memory.

"As it inevitably would," the immortal agreed, "though I suspect there was a certain childish turn of mind which took great pleasure in the idea of calling themselves 'The Destroyer' or similar. Alas, a lot of history's immortals have had a flair for the excessively grandiose. In the passing aeons, it simply became traditional, though, fortunately, the titles have become a touch more modest."

A companionable silence fell as Erebus took this explanation in, the pair entering the library quietly, their footsteps light enough to be ghosts even as Erebus' leg muscles protested viciously at this continued abuse, though, like most protests throughout history, the response was to crush it with extreme prejudice. Without a word, both men headed for a private room on the top floor, its four walls the only witness to many a whispered plot; The Swordsman, a man who took his paranoia seriously.

It was only once they were both safely ensconced within the room's walls that they resumed their conversation.

"The mercenary is more than just a student," the mage stated, certain enough in his own observations, that he didn't bother making it a question.

"Yes," The Swordsman agreed, "he has a rare natural talent."

"You've never taken on an apprentice before." Another statement of fact, Erebus' method of interrogation sublime as he let the person opposite fill in the details, avoiding questions where possible.

"I've been waiting for the right person. Someone with the same love of the blade." The answer was bizarrely defensive, the warrior aware that Erebus disproved of his choice for personal reasons.

"His moral compass is skewed." He didn't try to hide his dislike.

"More amoral than immoral," The Swordsman defended smoothly. "Not unexpected given his line of work."

"And if at the end of this apprenticeship I am proven correct?"

"I will kill him myself." He assured gravely, giving his solemn word upon the matter. "Now what of the boy?"

"What of him?" Erebus countered, seeking clarification of exactly what he was being asked.

"Out of an excess of a hundred people, why save only that one?"

"I didn't save any of them. Alec survived by his own merits alone." The failure one he would take to his grave with a heavy heart.

"Is he your son?" The Swordsman demanded, being far more direct in his enquiry.

"No!" Erebus protested. "Do you really think I'd leave my own child within the dominion of that mage hating bastard‽"

"It would be an ideal way to keep such a child hidden," he observed; the interrogation now reversed as the necromancer was caught flat-footed by the line of enquiry.

The magician snorted in triumphant amusement though, as he spotted a flaw in the immortal's theory, one sufficient to bring the entire house of cards built on it crumbling down, "That would only be a workable plan if I stayed out of the boy's life entirely. I've visited and wintered in that village in search of Ente's tomb every year for the last two decades; I saw it as a way of redeeming myself."

"And yet the boy claims to never to have seen you before the massacre," The Swordsman perpetuated, echoing Erebus' own ability to turn simple statement into a damning accusation.

"Of course he didn't. Do you truly think me so foolish as to walk within my enemy's own province wearing my own face?" he replied without hesitation, calmly clamping down upon the sense of affront this evoked. He knew his friend had to be thorough and explicit in his collection of the evidence.

"Then how did he find you?" The Swordsman abandoning his theory to ask the vital question.

"I wish I knew," Erebus confessed. He'd been quietly puzzling over that question ever since he'd first fled the village and had been drawing a blank upon it.

"Who knew where you'd be?" Seruatis' ruler asked, smelling betrayal like a bloodhound.

"Absolutely no one," the magician declared with certainty.

"You're sure?"

"Completely. I've avoided mirrors, my wards against scrying don't run out for another two months and I'd have noticed a telepathic bond or if someone had altered my shadow."

"You're assuming the means by which you were tracked were magical."

"I took precautions on that front," Erebus assured, bemused at being treated like a complete amateur at the dark art of shadowplay.

"Elaborate for me," The Swordsman demanded, seeking the flaw in Erebus' plans, something to explain how Lutan had located his lifelong foe.

"I never wore the same face for more than two days on the way there and kept my head down, the usual."

"You know how to keep your head down?" the immortal jested lightly.

"Naturally."

"And in Nusquam-in-ore?"

"An alias, well established and with no ties to myself."

"Then we may never know short of asking Lutan himself," The Swordsman concluded, "I assume you've no way of getting a message to the Necropolis?"

"None I would trust at this distance," Erebus replied calmly, "besides it's merely my word against his unless I submit to a memory scan."

"A dangerous task certainly."

"I don't think they'll react quite that badly," the necromancer said, though not with any great confidence.

"You killed a lich" the ancient being pointed out.

"He was out of his mind, I had no choice," Erebus protested vehemently. "Besides, it's not as if I'll volunteer that information. That particular incident will remain between you, me and the dead."

"You're not that naïve. There have been people dying for an excuse to get into your head for over a century, if you submit to a memory scan they'll pick your brain clean."

"If that's what is necessary to end this fiasco once and for all then so be it."

"It's nice to see someone with the courage of their convictions."

"Perhaps. But until I actually back my words up with action then all they are is words."

"Have you any other options?"

"Two come to mind. Either track down and kill Lutan and his supporters or travel to the Citadel at New Pax and present charges against Lutan to the High Paladin."

"Very risky, do you still have friends on the Council?"

"There are still one or two who would look upon me kindly for services rendered."

"Do I even want to know?"

"Nothing immoral, I just stopped a fae attack back in my youth and helped hold the line in the siege of Gerhultz."

"You've never told me about those incidents."

Erebus smirked, "The problem with being a confidante old friend is that you don't get to hear the things I don't mind people knowing."

"Are you going to tell the boy the truth about himself?" the change in subject exceptionally abrupt.

"This truth being?" the necromancer asked, hoping The Swordsman wasn't referring to his theory once again.

"He has power and a lot of it."

"I'm not going to tell him," Erebus said firmly. "And nor should anyone else. Magic needs always begin as a journey of self-discovery. He must choose his own path, only then may I, or anyone else, guide him."

"You're playing a very dangerous game if his powers have awakened. He could lose control at any time."

"I would hardly call it a game," the magician declared solemnly. "But Alec is the only one with the right to decide his future, and I doubt he'll lose control, the boy is one of the most naturally self-controlled individuals I've ever met. Possibly too controlled."

"So you won't set him up on your path?" The Swordsman asked, apparently convinced that the magician would, with sufficient questioning, admit to some deep-seated psychological urge to mould the teenager in his own image.

Erebus' laugh was dark and bitter, "Have I ever told you why I chose to become the man I am today?"

"You know you haven't," The Swordsman replied, calm in the face of melodrama.

"So no one else would have to," he growled. "I've thrown myself into every warzone and plague available so no one else would be forced to carry those choices around with them, to decide who lives and who dies, and though I'm pleased to say that the lives I've saved are at least tenfold the lives I failed to save and a hundredfold those I've taken, I would never ever wish this life upon another."

"Perhaps now is a bad time to point out that by path I meant school of magic," the immortal clarified with sheepish embarrassment.

"Still his choice," Erebus stated succinctly.

"Did you mean that speech just then?"

"Every word. I've made horrific decisions in my life, as you well know, often because the other options are even worse. Why?"

"Sometimes you worry me, I wonder what would happen if that immaculate self-control were to one day slip."

"You needn't worry about me. Ever. I've already taken precautions against that eventuality."

"I'm worried for you," his friend replied cautiously stressing the difference with great care.

"I've done nothing you haven't. Picked a code of honour and lived by it."

"Perhaps but people who live by a code of honour tend to die because of them."

For an instant, the universe seemed to hold its breath as Erebus held the immortal's gaze, allowing the ancient being to stare directly at the dark, writhing turmoil within.

"Only if they're very lucky," the necromancer declared as he left the room.

Chapter 13

Twilight bloomed gently upon the skies above Circulus Seruatis, softened greatly by the waning gibbous moon, its pockmarked matronly face the only witness to many a nefarious and malignant scheme and yet somehow remaining a beacon of light to mankind.

It would not be the sole witness to tonight's events, momentous only to those with a personal stake in the outcome as these select few assembled within the bleak, utilitarian confines of the infirmary.

Just four people present as they prepared to push the known boundaries of magic.

The gathering would have been larger if they hadn't kicked Saiko out, Erebus claiming that the fewer minds were in proximity to the spellweaving, the greater the chance of success. So it was just himself, Alec and Dus who gathered around Holly's bedside, the three determined to wake the poor dryad from her null-induced coma.

In ideal conditions, Erebus would have insisted the teen spent months exploring the deep magical bond he shared with the dryad, learning its nuances and how to control it, but alas, they hadn't the time. As of three days ago, the prognosis had been clear: Holly was dying, unable to draw the energy from her host which she needed to live in her current state, and if she died, then Alec would die with her if he was lucky — though Erebus had refrained from explaining what the graver alternative was.

The proposed solution was simple enough in

concept, for Erebus to enter the young dryad's mind and try to calm the torment within it. According to the necromancer, Holly had retreated into psyche to escape the agony induced by direct contact with nullstone, but her mind was too turmoiled, too tormented to attain a state of calm; something most had to meditate for decades to achieve in any case, and so the world of the mind in which she now resided was born of the worst fears and nightmares available to her. Anyone going in would have to unravel and resolve these fears to get to the part of her mind still aware of itself and pull it free, in theory.

Normally this would be a simple single person job, but after just one attempt, the necromancer had been bedridden for a day from psychic shock and physical trauma. The magics stopping his wounds killing him faltered as the agony in Holly's mind had overwhelmed the magician's exceptional mental fortitude, forcing him to rather rethink his approach to the problem.

And so now, two weeks after their disastrous arrival to this great sanctuary, the trio of travellers would be reunited, if only for the few moments until one of their minds burnt out.

The theory was simple, there was no way for Erebus to directly access Holly's mind, but Alec, by virtue of their soul bond, should be offered a measure of protection.

Alas, Alec lacked the prerequisite skill to take advantage of this and so a solution had been devised.

Erebus would use Alec's mind as a relay and thus, hopefully, benefit from the boy's protection when he entered the dryad's mind, the teenager being dragged along for the ride.

Dus' presence was merely for moral support, though it betrayed the lie which had seen poor Saiki so summarily ejected from his home of the last fortnight.

The Swordsman had politely declined on the basis of having personal business to attend to.

"Are you sure you're okay doing this?" Erebus asked one final time, knowing the boy had very little choice if he wanted to live but including a child in a magical experiment rankled greatly, necessity bypassing the usually ironclad morals.

"Yes," Alec replied though the quiver in his voice betrayed his uncertainty. "It's this or die right?"

"Unfortunately," his mentor admitted, "but if you're uncertain then I will find another way."

"How long might that take?" the boy enquired, suspecting he wouldn't like the answer.

"I don't know," Erebus said, electing for honesty. "Could be hours, could be years."

"How long until she… we… die?" he asked nervously, suddenly terribly aware that he was living on borrowed time, that the hourglass of his life could have scant seconds left in it, and he had no way of knowing.

"A few days at most before you succumb to the same condition, after that you'll be almost entirely out of the reach of anything within my power. Death should follow shortly after," Erebus explained as matter-of-factly as he could.

"So not much of a choice at all," the teen pointed out, voice hollow, unable to suppress the feeling that he was the victim of some great cosmic trick, a view, perhaps, not entirely unjustified.

"It's still a choice. No one ever said it was a nice one," the necromancer replied with sage regret. "Now I want you to meditate, do you know how?"

"Yes, there was a monk of the Stalwart Order who

taught everyone in the village," Alec informed him. "I enjoyed it, it was very calming."

"Good, open your mind to everything around you. It will make it easier for me to access your mind," Erebus said, sitting down cross-legged beside his patient's bed, clearing his own mind. Each exhale controlled and precise as he removed stress and distraction from body and spirit as he sought zanshin, the state of no-mind. It was a rare ephemeral thing, oft sought but seldom found, and the more it was sought, the harder it was to obtain.

Despite his two long centuries of life, Erebus could still count the number of times he'd achieved that state of total awareness, no past, no future, just now and the rich vibrancy of it.

The first time he'd achieved zanshin, the mere shock of realisation had been enough to jolt him out of it.

Alas, he doubted he would achieve it this time, and in that doubt guaranteed his failure, but fortunately, it was not needed in this case; a clear mind would suffice. Though that too was merely to ease the difficulties inherent to such a deep mind probe. The magician doing it had to take precautions not to leave traces of their own psyche behind after the spell was complete, a problem only exacerbated by Alec's youth, his mind far more malleable than an adult's. The young yet to build up the buffer of prejudices, convictions and other small things that set a personality in stone.

Upon attaining his desired state, Erebus looked up, observing Alec, the boy's posture for meditation very different to his own, the boy resting on his knees, hands over his stomach was an easier position to meditate in, the breathing exercises feeling less forced but far less comfortable than Erebus' cross-legged posture.

The necromancer waited, checking his protégé's breathing was slow and even before seeking out Alec's mind with his own.

At such close proximity, and with both in a prepared state, it wasn't hard.

Erebus' world tinged with nervousness as he entered the fringes of Alec's mind, not an unexpected occurrence; he'd been just as nervous the first time he'd communicated telepathically though not about the potential of imminent death.

'*Relax child.*' Erebus sent calmingly, entirely unsurprised as this produced the opposite response, Alec instinctively trying to remove the intruder from his surface thoughts. It was lucky he hadn't delved deeper, or both of them would be facing at least minor brain damage.

With an indomitable will, Erebus clung on, lurking in the boy's surface thoughts yet hard-pressed given the strength of his opposition, especially in the arena of his own mind, if he'd been fighting against an expert, he'd have been overwhelmed in seconds, but he knew how to deal with the instinctual approach. The necromancer insinuating his presence into the very thoughts trying to remove him, an eye in the storm so to speak, Erebus allowing his pupil to burn out most of his magical energy in the attempt.

'*Calmer now?*' he enquired politely. The second expenditure of magic was much smaller but still enough to raise the ambient temperature of the air.

Finally, the new storm subsided.

'*I'm calm.*' Alec replied, at last, figuring out how to thought-send intuitively. '*Sorry… I just wasn't expecting it.*' The message heavily overshadowed by guilt.

'*It's a normal reaction,*' Erebus assured him. '*We can talk like this for a while if that helps.*'

'*Okay. What did you want to talk about?*'

'*It's your mind kid, you decide,*' was the phlegmatic response. Erebus struggling to stop secrets hidden from the world for years from leaking across the mental link. 'Too old and too out-of-practice,' he chided himself, cursing the ravages of time upon his mind. To his horror Alec replied, the errant thought travelling across before he could stop it.

'*What's wrong?*' the boy asked, concerned at his mentor's doubt.

'*Just age,*' Erebus reassured. '*Though magic has conquered decay of the body, the mind is not so easy; we can prevent mental illness, for the most part, but that doesn't prevent centuries of memory from weighing you down.*'

Alec gave this due consideration. '*Why's that a problem now?*'

'*Have you ever tried, really, really, really hard not to think about something? Right now, two centuries of secrets are all but begging to flow across the link, and it's mentally exhausting, like being engaged in a form of mental combat against yourself.*'

'*Then how do professional telepaths cope?*' Alec asked, aiming unerringly for the pertinent question as the monk, and now the necromancer had taught him.

'*Decades of constant practise and meditation, alas, I am but a mere dabbler in the arts of the mind.*' Somehow Alec knew that wasn't entirely true but did not press further as Erebus continued with the conversation proceeding at the speed of thought; it was hard to believe that a mere handful of seconds were all that had passed thus far. One of the reasons for holding the conversation with eyes shut, neither of them could grow disjointed by the difference in the time they felt had passed and the time actually passed. '*Now, are you feeling comfortable enough with this mode of communication to allow me to delve beyond your surface thoughts?*'

'*I suppose so,*' the boy sent deliberately, though he lacked the discipline not to send his true thoughts across as well; a boiling mass of doubt and fear.

Erebus restrained himself from letting his frustration show; it was hardly the boy's fault. Alas trained telepaths underwent two years of training before they were allowed to receive mind-to-mind contact. To go as deep into the mind as Erebus intended, deeper than instinct, right to the heart of where primal magics dwelled, few could have done it, even fewer would have dared attempt it, and alas whilst the mage knew he had the nerve for the latter, even he doubted the skill to be included in the former. His trainer had been rigorous to the point of cruel, but even she hadn't imagined he'd have cause to go this deep into a mind.

Tragically, despite his assurances to the teen, there were no other options available if he wanted to save the boy's life.

He didn't voice any of this, mentally or otherwise, opting for a diplomatic. '*Suppose is insufficient I'm afraid. When you're certain, let me know.*'

'*Okay.*'

'*Do you want to take a break?*' the necromancer asked kindly — it was little less than a miracle that Alec wasn't bleeding from the eyes, though doubtless, his bond to Holly was providing some insulation from the strain. '*We can try again in a couple of hours.*'

Yes… please, Alec replied, finding the presence of a second set of thoughts in his own mind more disconcerting than he could put into words.

With great relief, Erebus carefully extricated himself from the boy's surface thoughts, removing any trace of his presence with a forensic attention to detail, leaving just the memory of the conversation; the last thing he wanted was to accidentally mould the boy into another version of himself.

Once this arduous task was complete to the best of his abilities, Erebus opened his eyes, noting the stillness in the room. With great deliberation to his movements, taking a few moments to get used to navigating back in what telepaths rather charmingly referred to as 'meatspace', the man rose to his feet.

"You can open your eyes Alec," he said softly; vocal communication might be less efficient than directed thought, but it was blissfully easier.

The boy opened his eyes. The world seemed strangely bigger after his brief stint within the confines of his own head, "Where's Dus?"

The necromancer had been pondering that himself, though aloud he said, "Back to her library I would imagine. Being present for moral support isn't particularly useful when the person you're supporting can't register your presence, and she's always been a practical thinker."

"You've been her friend for a long time?" the boy asked, pouncing upon the familiarity in his mentor's voice.

"Dus doesn't allow herself to have friends," Erebus replied evenly, "but I am pleased to believe she looks upon me fondly."

"Why doesn't she let herself have friends? She must be very lonely."

The venerable mage chuckled bitterly, "Sometimes loneliness is a preferable alternative to pain. It's not my place to say more than that."

"You admire her," Alec observed with the erratic insight of youth.

"Greatly. My art owes her more than we could ever repay, as does every being to live upon this world, and yet the memory of her suffering has all but faded from history."

"What did she do?" the teenager asked, wide-eyed at this unexpected aspect of that librarian who had been so kind to him these past two weeks.

"I can't tell you. Her wishes are to fade from history and despite a few literary protests in my youth the past few decades have brought me around to her point of view, some deeds, no matter how justified, or pure the intention, or good the result, are better not gloried."

"Surely people have a right to the truth, no matter how unsavoury it may be?" the boy demanded, Erebus barely able to restrain his shock at having his own ideology thrown back in his face.

"I said I understood, not that I planned to write myself out of history, though were I to be forgotten I would not be disappointed."

"What could you have done that's that terrible?" Alec asked, pondering what dark deed could have occurred.

"Nothing like that, I stand by my actions. But it's human nature that we hold our failures dearer than our successes," Erebus explained, or perhaps mused aloud to himself. "Each one, a vice-like chain about the ankle, weighing you down where'er you go."

"Are you carrying around a lot of chains?" the teenager asked, extending the metaphor. It wasn't asked in a cutting manner; Alec genuinely curious and eager for insight into his mentor's past.

"Yes, after two centuries I've more than I can

count," Erebus informed him matter-of-factly. "It is a burden of great magical power, a natural counterweight I suppose you could call it. Still I suppose there is a beautiful, terrible symmetry to it; that the punishment for an unnaturally long life should be an unnaturally long life."

"If it's so terrible why choose it?" Alec demanded, the conversation continuing its evolution from friendly discussion to interrogation.

"Are you asking why I chose it or why anyone would choose it?"

"Both I guess."

"It was a decision I made when I was young, well younger anyway, and thought time boon not burden. Regardless, I'd likely, given that choice again, still choose an extended life."

"You haven't told me why though," the boy pointed out.

Erebus smiled, "No. I haven't."

Alec frowned before rallying with a change of subject, "You told the Lord Protec- I mean Lutan that you'd used thirty years to hit him with the lightning, what did you mean?" his pupil asked, though he had more than an inkling as to the answer to the tangential question.

"Well, ultimately magic is simply the manipulation of energy, to get past the effects of the nullstone armour and Seruatis' wall took a lot of energy," Erebus explained amiably. "Now I'm a powerful magician, but I doubt any mortal mage has the innate power to use combat magic in that situation, therefore I had to turn to less traditional sources, so I burned thirty years of lifeforce in a single blast."

"Why would you waste that much of your life for

one shot?" Alec demanded, almost incredulous at the idea. "Especially when it did nothing?"

"To dent Lutan's confidence just a little. He was very careful to ambush us in a place with enough null dampening where he thought I would be harmless." There was a pause as the necromancer considered his next words with the care of a chess grandmaster peering over his board, "I wanted him to re-evaluate that opinion for the future. At the very least, I'll doubt he'll confront me in person again."

"You thought he'd survive?" Alec seemed quite surprised.

"I've learned to be cautious," Erebus dodged carefully, "and Lutan's oft proven harder to stamp out than any cockroach history's ever seen… he wasn't always like that you know? He used to be such a gentle child." There was a guilt-ridden sigh; fortunately, the undertones went over Alec's head.

"What happened?" Two such simple words, spoken in innocence yet loaded with dark potential.

"He lost his father at an early age," Erebus said flatly, not wanting to be drawn out on that particular subject. "Now we'd best find our patron, I suspect he's embroiled in momentous events."

The diversion would have been obvious to any outside observer yet was enticing enough not to draw Alec's attention to the fact he was being manipulated, the boy replying with his usual insatiable curiosity.

"How momentous?" the boy asked, trying, and failing, to feign disinterest.

"Enough for you to be telling your grandchildren a lifetime from now," he replied with sincerity ringing true for every word. "This only happens for two weeks out of every hundred years."

"What is it?" Alec's imagination conjuring great battles and historic duels.

"The Confluence of Immortals," Erebus announced with a sweep of his arm as if unveiling a great secret, which technically he was.

It didn't get the expected response, the teen's brow merely furrowing in bemusement for a moment. "What's that when it's at home?" he asked, a touch annoyed at the magician's showmanship.

Erebus sighed. When revealing some of the world's greatest secrets, mild snark was not an expected nor appreciated response. "Once a century, the world's immortals meet up to discuss their affairs, as well as make sure none of them have gone mad in the interim."

"Does that happen often?" he asked, picturing their benevolent benefactor as a frothing-at-the-mouth murdering maniac. It was a difficult image to hold on to, at least until he remembered how calmly he'd slid the blade through the paladin's spine.

"More often than people are comfortable with," the necromancer answered phlegmatically.

"What do they do then?" the child enquired, pondering, as had countless before him, how to disable a being who healed soon as injured, had the strength to treat best steel like mere talc and could not by any known method die.

There was a pause.

"…no one actually knows," Erebus admitted, "though theories abound. They just disappear."

Off in the distance, the distinct melody of steel on steel rang out, it was a surprisingly dull sound, dampened rather than the expected clear, pure ring of vibrating metal and yet, despite having known it barely a month, somehow the sound was so distinctive to the human ear that Alec found it unmistakeable; Erebus certainly had a similar moment of recognition for a hand was placed firmly upon the boy's chest, palm open, preventing him from taking another step.

For Alec, it was like walking into an iron bar. Surprised, he turns to face his mentor, "You think they'd hurt us?"

As if in answer, a bodkin stopped scant inches from the boy's chest, almost pinning Erebus' hand in place, the shaft held firmly in The Swordsman's grip, the immortal appearing from apparently nowhere, a sound like a thunderclap accompanying him moments later. A second look at the arrow would reveal its sudden deceleration had made it catch fire.

"No, but they might not notice us until it's too late," Erebus commented quietly. "I see the Huntress has arrived and is as cavalier about collateral as always, anyone else?"

"The Smith, The Artist, The Ancient and The Cursed Wanderer," The Swordsman replied, one eye fixed cautiously upon the treeline. "Might I suggest I escort you to an area of designated safety if you wish to observe?"

Erebus laughed darkly, noting that Alec was still in a state of mild shock from his narrow brush with death, "I'd certainly appreciate it, I find getting hit by arrows bad for my health, though you'll have to ask Alec again once he snaps out of his fugue."

"Perhaps it would be best to wait for that in relative safety."

"Only relative?" Erebus asked, concealing a grin with some effort.

"Well, you might spontaneously have a heart attack,

nothing I can do about that," The Swordsman pointed out graciously, beginning to lead them to proclaimed 'relative safety'; which proved to be a section of grass fifty metres from the wall, sectioned off by four roughly hewn wooden posts, currently occupied by Saiko and the oldest man Alec had ever seen.

"The Ancient," Erebus whispered in response to the unasked question.

Old eyes snapped to them, a burning intelligence behind the faded orbs as what appeared little more than a desiccated cadaver examined them in turn. "I know," he croaked, "aren't I a horrific sight? Still, you would be lucky to look half as good at my age." There was the very smallest hint of a smile behind the wrinkled lips, "Hello again necromancer."

"Ancient One," Erebus respectfully intoned, eyes back on the five-way duel that had re-erupted, though, at such speeds, the combatants were little more than blurs.

"How many times must I ask thee not to call me by such a ridiculous moniker? Edward will suffice," the man croaked from his chair. "And you boy, if you're done gawking, there's a cigar in my right jacket pocket. Would you kindly remove it for me and have the necromancer light it?"

Timidly Alec obeyed; the skinny figure, little more than a well-dressed skeleton that had been lacquered in flesh with the occasional wisp of long white hair, was somehow greatly intimidating. Finding the vice in question with little difficulty, he removed it with agile fingers and offered it to Erebus, who simply stared disapprovingly at it.

"What's it going to do? Kill me?" the old man wheezed irritably. "Permit me a few mild pleasures in my life."

For several surprisingly long and tense seconds, it looked like Erebus would refuse, but slowly and deliberately, he took the cigar from Alec and gripped the end delicately between thumb and forefinger. For a moment the fingertips glowed white with heat, lighting the cigar with ease before placing it in the immortal's mouth.

"Thank you," Edward said, rolling the cigar to the corner of his mouth, "love to have done it myself, but it's just a bit too painful, my arms you know." The pair of twigs that were theoretically arms gave a lacklustre shrug; he let out a mirthless chuckle, "Don't suppose you could knock a few decades off by any chance?"

"Ed, you're over six thousand years old, I could knock centuries off and you wouldn't even notice," Erebus told him sadly.

Edward sighed forlornly, "Can't blame me for asking." The burning intelligence turned its gaze upon Alec, "Word to the wise kid, when making deals with daemons, always check not only the small print but also what you've actually asked for."

"Why? What did you ask for?" Alec questioned as politely as possible.

"To live forever," The Ancient declared or perhaps admitted. "Unfortunately I forgot to include eternal youth in the bargain, and so, despite dodging successfully the various snares for my life, soul and service in the first set of conditions, ultimately I lost."

"How do you actually make a deal with a daemon?" Alec asked inquisitively.

It was an oft-spoken practice in the annals of folklore, but no legend or myth ever explained the actual process for obvious reasons, instead opting for the equally foolish option of expressing the dangers and the forbidden nature of such an act, thus ensuring most teenagers throughout history attempted it at least once; fortunately most failed utterly, though occasionally an innate eldritch intuition allowed them to summon something, and even more rarely survive the encounter. Though developments of the last few centuries had greatly increased the survival rates of fledgling demonologists, most daemons now, instead of murdering the poor summoner, and through the application of some truly excessive bribes, would simply contact a member of the Path of Summoning and inform them of the newcomer's location.

It was a matter of opinion whether this was an improvement; the Path had been born out of very different circumstances to its fellow' dark arts', not as a defence against a world that hated them like necromancy and shadowmancy — though the world more certainly hated them — nor did it arise out of the enterprising spirit of academia like nexomancy, but out of a deep-seated paranoia and fear of each other, or rather to try and prevent said fear.

It hadn't worked, the new unity simply leading to factions of demonologists killing each other rather than the singular. It was a situation no observer was particularly inclined to remedy. Megalomania ran high amongst such summoners, and if it wasn't there to start then, their demonic 'servants' would soon cultivate it.

Technically it wasn't their fault, even if even more technically it was, but since the last great daemon war, the demonic population had settled for war against the world by proxy. The summoners thought themselves to be in control, but so did the daemon; usually, the daemons were right.

All of this flashed through the Ancient's mind as he

formulated his answer; it was important to be delicate…

"You don't," Saiko interjected coldly, not out of dislike of the people involved, just a deep foreboding when addressing the subject. "Not if you intend to live long."

"Why not?" Alec asked, seeing this as the innate fear of an outsider addressing a subject they didn't understand; afterall, it's not like the mercenary had magic.

"Because they will betray you; and then one of you will kill the other," Saiko declared solemnly.

"So says the voice of experience," Erebus observed, watching the mercenary with a careful mix of amusement and interest.

The Ancient laughed with mild derision, "Don't tease the lad Erebus, as I'm given to understand it you yourself spent time in service to such a creature in the very heart of their own realm."

"I'd use the term apprenticeship rather than service." The necromancer replied calmly, "And the terms we parted on were quite amicable, I'd even go so far as to say pleasant."

This last proviso didn't change the amused, knowing looks the immortal and the mercenary were giving him.

"And this daemon would be?" Saiko asked, trying to sound disinterested.

"I knew her as Sara," Erebus replied, tone wistful and gaze distant. "It was a much… simpler time I suppose."

"Knew?" the Ancient, or as he preferred to be known, Edward, seemed surprised by this, "Something happened to the young lady in question?"

"Lutan."

"This would be the paladin everyone keeps talking about? He must bc a skilled member of his order to defeat even a succubus in single combat."

"She's not dead, just contracted to non-interference," Erebus complained by observation. "I love how everyone is just assuming that my daemonic contact is a succubus."

"Male magician, female daemon. It's not a great leap of imagination," Saiko pointed out.

"She was a quod-frequentat-somniorum-malorum-pressum."

That earned a wince from Edward, "And you're still sane?"

"Debatable," Erebus declared dryly.

"What's a quad-frequentat-somnorum…?" Saiko asked, trying to recall the long fluid string of syllables.

"Possibly one of the evillest daemons to ever exist," The Ancient said quietly, taking a long draw on the cigar as he awaited Erebus' response.

"Evil is a poor choice of words; dangerous or predatory would certainly suffice," the necromancer mused aloud, not overly taken with the immortal. In his opinion, the Ancient abused his infirmity by using it as both shield and weapon in arguments where people were too considerate to call him out on his abrasiveness.

"What's so dangerous about them?" Saiko enquired, his own experiences with the genuinely otherworldly rather limited beyond a single close friendship, and even if he had been taught about their home realms, the loose linked set of realities that mankind collectively referred to as the Infernal or The Hells, the number of distinct species and sub-species of daemon which had been identified numbered in the thousands.

"Well firstly," the Ancient was far too happy to explain, "they know your worst fears simply by looking at you, secondly they can make you hallucinate those fears from up to a hundred feet away, thirdly they can drain your life with a single touch, and finally they take great pleasure in doing all of the above."

"A trifle unfair," the necromancer said calmly. "They can't help their abilities any more than we can help ours."

"They are also semi-insubstantial, an unholy combination of flesh and shadows."

"I have trouble with the word unholy," Erebus snapped.

"As do I," Saiko chimed in, much to the magician's surprise. "One of my best friends was a daemon remember?" he continued in response to the mage's enquiring glance. "And I won't hear a word against them."

"This would be the daemon you were forced to kill?" asked Edward, earning himself no karma points in the process.

"Yes," Saiko declared with sufficiently violent vehemence in his voice to end that avenue of conversation.

Alec pressed his lips together in a frown, not liking the verbal warfare's sudden viciousness and deciding to turn the conversation back upon his mentor. Erebus might not appreciate it, but at least he was sure the necromancer had the patience to withstand it.

"So why apprentice yourself to a quod-frequentat-… a demon?" the boy finished lamely.

"She had knowledge I needed," he replied, not quite hiding the deep regret he felt, though at what specifically he didn't elaborate upon.

"What knowledge would that be?" the elder amongst them demanded.

"How to inhabit the line between shadow and reality, and stay there safely," Erebus' voice grew quieter, the words appearing almost to choke him.

"And why would you want to do that, hmm?" the Ancient smiled cruelly. "To the best of my knowledge only one creature inhabits the shadowgate…"

As leading questions went, it wasn't even subtle.

Erebus took a moment to master himself before answering with consummate calm, "To honour a friend." There was something in the undercurrents of the words, a hint that there would be severe enough consequences for any further enquiry that even the immortal backed off.

Instead, the group's attention turned to the war in microcosm raging before them, though Saiko's attention had, in truth, never entirely left it, gaze peering intently from the protection of their four wooden posts as he tried to interpret the actions of people who were little more than blur and afterimage.

"I was being toyed with," He concluded aloud, then realised that statement needed some clarification, "When we fought I mean."

"To an extent," Erebus admitted, "though not in the way you're thinking."

"And what exactly am I thinking?" the mercenary asked, calling the mage's bluff on the façade of omniscience the necromancer tried to exude at all times.

"You're thinking that he deliberately slowed himself down to a speed you could cope with," Erebus said, quoting Saiko's internal monologue almost verbatim. "Which to the best of my knowledge is simply untrue."

"I'm watching him move at speeds my eye can't even properly track right now," the swordmaster pointed out, finding his title more and more dubious by the second.

"Yes but right now he's not right outside the barrier and next to two suits of null plate, nor having to worry about a spellbreaker blade." Erebus smiled slightly, "You had the first even fight with him in over six millennia and held your own for a while. You should be proud of that."

"It's the 'for a while' part that bothers me," he complained.

"Why so glum about it? You've managed to impress someone who's been using a blade for most of recorded history, and he's not the only one you've impressed, I've heard good things from Alisha, and she's notoriously difficult to please."

"Why do I get the feeling everyone is in the know here other than me," Saiko grumbled.

"Because it's true," Edward quipped. "The problem with the long-lived is eventually it ends up as a bloody clique. Everyone knows everyone and everyone tells everyone everything, even if they don't particularly like each other. I've no doubt half the population of this dreary hellhole knew about your sword's secret within a day of its discovery."

Saiko frowned, "So basically this place thrives on gossip."

"Understandable given its isolation," the magician pointed out. "News of the outside is rare enough to practically be hard currency."

"If it's any consolation no one tells me anything either," Alec proffered with only a hint of resentment before attempting to draw the subject back to the battle before them. "So who's actually fighting?"

"The Swordsman, The Huntress, The Smith and The Cursed Wanderer." Edward sighed, rolling his eyes to the heavens, "Pretentious nonsense."

"Perhaps. Perhaps not," the necromancer said evenly. "There's power in a name, and distance, and they certainly need both. And I'm sorry for keeping you in the dark Alec, I'm doing my best to introduce you to the nuances of the magical community slowly to minimise the shock, and this really is not a good place to be doing that. Not that that seems to be an issue."

"It's okay I guess…" There was a significant pause as the boy tried to put into words an insecurity he'd been quietly nurturing for weeks now. "What's going to happen to me once you've left?"

The necromancer frowned; he'd been deeply hoping that he wouldn't have to address this so soon, that he'd be able to acclimatise the teen to magic and its many supplicants before revealing his own sorcerous abilities. Still, he'd been backed into a corner, if unintentionally so, and should the boy pursue this line of enquiry beyond its surface, he'd be left merely two choices, the truth or a bare-faced lie. Neither were palatable options.

"If circumstance permits I would bring you with me," he informed Alec honestly. "Provided you have no objections of course."

"I do like it here," Alec replied contemplatively, clearly attempting to weigh his options. "So what happens if I travel with you?"

"Then we would travel to the Necropolis, on foot for the most part… it would take a long time and not be an easy journey. I have enemies, some of whom I would have to take significant detours to avoid."

"I see… then why shouldn't I stay here?" the boy asked, seeking the catch he knew had to be there.

"This is a beautiful place, an oasis of calm, peace and sanctuary which cannot be equalled anywhere on this verdant world," Erebus said solemnly, forced by his own principles to give a balanced argument. "But it is a place to grow old, not a place to grow up. Every day you will be regaled with some of the greatest deeds ever to fade out of history by the very legends who performed them, but never will you have the chance to commit any of your own."

Alec thought about that for almost a full minute, mulling it over. "Then I would prefer to go to the Necropolis," he concluded, returning his attentions once more to the fighting, which seemed to be slowly winding down as the participants returned to speeds which could be seen with the naked eye rather than the pure blur they had been until then.

It wasn't a pretty sight. Two of the participants bore a close resemblance to pincushions, a quiverful of arrows shared between them. The woman responsible was engaged in a frantic duel with The Swordsman, both still ablur even as their peers departed for the safety of the square.

Going from the hammer one of them was carrying, an artefact found in any blacksmith's, it was not an unreasonable deduction to conclude he was 'The Smith', which by elimination would make his companion 'The Cursed Wanderer', the latter a thoroughly intimidating figure in a type of armour and mask that was entirely unfamiliar to both Saiko and Alec, red-lacquered leather plates in an overlapping pattern and the mask in the same style. Despite his appearance, Erebus greeted them both as if they were old friends. Only the Wanderer replied in kind.

"I see you both proved lacking in martial zeal on the field of battle," Edward commented abrasively, clearly seeking a rise from them. Both declined to give it to him.

"Huntress must have spent years perfecting that trick," was all the Wanderer would venture on the subject.

"I'm afraid none of us has the skill to see what trick you are referring to," Erebus said smoothly.

"Liar," the Ancient snapped.

The necromancer frowned, "Is there any detail of my life he hasn't shared with you at some point?"

"Most likely but, for reasons I won't even pretend to understand the rest of the immortal community regards you as a person of interest," Edward all but snarled.

"Please excuse him necromancer," the Wanderer interjected head bowed respectfully towards the magician. "He is in great pain and thus common courtesy escapes him betimes. But in answer to your question we have indeed been regaled with tales of your exploits, the more humorous ones at least, please do not blame The Swordsman. Time has made us easily bored and your misadventures have been of great interest to us, and no tale was shared without the understanding that it shall not pass beyond timeless ears. Your secrets are safe with us."

"You needn't fear on either front, I am quite familiar with Edward's abrasive charm and I knew the risks of taking The Swordsman into my confidence," Erebus assured probably the most humble of the immortals. Or at least if there was one more humble, they hadn't made it known. "Now I believe you were going to enlighten us as to the Huntress' latest trick?"

"Three arrows to the strings at once," the Smith grumbled, "it's hard enough blocking just one. I never should have designed that bloody bow."

"You're not going to receive any dissent from me," the Wanderer replied, trailing off with a pained grunt as he tore an arrow from his chest. "I do however have one question pertaining to her choice in projectile. Why, when knowing we would be her only foe, does she insist on using barbed arrows?"

"Latent sadism perhaps?" the Smith quipped, though only half in jest. "Or more likely as each landed shot reduces our manoeuvrability slightly… though for that theory to be valid she'd have to be targeting our joints… which just leaves sadism."

"One of you seems to be coping rather well," Saiko pointed out, still trying to make out what was going on, apparently having decided that if he just squinted hard enough he'd achieve what magic should not.

"That is because he predicted this three centuries ago," the Ancient pointed out. "The mewling children here were warned."

"It still doesn't explain why she has yet to land an arrow on him," the Smith grumbled, partly to himself.

"Simple geometry," Erebus told them with a wry chuckle, glancing around to make sure Alec was paying attention, not that there was much danger of him doing otherwise, the teen very much in learning's thrall. Forbidden knowledge held a great allure, particularly at a young age, not that the paladins held a monopoly on the repression of information. Some of the things Erebus had learned during his youth the magical community had had to come up with punishments far worse than mere death to ensure the knowledge could not be passed to another, as well as as a deterrent to prevent the same.

"You see," he continued, "any two points in three-dimensional space can be mapped and joined by a line, and a sword could technically be counted as a line segment, which is to say a line of finite distance. Alas, three points count an area provided they aren't along the same line, and thus can't be met by a single sword. Which is why he's using two."

"I thought he was just showing off," the Smith grumbled.

"He's also showing off," Erebus remarked. "Now if you'll all forgive me I'm afraid whilst time might be willing to wait for you three, it won't do me the same courtesy and I have work to do. Good to see you."

"And you my friend," the Wanderer replied, though whether he was speaking personally or for the three of them was unclear as the necromancer slunk off back towards town.

"That was abrupt," Saiko remarked.

"He's stressed trying to find a way to save the dryad and the boy." The Wanderer replied simply. Alec frowned in surprise and confusion, "How could you know that?"

"My mask is enchanted to observe the souls present; it's more useful than you'd think. I noticed an irregularity in yours. A mixture of human and non-human souls, and not a stable one. Madness inevitably results, usually death follows. According to The Swordsman, Erebus arrived with a comatose dryad in tow. He clearly has a level of emotional attachment to you. The rest is trivial."

Alec smiled, "I noticed Erebus does that analysis thing too, how long does it take to learn?"

"A difficult question. Ultimately it is dependant upon the student. A rare few develop it naturally without apparent effort or learning, some take years, some decades, some try their whole lives but never learn it. What I will say is it that before you try and walk that path yourself, know that with it comes a cost, once learned it cannot be unlearned. You will see more into people than they like and that earns enemies, and sometimes you will see more into people that you would like and that earns melancholy."

"Then why learn it all if it just makes you miserable?"

There was a saddened mirth in the man's voice as he answered, "Even if you refuse to see something it is still there. The young necromancer taught me that."

"Erebus taught you? I would have thought it would be the other way around, with you being immortal and all," Alec's voice cracking slightly as surprise and youth combined.

"Clearly you haven't been told my tale quite yet. For now let it suffice that a hundred and thirty year ago, going by planar time, I was in a very sorry state, taken to isolation in the deepest pits of the mirror network when a young magician, hounded and upon the brink of death, stumbled upon my hiding place. It took him three months to recover," the Wanderer recounted fondly. "In that time there was shockingly little to do but talk."

"I assume you're meandering to a point," Edward snapped with annoyance. "And for the record, I rather enjoyed your absence." He turned slightly in his chair to address Saiko directly, though even that visibly pained him. The mercenary, he hoped, the most likely of his audience to be receptive to the spiteful aside prepared, "He was always spouting pseudo-philosophical babble, and since that blighted magician turned up he's become even more longwinded in the telling. One can only hope that when he finally has the decency to shrug off this mortal coil he'll revert back to insufferable rather than intolerable."

Saiko frowned before pointedly ignoring the irritable cadaver impersonator, "You were saying sir?"

"Thank you young warrior. Now where was I… ah yes, Erebus was a surprising companion, at once impatient to be back to the fight and yet somehow very tranquil and accepting of his injuries. As much as he wanted to return to normal reality he never hurried or risked a worsening of his wounds. Once I asked him how, when every day still in the mirror was clearly a trial, he could suffer through it without complaint."

"What did he say?" Alec asked eagerly, keen to gain a better sense of the man who saved his life.

"That a man should not lament that which cannot be changed, for there is nothing to be done. As the past cannot be changed one should not regret it only learn from it and so focus on what we can change. The future," the Wanderer explained.

"Nonsense and poppycock. The past makes the damned future. Our mistakes are what define us!" Edward spat. "Some more than others."

The Smith frowned. "I think," he began carefully, "that it's time you and I visited the Vault, paid our respects."

The Ancient protested fiercely, at least verbally, physically the man didn't, or likely couldn't, offer any resistance and, were they not relieved to see him go, both Saiko and Alec would likely have felt a great outrage at the manhandling of the venerable grouch.

The Wanderer, for his part, merely sighed, "Please forgive Edward; if my curse is great, then his is greater, and the pain he is in keeps him from adopting a stance of acceptance to his fate. Now let us please return our attention to the entertainment so kindly provided by our patron and his rival."

"Tempting, but neither myself nor the boy is gifted with your senses," Saiko lamented albeit politely. The softly spoken warrior had been nothing but gracious thus far, and the merc was warming to him rapidly, strange armour and all.

"Gift would be correct," the Wanderer replied, fiddling idly with his gauntlets. "Unlike most of my brethren, I have no intrinsic magic of my own beyond my curse."

"You seemed to be keeping up with them quite well," Saiko observed smoothly, allowing the implications to ask the question for him.

"Indeed," the armoured man agreed, finally working a finger free from his gauntlet; or so it seemed, for the instant before he worked it free the finger collapsed into several pieces on the ground, the gauntlet just a series of metal rings.

"Enchanted?" the merc asked succinctly as he helped pick the small hoops out of the dew-moist grass.

"For moving and perceiving at greater speeds than the human body can normally," the immortal confirmed with mild approval. "No more than two a hand, unless one of you is a mage in disguise, I'd rather not explain how I managed to poison you both with mana saturation. And don't wear them for more than half an hour unless you want to cook in your own blood."

"I've worn more than four enchanted objects before," Saiko stated as he and Alec put on the rings. Despite the very mild complaint, he only put on four rings, immediately noting the sharpening of vision as the two figures fighting in the background came into focus, now moving on the very edge of his eyes' newfound resolution.

"Not like these you haven't. The Smith and The Runemaker made them so we could spar with the two stooges over there," the warrior explained, watching with gentle mirth as shock overtook them both as the magic set in. "Witness and marvel," he declared in mock awe, the words sounding slurred and slow as he messed up the time differential.

There was a wry chuckle as he gleaned his mistake from their bemused expressions. "I'll leave you youngsters to observe those two showoffs. It's honestly ridiculous those two have been feuding since I met them; it's like they enjoy it." With a last shake of his head, the world's oldest ronin stalked off in the direction of the town, doubtless intent on rejoining his brothers-in-arms who'd already elected to retire from the field of battle as well as those who lacked his interest in martial pursuits.

An unexpectedly amiable silence descended upon teen and sellsword as they watched the fight; their animosity, as one-sided as it had been, had been quick to dissipate. As Alec had gotten to know the swordmaster (however inaccurate Saiko was beginning to view that particular title) he'd realised there was no malice in the man, in fact, his newfound tutor in the ways of the blade seemed to be going out of his way to be nothing but kind and generous around him.

Saiko was particularly attentive to the duel unfolding before him, noting with surprise how the Huntress was using her bow as both club and stave with great effect, a promising style that, were sharpened steel not his one true love, he'd be tempted to learn for himself.

For a brief moment, the duo disengaged, cautiously assessing their foe as they circled, their martial prowess sufficient that, for a span of seconds as they stood in relative stillness, wounds showed through even their ludicrous healing.

The Huntress, for her part, bled from over a dozen scratches on her arms whilst The Swordsman was haemorrhaging blood from a broken nose, the rest of the blunt force trauma hidden beneath his jacket.

After an eternity, at least through the stiletto lens of adrenaline, The Huntress saw an opening and the fight broke into a frantic flurry once more though not for very long. This last attack proving both decisive and brutal. The Huntress swayed under her foe's counter-stroke, calmly absorbing a punch in the ribs as she closed in past his guard to kick hard against The Swordsman's knee, dislocating it with a fleshy pop whilst in the same movement stepping past him to avoid the backswing, the string of her bow pulling tight as she looped it about the man's throat, the garrotting to the accompaniment of the sticky wet shlick of metal biting into flesh.

They both froze, nemesi in a bloody tableau. The Huntress stood behind her opponent, bowstring digging deep enough into his throat to fountain blood, but she hadn't come through unscathed.

From their vantage point, Alec and Saiko could see half a foot of bastard sword sticking through from between her shoulder blades, the blade having been reversed and driven back under his armpit once he realised his foe's true intent.

"A draw," the Huntress said evenly, loosening the string from about his throat.

"A draw," The Swordsman replied gravely once the wound closed, pulling his blade free and flicking blood from it with a practised motion of the wrist. "Until next we meet," he intoned formally, bowing to his opponent before sheathing his blade and retrieving the other before beginning the walk back to town at a normal human pace; the sight almost comical until the two observers quickly removed the Wanderer's rings, falling into step beside him, taking his choice to share their time frame as an invitation for conversation. Correctly as it happened, the tattooed menace turning to regard them with a kindly eye.

"Your thoughts?" he enquired, not breaking stride.

"I don't understand," Saiko said, apparently having mastered his mentor's ease of generality.

"Good. Violence for the sake of violence should never make sense," he replied with an approving nod, waiting for the inevitable second question; not the first or even thirtieth time he'd had this conversation.

"Then why do it?" Alec asked, interjecting smoothly into the discussion.

The Swordsman smiled at the subtle ways in which life could prove predictable and yet so surprising at the same time; right question, wrong source. Maybe he was just getting old.

"Why do anything?" There was a weary half-shrug before he continued with the actual answer, "Habit mostly. Because it's what we've always done, for as long as any of us can remember. I think there was a reason once, I remember that much, although the tradition was well established long before I was declared immortal. I think it was partly because rare was the mortal who could match us, even without magic on our side. Not to mention that if rivals were thick enough on the ground to be likened to wheat in a field, there's our non-interference pact so we probably wouldn't even be allowed to fight. And our actual enemies would be playing for keeps so who else could we practise against? But mostly it's because we've always done it; relics of a bygone age reliving old triumphs and unable to make new ones."

The Swordsman shook his head, "The folly of humanity is always to want more, no matter what you already have."

"That's… sad," the boy replied, not expecting something that bordered upon an emotional outburst from the simple question.

"What pact?" Saiko asked, apparently unmoved by the show of emotion, perhaps suspecting it for a sham.

"One of non-interference, but for a few specific circumstances, we're not permitted to meddle in the politics and wars of mortals. Can't have unkillable soldiers altering the balance of power, though fortunately most of us lack any intrinsic magic."

"I can see the logic, but it sounds nearly impossible to actually enforce," the sellsword observed. Though he'd acted as a bounty hunter for — and against — the supernatural, this would certainly be a job he'd have turned down out of hand; as much as he enjoyed a challenge, there were limits.

"You could say we're prisoners of conscience," he replies wryly. "Or each other."

"My condolences," his proto-protégé replied. "What are the exceptions?"

"This place is possibly the biggest exception, though I prefer to view it as mortals meddling in our affairs rather than the reverse," he snarked though there was a smile to it, the few square miles of peace, tranquillity and safety a source of great pride.

"Any others of note?" Saiko enquired. As world-weary and battle-worn as he was, he couldn't entirely withhold a sense of wonderment strong enough to pierce the 'seen-it-all-done-it-all' attitude that had served him so well through the years. As much as it tended to dent the opposition's confidence if you made a show of taking everything in stride (even if deep, deep down inside you were fiercely wishing you'd remembered to wear your brown trousers) somehow, within Seruatis' wall — the lack of plural required a conscious effort much to his annoyance — he couldn't muster the effort, it not only didn't seem worth it, but it seemed the very height of hubris when brushing shoulders with actual myths and legends.

"The other major possibilities? How good's your history?"

"Passable."

"You're familiar with the Era of Invasion?"

"Only as a mythical footnote."

"Think non-mythical," The Swordsman said flatly. "I know people who lived through it, well most of it. It's complicated."

"That nonsense was real‽" the merc exclaimed in both horror and shock.

"Indeed. Armies of fae, daemons and creatures from beyond the sundered veil we don't even have names for, possibly even can't have names for — a memetic hazard would explain a lot about the accounts. Each army stretching as far as the eye could see. That's the sort of situation where they let us off our leash."

"Sounds terrible," Alec said quietly, envisaging a plain filled with slavering fanged monstrosities, some taller than the Seruatis library, and each consumed only by the need to kill and maim. Whilst alongside them shapeless beings oozed across the landscape like a flood, consuming and extinguishing every spark of life in its wake. The picture in his mind's eye disturbing and unnatural in its clarity.

"It was. Though at least we survived, the dwarves and the trolls weren't so lucky," The Swordsman replied wearily.

"The what?" the boy asked gormlessly.

"Exactly," he replied as they reached the outskirts of town. "Fortunately, the world is a lot safer these days, or so I'm told."

"How often do people tell you things?" Saiko enquired with false sweetness.

"How else am I meant to find things out? You and your employer are the first legitimate reason I've had to step beyond these walls since the last Necromancer-Paladin war."

"And illegitimate excuses?" he asked, an amused twinkle in his eyes as he seized on the choice of words. He'd figured the man out, or at least he felt he had, The Swordsman too honest, or perhaps too clever, to lie outright, instead relying, with practised fluidity, on concealment, misdirection and implication.

"Von Mori and I might have been holding clandestine poker games until people finally caught on." The Eternal Swordsman confessed with a chuckle.

"Dare I even ask what you both used for stakes?"

his protégé inquired, titillated by the revelation. Though his encounters with the great dryad were brief, the second lasting literally as long as it took to bind her, Saiko had found her an imposing presence; it was hard to see her lowering herself to games of chance, no matter how illustrious the opposition.

"I'm afraid that is a secret that will remain between myself and the other competitors. Now, if you'll excuse me, I'm afraid I'm chairing the Confluence's meetings for today," he evaded, peeling off to disappear in the Seruatis library, the trio left a duo. The two staring numbly at each other as they sought to fill the silence now the main topic of conversation had walked off.

"I don't think I could be immortal," the teen said finally, "they all seem so lonely."

"Thousands of years' worth of survivor's guilt," his teacher observed. "It's hardly surprising."

"It's more than that," Alec said slowly, brows furrowed as though solving a particularly thorny puzzle in his head. "I think it's fear of survivor's guilt, and pain at its inevitability. To know that everyone you call friend will become no more than dust whilst you shall live on to see it happen again and again."

Saiko gave him a look of concern, "You are *far* too young to have to understand these things." There was a pause, "Scrap that, I'm too young to have to understand these things."

"Ignorance is only treasured by the ignorant," his student answered off-handedly.

"Now that's got the air of a quote to it. Who's it by?"

"My teacher, back home. He's always coming out with stuff like that, or rather he was." There was a touch of accusatory bitterness to the statement, not that the mercenary could blame him. He may not have given the order, he may not even have liked the order, but he'd carried it out all the same.

He sincerely doubted that if the situation were reversed, he'd have been able to be so understanding or restrain himself to the odd glare and verbal jab. It was a worrying thing to realise a fourteen-year-old was more emotionally mature than himself, that, or far far more emotionally repressed.

"Sounds like an interesting guy," was all he said, intoning it as an apology.

"He was," Alec sighed, picturing the monk's kindly, wrinkled smiling face. "Um… he would have been wearing a brown monk's habit, woollen — you practically itched to look at it. Old, weathered skin, like he'd been left outside for most of summer and shrivelled." No question was asked; no question needed to be asked.

"I don't remember him," Saiko answered truthfully, noting how a metric tonne of tension seemed to life from the teen's too-old eyes and shoulders. "He might have survived."

The boy's expression was grateful but hard, "You know that's a lie."

"Yes," the man admitted, "but I hoped you didn't."

"Thank you," Alec said and meant it. "You know Erebus reminds me of him sometimes."

"Perhaps, but all necromancers have another side; a darker side," Saiko said, quiet and soft. "No one can wield that sort of power without one of two things. Madness or utter faith in a set of values, which is basically madness in nice clothes."

"He's a good person," the teenager insisted. Somehow the necromancer had become the rock upon which he'd built his world. It was as unsurprising as it was obvious, Lutan had torn down the edifice atop which his life had been built upon just a month ago; it was almost natural that he should latch upon the man who saved his life and his values."

"They all are," the swordmaster-once-more-in-training agreed, "right up until the moment they aren't."

"How many mad employers have you actually had?" Alec enquired, sadness ephemeral and mercurial with the vaunted curiosity of youth.

"Depends how much I've had to drink," the merc replied. "Or if I'm feeling cynical."

"And when in a good mood?"

"Maybe four; including Lutan. At least if you're only accepting certifiable and diagnosable insanity." He shrugged helplessly, then began listing, "There was my third employer, egomaniac vampire who wanted bodyguarding in the daytime. Then there was a healer — more bodyguard work — cracked under the pressure and began going all angel of mercy on some of his patients." There was a small sigh and shiver at memories best left behind, "Fortunately when I reported this I got the order to put him down. Some things a mage can do are simply wrong. Lutan got that much right."

"Erebus agrees with him on the subject of dread healers," the boy agreed by proxy; he may not have entirely understood the history of dread healers or the nuances of their power, but anything which scared Lutan and Erebus was something he never wanted to meet.

"Everyone does. It's one of the few major things all major factions agree upon."

"I thought it was just the Mage Alliance and the Paladin Order."

"With the best of respect you've spent most of your life living in a small backwater deep in Paladin territory, there's no reason you should know," he explained, not unkindly.

"So what are the major factions?"

"In Contenmere? It is mainly the Paladin Order and Mage Alliance, though there are a few others. Fortis Umbra, The Court of Stars, Aegis Borealis, couple of other really minor ones. Few major global groups, though they're mostly extradimensional factions looking for a permanent foothold."

"What are they all about?"

"Globals or non-global?" Saiko asked, using the question to buy a couple of seconds to dredge up old memories; as varied and chequered as his past was, he'd had very little to do with the groups he'd named.

"Non. Even I can guess a few of the others." The sentence definite if mildly butchered.

"I don't know much about the Umbra," Saiko confessed. "They tend to keep to themselves, only thing remotely close to public information is that they split from the Alliance eight hundred years ago to deal with something they called 'The Great Threat'."

"What does everyone else call it?"

"Gross paranoia."

"And the others?"

"Well," The merc-turned-surprised-geography-teacher began, moving to more familiar ground, "the Court of Stars is little more than an independent nation of gorgons which the Paladin Order has never had the time or spare manpower to crush; very insular even to necromancers."

"What makes gorgons think necromancers are special?" Alec demanded, a glimmer of old biases reasserting themselves.

Saiko snorted, "If you ever get a straight answer to that one, tell me."

"And the last group? Aegis means shield right?"

That earned a blank look, "I have no idea. But they're the only large faction on the continent I've had direct contact with beyond the obvious two. Maniacs for the most part, largely mages, some kind of big fortress way to the north. They're coldly calculating, as befits their element." He paused for but a moment, catching Alec's questioning glance, "Cryomancers; ice mages," he explained. "It's always a source of amusement how often the mages grow to stereotype their element, though I'm told there's a good reason for it. Something about ease of channelling."

"Channelling?" Alec asked laconically.

"Using the body as a focus and vessel for elemental energy… though that's just what I remember from a very, very dull lecture on the nature of magic. Apparently being 'in tune' with your element makes the spells easier."

"Okay. I guess that sort of makes sense."

Saiko shrugged, "Guess you'd have to be a mage to be sure. Now enough idle chatter, have you been practicing the sword drills I showed you?"

"Yes sir," Alec replied smartly, standing straighter and more respectfully as he transitioned from talking to Saiko, battle-hardened mercenary, to Saiko, his swordplay teacher.

"Good. I want to find you a sparring partner for an hour from now; is that acceptable?" he asked the boy, not quite making it an order as the warning of a masked lunatic played in stereo inside his head. It was probably for the best given how his own training had gone, way back when he'd first grown enamoured by the subtle nuances of blade work.

He still remembered his first day, and sometimes, in the heart of winter, the phantom pain of those long gone bruises would keep him awake.

Saiko's mentor, Jonen McLathe, now long dead and begrudgingly much missed, had not believed in regimented styles, preferring to let his students hone their skills by constant sparring once they'd grasped the basics and no one got in without having grasped the basics. In the grizzled ex-sergeant's own words, "Once you can beat one clockwork soldier you can beat them all."

Alas, the methodology lacked the encouraging nature of the philosophy. Saiko had spent most of his first day being beaten to pulp by two far more experienced students, his only respite being meals and those brief periods where he'd been retrieving his training blade from the sun-baked ground.

For his part, Alec was, in Saiko's opinion, the ideal student. He listened, tended to understand things the first time it was explained, and when he didn't, he asked. The big problem was on his end, having to pick which styles to teach the boy with so limited a time until the necromancer would likely leave, and, if his own mentor were to be believed, the boy with him.

As Alec walked away, Saiko couldn't suppress the feeling that despite his very best efforts, Alec was inevitably heading for a date with an early death.

Chapter 14

Pride was a terrible, difficult thing to swallow up until the point you chose to do so. This was not the first time Erebus had been forced to face this hard truth, but it was definitely the most bitter as he stood outside the ancient enemy's door. Fortunately, with the choice came determination and acceptance, enough, he fervently hoped, for the task at hand.

With great disgust, he rapped firmly on the stout oak door before him, the wood so old it had all but fossilised, and the sharp crack issued forth could have just as easily been the sound of his knuckles breaking.

It was almost two minutes before he heard the sound of footsteps past the threshold; doubtless, the wait was a calculated insult by the owner. The necromancer knew there was no way the creature behind the door hadn't heard the knock and, by other, more esoteric senses, been expecting him for hours.

A dreamy-eyed man opened the door, his stare managing to take in Erebus whilst also gazing into the middle distance. "Hello again necromancer scum. Please do come inside," the man said without preamble before gliding back inside with a swish of his tartan toga and long, flowing auburn locks.

"A pleasure to see you too Pheus," the scum replied dryly, acutely aware the creature was making an effort to be polite. "I'm here to-"

"Get me to save the dryad girl. My answer is no." The man smiled, exposing too perfectly white teeth. "I will see you and everything you care about rot, now would you like a drink?"

"Whiskey please, whatever Agh'zak recommends," Erebus replied. "I am prepared to bargain for her life."

Pheus smiled unpleasantly, "Then perhaps we might come to an arrangement. From your desperation I presume your library search was utterly fruitless."

"As you knew it would be," the necromancer replied evenly. "Your terms?"

"Of course it wouldn't work." Pheus sneered, "Foolish boy, like all your kind, looking to the past to find the future. How you defeated us I will never understand."

"You only fought for yourselves."

"Spare me the heady idealism," his host declared in disgust. "You want terms, here are my terms. Your dreams and a month of nightmares visited by me."

"A steep price," the mage observed. "For the attempt or the successful completion?"

"They are the same. That is why you came to me when all other options were exhausted." Somehow the statement was utterly without ego, a fact and nothing more.

"No one knows nightmares like you Pheus."

"And no one ever will," this time there was ego.

"Why my dreams?" the necromancer asked.

"Boredom. You and the paladin are the most entertaining show for a thousand miles and everyone gets to watch but me."

"And the others? How do they watch this?" Erebus asked, voice growing softer still.

"Nem sees the paladin. Jay sees the choices, but both of you keep your dreams from me."

Erebus laughed, the sounds utterly humourless yet

filled with a near bottomless well of viscous hate. "To know you are reduced to mere voyeurs. Very well o'lord of Dreams. The pact is made."

"The pact is made," Pheus echoes, getting up to fetch two glasses, each glittering like the finest jewels in a king's ransom and pouring a generous measure of amber liquid into each from a jewel-encrusted decanter. "Do you know there's a huge expanse of land across the western ocean which has never known our guidance? A tribal people, rich in oral history and trusted by the spirits of nature."

"Am I supposed to applaud?" the necromancer snorted.

"I haven't got to my point yet," Pheus chastised. "Just south of this place there is an empire, built upon human sacrifice by the bloodiest of my kind ever known."

"And you are telling me this because?"

"Simply enjoying the irony, that we were cast down for our excesses, yet they persist." The man shrugged, "Sometimes I consider making a clean break, letting go of my hate and rage. And then I remember your people had my family killed."

"And all the families they had killed?" a harsh, bitter note in Erebus' voice, quite in contrast with the whisky.

"Weren't mine."

"Very well." The magician sighed, downing his glass in a single burning gulp before continuing with a hint of hoarseness, "Our business is concluded."

"Don't let the door hit you on the way out."

In the two days since Alec had failed to enter Holly's mind he'd had very little free time, either stuck meditating, which wasn't particularly conducive to a clear mind, or learning how to fight with Saiko, the mercenary growing more visibly worried each day and the training more intensive and eccentric.

Yesterday he'd been training against Agh'zak, the orc proving an amiable and patient teacher when kitchen utensils were kept out of reach. This afternoon he'd been tutored by a retired paladin Saiko had managed to dredge from amongst the populace. A fact Alec had come to regret by the third hour of drills, when the wooden gladius in his hand may as well been purest lead. Still, the boy didn't shirk from the training, a fact Saiko found as disconcerting as it was helpful, the mercenary certain that one of the demons the boy was to fight was, in fact, the very same he was being trained to fight.

It was bound to be a fruitless task; Saiko knew Lutan, his style, his weaknesses, his strength. He also knew it wouldn't make a jot of difference if it ever came to a fight. There was no way a couple of months of training, no matter how well targeted, how superlative the teachers themselves or how dedicated the student, could overcome decades of training and experience, not withstanding the better weapons and armour or the greater strength, speed and reach.

Agh'zak had been a lesson in dealing with superior strength, the orc quite reasonable about playing the thug once the motive behind it had been explained. Whilst, in Saiko's experience, orcs were seldom the bloodthirsty, bloodsoaked berserkers of legend, Agh'zak was laid back to the point of pure zen by comparison.

The retired paladin, Sir Antimony, had been a stroke of luck in the discovery. A silver-haired, eye-patched rogue, Saiko had taken an immediate liking to the old man, his first impression one of roguish humour, lazy amiability and razor wit. A mental picture neatly framed by an evening of drinking as they lied outrageously about their exploits.

The paladin had proven a less able tutor than Agh'zak, at least by Saiko's definition, friendly yes, considerate also yes, but an uncreative taskmaster, though that wasn't why he'd recruited the age-silvered swordsman. He'd needed a paladin to teach the boy the basics and, by fortune or fate, had found one. And for all Sir Antimony's creative recounting, his time amongst the townsfolk had proven the old knight's tall tales to be a mere appetiser.

Which led to tonight.

Alec had never had a training session at night before, but there was a certain frisson of expectation on the air and a subtle sense of motion in the shadows as well as gliding silhouettes amidst the umbra, just outside the reach of the magelights. Apparently, Seruatis never truly slept.

Saiko had told him to turn up at the patch of dying grass and moist earth that served as their training ground at midnight, a time he'd interpreted, never having had access to a clock, as a few hours after dark until now. Fortunately, especially given they'd only recently passed the Winter Solstice, Dus had elected to time it for him.

Days at a time of solitude had given the gorgon an uncanny time-sense, or so Alec had come to believe. The truth had proven a touch more practical though not as prescient. The slender beeswax candles that burned in a bowl on Dus' desk burned for an hour and no more, with a ten-hour candle for when she slept, though how she knew if they remained lit when her mask was on Alec couldn't fathom.

The patch of warm earth proved eery in the night air, the shadows giving it the greyish hue of old grave dirt, and each chirp of an insect or faint mammalian rustle was a clarion call to the small nub of neurons in the back of his head marked 'Fear.'

As he began to relax, gaze flitting from shadow to ominous shadow, a hand came to rest gently on Alec's shoulder.

The teen's terrified scream was muffled by the gloved hand across his mouth. "We're going to have to work on your awareness," Saiko said quietly, letting him go. "Allow me to introduce tonight's sparing partner; Anita Vasghoul."

Alec looked around for his foe, whilst pondering why the nocturnal duel, he'd figured out already that each new trainer or foe was intended to teach a lesson. Finding out what the lesson was, on the other hand, and understanding it was another matter.

A small petticoated girl stepped out from behind Saiko, almost a full head shorter than Alec, but he judged to be about his own age, her skin unhealthily pale if belayed by the vitality in her eyes.

Short as she may be, Alec was overcome with a certainty she'd be able to pound him into paste.

"She's kindly agreed to be your sparring partner tonight," Saiko continued.

"Thank you?" he replied hesitantly, mind split between the inevitable beating he was going to receive and the reasons for the subterfuge and misdirection. Another infamous invaluable lesson from his old mentor: The only thing better than spotting and understanding a trick was to not let anyone know you'd done it.

Alec had suspicions as to what the catch was with tonight's lesson, a growing theory. With the bare minimum of flourish, he brought his wooden blade up to a guard position, arms still aching a little from earlier today, the tip aimed at Cassandra's pale throat.

"Ready when you are," the teen declared evenly.

Saiko nodded approvingly, regarding his pupil's stance and movement with the same calculating critical eye he would a potential opponent and despite a few minor problems with his stance — weight slightly too much on the forwards foot — and his grip on the blade a bit too stiff in the wrist — found it passable.

In the mercenary's experience, most people first learning to use a blade had a tendency to grandstand and flourish, more focused on looking heroic than being effective in the belief the two flowed together.

There was an art to fighting for style; arena fighting was a discipline in itself, but it bore little resemblance to one-on-one duelling and even less to a pitched battlefield.

As his mind wandered Saiko kept part of his attention on his student as with steady exactitude, the girl bowed low, and Alec struck, stepping forwards to bring the flat of his blade towards her exposed head, aware the surprise attack could be lethal if it landed edge first even with a training blade.

Saiko smiled briefly, watched as with an adroit sidestep Anita span in under Alec's guard in a neat half-circle, taking him by his overextended wrist and flipping him over her hip into an embarrassing sprawl in the dirt.

The girl stepped backwards, out of reach of a desperate grab or kick, though none was forthcoming. "You fight without honour," she stated as Alec pushed himself back to his feet. "Good. You might just live."

Five minutes later and Alec had had enough, body a mass of stinging welts. As he'd suspected, Anita was most definitely not a young girl, she was too fast, too strong, and even without a sword, she'd beaten the crap out of him. Little more than a blur when she decided to strike, and she'd struck often.

Frustrated, he threw down his blade. "I give up! what's the point of this? I'm getting nothing out of this other than hurt," Alec declared, anger echoing out into the darkness. In any other city, this would have caused a chorus of rage back from freshly awoken residents, but fortunately, as he'd already figured out, the day-night cycle wasn't even given lip service.

"You tell me what the point is," Saiko told him. "You've a decent head on your shoulders, use it."

"And I'm telling you I haven't the slightest clue!" the boy protested loudly.

His teacher frowned, "Very well. Then we shall end this lesson early. Think on what this was meant to teach you and when you've an idea find me and I'll set up another lesson."

Alec scowled but didn't protest further, picking up his blade before saluting his foe/partner as curtly as he felt he could get away with before stalking away to go to sleep.

Saiko shook his head as the boy left, noting the sullen sunkenness in the boy's shoulders, "That could have gone a lot better."

Anita shrugged, "Could have gone worse. It can always go worse."

"It can always go better too," Saiko riposted. "Don't be such a pessimist."

The vampire shook her head, "I'm an optimist at heart. To expect the worst from any situation means you can never be disappointed, all the surprises are joyous ones." She smiled warmly at him.

The merc couldn't suppress a shudder; child vampires creeped him out. Though not the norm, they were popping up more and more often, at least according to some of his friends in the monster-hunting business. On the mage side of the border.

Something about the increasing social acceptability of the undead in modern society, though that was just what the younger hunters said, the old ones, grizzled steel-stubbled bastards to a one, the ones who had stopped being quick a very long time ago and had to settle for smart and underhanded, they simply smiled sadly when the subject was broached, but they wouldn't talk about it.

Usually, child vampires were 'mission of mercy' cases though Saiko couldn't see anything merciful about it. True, their lives were being saved, but saved for what?

Eternity trapped in a child's body, unable to form adult connections, forced to watch your friends and peers age and grow, and eventually wither and die, whilst forever trapped in a body their mind had long outgrown. A lot of adults weren't equipped to handle that sort of trauma. He'd heard almost a quarter of vampires chose to greet the sun within their first three decades though Saiko doubted that. In his experience, when a vampire snapped, they *snapped*, and it was time to clear out or arm up before your corpse was part of an art exhibit with a central theme of red.

From what he'd heard, child vampires were worse.

Anita met his eyes and, he judged, read rather more than he'd have liked from them. "Don't worry. I haven't killed anyone in years."

"That's reassuring," Saiko said dryly. "Sorry your practice got aborted."

"Hardly practice, barely even qualified as fun," she complained, raising a hand that was rapidly turning into claws. "Care to go a few rounds? I'll take it easy on you."

"I'll be sure not to return the favour," Saiko replied smoothly.

The best part of an hour later, nursing a swollen eye, a split lip and some stinging of light cuts, he found himself approached by the necromancer.

"What do you want?" he demanded. He'd been aware of the magician watching for some time, though he'd been courteous enough not to interrupt. Black always showed up bizarrely well in darkness.

"Just curious as to why Alec can almost be classified as a walking bruise," Erebus said.

"He came to you to complain?" the merc revising his estimate of the boy downward.

"Nothing so dramatic. The boy stopped by the infirmary to get some salve for his bruises, I merely happened to be the healer on duty."

"And here you are to question my methods," the swordmaster pointed out, voice sourer than acid.

"I understand your methods. It's an unfair world so you've given him an unfair opponent, someone he would not normally consider a threat then have him crushed mercilessly and repeatedly so he'll treat all opponents no matter their lack of stature or obvious physical prowess with wariness and respect." Erebus paused just long enough for Saiko to nod. "Have you considered that the boy's spirit might break under such methods? He's been through a lot lately."

"I have," the swordsman answered with defensive haste and testiness. "Personally I'd say Alec is made of sterner stuff than that. And if he isn't… then better he breaks here than out there."

"I agree," his former foe replied. "I just wanted to make sure you were thinking about these things."

Saiko nodded, prepared to accept the olive branch on offer, "Why all this interest in the boy? Don't get me wrong, I like the lad but you've gone to great lengths to protect him and at great risk to yourself."

"Our host has been sharing his theories I see," Erebus remarked, rolling his eyes.

"Not even slightly. Why? What does he think?"

"That Alec is my son who I've kept hidden for years under Lutan's nose."

The some-time assassin gave that a moment's thought, "No."

"My thoughts exactly."

"Still doesn't answer my question though."

"Maybe not but let me ask you a question, why should I not have saved the boy?" Erebus smiled slightly, the guise of amateur philosopher one he wore with the familiarity and comfort of an old coat.

"I'm not your apprentice. Nor am I an idiot. Please stop evading."

"Very well," the necromancer replied with steady finality. "My reasons are my own and shall remain so."

"I can respect that. I've some other things I've been meaning to ask you, if you've no objections."

"I will listen to your questions, though I cannot promise you answers," Erebus replied, hedging his bets, still unsure where Saiko's loyalties lay and finding the sellsword both perceptive and likeable, always a dangerous combination.

"Very well," Saiko agreed and the sotto voce negotiations over, ploughed on with his question. "What exactly is a grey mage?"

The necromancer laughed, "Technically I am, as

I'm sure Lutan said many times. Let me guess you didn't want to appear ignorant in front of your employer so just smiled and nodded whilst making appropriate defamatory remarks, possibly concerning my parentage?"

"It tended to do the job."

"It's a rather old and dated title, seldom used since the line between healing and necromancy got really blurry," Erebus explained. "It refers to a magician who is an acknowledged master of a 'white art' — usually healing — and a 'black art' such as necromancy."

"With white representing good and black representing evil," Saiko observed.

"Naturally, though the original reason many of the more morally murky arts were called black magic is that their practice traditionally took place under the cover of darkness, and thus for purposes of juxtaposition any magic that was perceived as good became white. Next question."

"Very droll. Here's a question, I thought most mages only focused on the one art so why would you split your attention between two magics which are antithetical to each other?"

"Because they aren't, or at least the traditional combination of necromancy and healing aren't, they compliment each other magnificently, and the longevity both give gives more than enough time to study both. Both require a near unrivalled knowledge of anatomy and both in times of war have the effect of keeping as many troops in fighting condition as possible."

"Very pragmatic."

"The magicians who survived the constant warring with the Paladin Order had to be pragmatic. The peace we are enjoying now, the same peace Lutan would see shattered is a result of that pragmatism."

"I know my history." Saiko growled, "Just because I'm a mercenary does not mean I'm an idiot."

"Never said you were. Lutan's no fool and unless you're the secret heir of some lost kingdom I can't think of any reason he'd keep a sellsword for an advisor other than that you give good advice."

"You never had the pleasure of Lord Owen's conversation," he replied dryly. "I assure you his swordsmanship was superior in all aspects."

"The knight?" Erebus hazarded.

There was a nod and a smile, "Made advisory meetings all but intolerable."

"What exactly would he suggest?"

"Oh the classics. He really believed the whole 'down with magic' spiel Lutan preached, particularly the concept of tainted by association."

"I presume from your derision that you weren't a believer?"

Saiko gave him a hardbitten look, "Of course I believe, I believe whatever I'm paid to."

The smile shared wouldn't have been out of place on a pair of sharks.

Silence reigned briefly between them until "What are the boy's chances?" the mercenary asked.

"Good. I've found a… specialist who should be able to solve the problem."

"Shouldn't you and Alec be with him then?"

"If only it were so simple, unfortunately Pheus requires Alec to be sharing Holly's nightmare state."

"I know it probably doesn't change anything between us but I do regret the null collar and I did speak out against it."

Erebus closed his eyes in contemplation, "You're right, it doesn't change anything."

"Shall we part ways now?" Saiko said quietly. "It would be a pity to end on a note of discord."

"There is no discord," Erebus assured him. "There is nothing to be done about the past, just have care for your future." The master magician lowered his voice to the deep quiet of a conspirator, "Our dear patron has plans for you, and as I respect him I would play nice even if I despised you, which for the record I don't."

"What sort of plans?" the mercenary queried as a cavalcade of red flags danced in his mind's eye.

"Well the term 'apprentice' may have been tossed around, as might have been 'successor."

Erebus had seldom had just cause to use the word flabbergasted, but this certainly seemed to qualify as Saiko seemed to be giving his best impression, and it certainly was a convincing one, of a freshly landed pike.

"But he's the finest swordsman on the continent!" Saiko managed after the best part of a minute stammering over the first letter.

"Which makes him rather qualified to make such a judgement. He think's you've a natural talent which needs refining."

"Why are you telling me this?" the mercenary asked.

"I think you can guess."

"Lutan," Saiko answered.

"Indeed. I felt, though The Swordsman disagrees, that knowing the opportunity available to you might affect your choices should agents of your old boss come a-calling."

"So you don't actually trust me."

"I trust you to act in your best interests and so I felt it only fair you were able to make a well-informed choice."

"As I said you don't trust me."

"I trust you the same as I trust anyone else, I trust you to act within the confines of your personality."

"But you don't know me," Saiko objects.

"Are you familiar with the phrase 'know the man, know the method'?"

"Yes…" the sellsword replied, not sure where the necromancer was going with this.

"Then by the same virtue to know the method is to know the man, and so you'll find I do in fact know you rather well sellsword."

Saiko glared, "How do you know Lutan's people aren't already here, laying in wait?"

"You'd have told us." This was met with a doubtful look, "I said I know you. You're a natural survivor, you'd tell us just to hedge your bets. I get assassinated and we can't blame you and you remain in favour with Lutan. Whereas if we foiled any such attempts then you gain favour in our eyes and Lutan never finds out."

Saiko considered protesting, but unfortunately, it was all true. "You're disturbingly perceptive for a necromancer. The ones I've met tended to spend all of their time wittering on about if truth is beauty then is beauty truth and whether it's possible to hear falling trees."

"I'm the other kind of necromancer," Erebus replied with a quiet smile. "You remember those evil bastards who starred in the old tales? I'm one of them."

The mercenary laughed nervously, "I'm beginning to see that."

"One last question before I leave you in peace. Did you know what Lutan had planned for Von Mori?" There was an edge to the question, and despite Seruatis' ban on non-consensual violence and Erebus' earlier assurances of good intent, Saiko knew that if he gave the wrong answer, then the peace he'd be left in would be a final one.

"I knew he had a plan but I didn't even expect what it involved. My guess was some careful legal obfuscation under the auspices of the Accords."

The mercenary shook his head in disbelief, "If I had any idea at all well… contract be damned I'd be being led blindfolded through the Stonegaze mountains right now."

"What do you know about the soul binding he used?" Erebus asked, sallow and troubled.

"Well, emerald focus, but you already knew that and I've no idea where he got one that large, but very intricate runes inside it, four dimensional layering."

"Four?" the necromancer spluttered. "Are you absolutely sure it wasn't a trick of the light?"

"Beyond a shadow of a doubt. I even asked."

"Most troubling… and Lutan had his armour on during the activation?" This was met with a curt nod, "Very troubling indeed, the only way to get a spell-trap that intricate in the presence of nullstone is to use enchanted null for the runes."

It was Saiko's turn to splutter, "Impossible. I've never even heard the legend of a craftsman that good."

"I know of just two able to pull off such a work of power and skill. They're both here as it happens."

"The Smith," Saiko guessed, glancing at the currently inactive acceleration rings on his fingers, "and…?"

"The Runemaker; what you've described is exactly his area of expertise."

"I can't see it if I'm honest. How would Lutan even know he existed?"

"I'm not allowed to tell you. There are confidences I can't betray."

"Can't or won't?"

"Does it matter?" the centuries-old mage replied, smile terribly sad and desperately weary. "You know how the game is played."

"Blood contract or worse?"

"Does it need to be worse?" Erebus replied. "I think I'll take my leave now, though I fear your candour has merely spawned more questions."

Saiko watched the necromancer with a mixture of dark amusement and respect.

He wondered what guesses the magician was keeping to himself. He'd certainly been right about most of it.

Once he was sure Erebus was gone, he split into a full grin; it was time to hedge his bets.

Chapter 15

It was with a heavy heart that Erebus stood silent vigil over Alec's sleeping form, though sleeping was a poor descriptor for it. The boy's brow drenched in a cold sweat as he twitched and moaned with agony, in perfect synch with the dryad in the cot beside him. It had taken a full day longer than Erebus predicted, but Alec had finally succumbed to the nightmare leaking across his bond with Holly.

Holly herself was in a worse state and, in many ways, the necromancer's primary concern. With the soul bond in place, to lose one patient was to lose both of them and even at a glance, it was clear that the dryad was on the cusp of death, her bark hewn skin drawn, cracked and weeping from dehydration despite Erebus' best efforts.

The door opened with a gentle creak, Pheus stepping in quietly, but for that, there were incorporeal spirits that moved louder.

Slowly Erebus turned to face him, fight or flight instincts warring across his face before they could be forced behind a barricade of calm and collected dispassion.

"I expected you earlier," the necromancer stated, an opening salvo of reproach.

Pheus narrowed his eyes, "You were a low priority. Now allow me to see my patients."

Begrudgingly Erebus stepped aside, trying not to antagonise the creature further.

Pheus moved nimbly to the bedside, placing his

hand on Alec's forehead. "His natural mental defences have almost completely crumbled. Once the last barriers have fallen I can begin."

"Why do you need him in such pain?" the magician enquired.

"Better access," the thing-in-human-form half-explained. "I will need optimal conditions for this to work."

"And what exactly do you intend to do?" Erebus not quite demanding.

"Well, like you, I have no idea how to even begin healing the dryad. Normally I would simply consider her a lost cause and spare her not a second thought, but the boy opens up a line of approach.

Erebus folded his arms, less than impressed by the grandstanding even if it was relevant.

"The boy's condition on the other hand I could solve in a heartbeat but for the fact the problem would retransmit back to him in a matter of days. What I can do however is build a general spell template using the boy to specifically cater to the nightmare in question. Then I simply use the template on the girl, she wakes up and then so should he."

"Clever," Erebus conceded. "But what if the difference in species causes an adverse reaction? No one can build a spell that affects magical and non-magical beings that fast, it takes decades of research."

"Then they both die. I don't care either way what the result is."

The magician took a deep calming breath but held his tongue, "How long will it take?"

"As long as it takes," Pheus replied, eyes now closed, his hand still on Alec's forehead.

"That isn't helpful."

"Helpful wasn't part of our bargain. Now leave me to work."

"There is no way in the hells that I'm leaving you alone with them."

"Very well, if your paranoia extends that far but be warned: I shall require complete silence whilst I'm working."

"I can do that," Erebus assured him solemnly.

"Starting now."

Outside, a small audience waited, Saiko, Dus, Agh'zak and Alisha, each with their best impressions of patience, disrupted only by the occasional bout of conversation.

With an amused smile, the mercenary-turned-honour-guard swept his gaze across the motley crew, biting his tongue gently in concentration before speaking.

"Well I know why I'm here but the rest of you I can't quite figure out," Saiko drawled in transparently feigned disinterest.

"I have grown fond of the boy and thus am standing vigil lest the creature attempts something," Dus all but spat.

"I take it you don't like this Pheus guy?" the swordmaster hazarded.

"No. You I dislike sellsword. 'Pheus' as he now calls himself, I loathe and revile with a burning hate. I have waged wars and toppled empires to kill him and all those like him."

"What is he exactly?"

"In terms you would understand? A god, ancient and terrible," Dus replied. "You could honestly say they made me the woman I am today."

"But gods aren't real," Saiko said dully. "Everyone knows that. They're a fairytale for children."

"And we have worked extremely hard to make sure it stays that way," the gorgon growled.

"If he's a god, then what would you possibly hope to do?" Saiko demanded as he struggled to comprehend this new paradigm, not even half-convinced that the gorgon wasn't simply pulling his leg.

"Kill him, if he breaks the rules then he's fair game," the glee in her voice was quite worrisome. "I have waited so very long for him to step out of line."

"I thought gods were supposed to be immortal?" Saiko pointed out the obvious problem.

"As our patron is so fond of saying, 'Immortal simply means no one has found a way to kill it yet'. The necromancers found a way, if you ever earn Erebus' trust, unlikely as that is, ask him about the Ascended Martyr."

"Why can't you tell me?"

"Because I don't trust you."

Alisha sighed, rolling her eyes, "For inspiration's sake Dus, you've told him this much, you might as well tell him the rest."

The gorgon scowled behind her mask, "You tell him then. It's bad enough the necromancer figured it out."

"Hardly figured it out, if you didn't want anyone to know you'd have destroyed the damn book rather than burying it in the back catalogue," Alisha snapped, clearly an old argument.

"No one ever read the back catalogue!" the gorgon grouched emphatically.

"He did," Agh'zak observed, the orc's deep bass rumble bringing the matter to a close.

"So is anyone going to actually tell me whatever it

is you all keep alluding to?" Saiko demanded, "Or do I need to know the secret handshake first?"

The orc chef placed a hand on his shoulder, "It's about trust lad. Now I want to trust you and Alisha wants to as well, but we ain't had the time to get to know you properly."

"Joy. So hurry up and wait essentially."

Alisha smiled, aiming for reassuring, "I'll tell you what I'm allowed to when we next spar."

"Allowed to?"

"An unwritten rule you don't share secrets that aren't yours," she explained.

"Are you able to tell me who can tell me?"

"Yes but they won't. Erebus is the most likely to share some of it, but he doesn't know everything, and he obeys the same strictures."

"So I get why the snake-haired psycho is here but why are you two?"

Dus bristled, snakes extending out from her hood, hissing and spitting venomously as Saiko backed away, slightly pale as he looked plaintively at Agh'zak and Alisha.

The orc laughed, fully content to let things fall as they would.

Alisha was less accepting, "Control yourself Lady," she snapped with acid ire.

Dus paused, then slowly the serpents withdrew back into the shadowy recesses of her hood and then the last sound Saiko could possibly have expected from the raging gorgon — a quiet sob.

In moments Alisha was beside her, arm around her shoulders, "It's okay my lady," she said quietly, leading the robe gorgon away with a gentle hand, "deep breaths."

As Saiko watched them walk away, he noted

Agh'zak, the orc watching him in turn with a chill look of calculation behind his perpetually bloodshot eyes.

"Was that deliberate?" he asked quietly. The question, while soft, was devoid of his usual warmth. For the first time since meeting him, Saiko actually saw the orc as a threat. Sure he'd seen him cleave through a carcass with a single casual swing of his cleaver but thus far, he'd never once imagined what might happen if the jovial behemoth turned that herculean strength upon him. It wasn't a mental picture he relished.

"No," he said with slow caution, "I'm not even sure what just happened."

The orc's expression softened, "You don't live in Seruatis unless you're a monster of one form or another. For a few that's a more literal statement than moral."

"That is either a deep philosophical statement or utterly uninformative, maybe even both."

"It's part of her curse. Anger, rage and hate boil to the surface easily and with Pheus so close it's particularly raw. If she didn't hate you before then she probably does now."

"Oh joy. You're telling me she was giving me regular death threats but didn't hate me?"

"From Dus that's basically hello," the gourmand gourmet assured him. "You weren't really worried were you?"

"Absolutely terrified," Saiko admitted, leaning in and lowering his voice further. "She said she would-" he glanced around nervously, reducing himself to a whisper as he relayed the threat.

The orc warlord turned a shade greener than usual, audibly dry-heaving. "I take it back. That threat she meant."

"Wonderful. So is there anything I should know about how to avoid disproportionate snakey vengeance?" he asked the orc, looking somewhat queasy himself.

"Just… try to stay out of her way. Dus has far bigger prey on her mind than a mere human mercenary. No offence."

"Some offence taken. What's all this mere human malarkey? Even Alisha's pulled it on me once or twice."

"It's well.. how to phrase this nicely? It's your lifespan. When so many people here will never die of old age there's a certain disconnect, a level of insulation."

"You're saying they view me as a child," Saiko interpreted sourly.

"Nothing so dismissive," Agh'zak assured him. "But see it from their point of view, any of them who befriends you is going to watch you get old and die. When you live thousands of years that's a lot of heartache. After a couple of lifetimes most just don't bother getting to know anyone who comes with an expiry date attached, less hurt in the long term."

"You don't do that, The Swordsman doesn't."

"Oh orcs get old, it takes slightly longer than with humans but it happens, it's just so rare, what with the whole constant tribal warfare problem, not even most orcs know it happens. An orc is referred to as 'Elder' if they make thirty."

This drew a tight-lipped frown across Saiko's narrow features, "But I've lived amongst orcs, two years with the Bloodtide tribe, and never heard of this."

"That is because of how rare it is. My people have based their entire culture around war. It's a practice that has made us exceptional in terms of strength and resilience. Life expectancy not so much."

"Sounds tough," the human replied, trying not to sound uncaring. "I can see why you gave it all up."

Agh'zak stared at him, or possibly through him, large, deep-sunken eyes not unkind, "No. You can't," the orc answered, gravelly voice coming across even graver than he'd intended. "I forsook my clan, my family and my honour by leaving."

"Then why do it?"

"For friendship. Matters of leadership in my clan were dealt with by an honour duel to the death."

"Not much of a friend if they challenge you to a fight to the death," Saiko interjected, stopping as Agh'zak pierced him a look of pure venom.

"He was a good friend. He simply disagreed with the direction I was taking the clan." The orc's voice was a fire of barely suppressed rage, "He was a good orc, an orc of strong principles, that is why he was my friend and that is why he felt he had no choice but to challenge me for the leadership of the clan. You know nothing of our way, so don't presume to."

"I know you're a very lucky person. I've never had a friend I wouldn't be willing to kill if I had to."

The orc frowned, "You are either a terrible person or have had terrible friends."

"Probably both," Saiko admitted shamelessly. "So is there anyone in Seruatis who isn't fleeing something?"

"There's you."

"Perhaps. Though running to is not so different to running from."

"And what exactly are you running to?" the old orc asked, surprised and perhaps even mildly suspicious of this introspection.

"Being a better version of myself I think. I haven't been in this place long, I only actually met my room-mate a couple of days ago for example, but I can feel it changing me. When I spar with Alisha I know I've never been this fast or this skilled."

"She tends to have that effect." Agh'zak looked thoughtful, deep furrows travelling across his brow, "Been a while since I gave the old armour a good airing. Mind if I join you tomorrow?"

"I don't have a problem but she's a bit tetchy around other people."

The orc nodded, not rising to the inherent question. "I'll ask her. See you then."

"What about this whole keeping an eye on this Pheus guy?"

"That's Dus' worry, not mine," the orc called back, beginning to head towards his siege-proof kitchen. "I just wanted to back up a friend; she's not here so my job is done."

As he watched the orc walk away, it occurred to Saiko, and not for the first time, that Lutan had played him for a fool and that, rather naively, he'd assumed himself invaluable.

The concept of atonement was a new one for him; previously, a mistake was something he'd simply survived then avoided in the future.

Still, there was another concept, far older and easier to grasp, running parallel to the blossoming of his newfound conscience: Revenge.

Lutan had set him up; there would be a reckoning.

Chapter 16

When Pheus opened his eyes, he was, for a brief moment, in two places at once, two images flickering between each other for just long enough to get a vague impression of barren trees before the other image won out, the ancient creature finding himself in an apparently deserted village, the entire place a patchwork of foreboding wooden and thatch buildings and deep shadows, so thick and absolute a man could get lost in them.

A brief check of the horizon showed the absence of the sun, though the faint glow promised it had either left recently or was soon to arrive.

"It's dusk," Erebus said firmly, "though you should have known that. This is a nightmare afterall."

Pheus whirled around, eyes narrowing at the black-robed silhouette as he rested nonchalantly against the timber wall of what appeared to be a butcher's shop.

"You shouldn't be here," the master of dreams declared. "Your presence in the boy's mind could contaminate my investigation."

"Fortunate then that I am not in Alec's mind, nor in Holly's," the magician answered evenly.

"Impossible," Pheus scoffed. "A mere instant in my thoughts should drive you to insanity."

Erebus chuckled lightly, the sound jarringly out of place in the soon-to-be night air, "It's cute that you consider me sane in the first place, besides your mind is far less alien and inimical to mine than say a fae or a daemon's."

"How are you alive? It's like you read a book titled 'Really Stupid Things To Do' and treated it as a checklist," the lord of dreams muttered, returning his attention to his surroundings.

"Lots of practice," the magician replied, resuming his own observations, "And my master was a daemon, and we had to cover mental defences, so… that wasn't fun. Lots of therapy afterwards."

"Very trite. But I still wonder what they all see in you, a mere mayfly before a mountain. What makes you so special that The Swordsman would risk war? That the Wanderer would be moved to return to the world?"

"Perhaps, to use your own metaphor, because the mayfly was given the option of being a mountain but chose to remain a mayfly. Now I believe that we are here to help Holly and Alec, not bicker like petty children."

"It is as you say," Pheus conceded, "though I am confused as to the relevance of this place to the girl."

"None that I know of. Why?"

Pheus frowned deeply, dark creases of annoyance across an otherwise perfect face, "It means the nightmares aren't shared, merely parallel."

"Can you still do it?" Erebus asked after a moment to digest this information.

"I don't know. A generalised spell was one thing, a single fact, a single point where it could fail. I could accommodate for that with the right runes, but a second generalisation does more than double the risk and the energy needed is greater. You'll have to accept there is now a very good chance that the spell won't work."

This was met with a simple nod from the necromancer, "I presume the difficulty is one of complexity and not power."

"Indeed, though I'll need someone to contain the fallout."

"I'll do it," the mage declared without hesitation.

Pheus laughed in his face, "You're a battlemage, I need a specialist in warding and defensive bindings."

"Present."

The ancient creature looked surprised at this, "I assumed the Necropolis' favourite attack dog would be more aggressive."

Erebus met his gaze with cold compassion then began, with an air of quiet indignation, "It matters not the strength of the blow, nor how many are thrown, simply that-"

"Your's is the last," Pheus finished for him. "A practitioner of Endurance Vile. Very well, you're qualified."

"How much inefficiency are you expecting from this spell?" the centuries-old youth asked, tone no longer bitterness and hate but that used with a respected peer as he focused on the task at hand.

"Up to half."

"That's pretty crude for an intricate spell. What's the expected backlash?"

"Enough to turn the infirmary into a smoking crater."

Erebus winced, drawing the air sharply through his teeth.

"More than you can handle?" Pheus enquired dryly.

"No. Just enough that I hope you work fast. What do you need to complete the spell?"

"An intimate knowledge of the fears that built this ghost town. I'm rather surprised actually, normally in a nightmare something has jumped out and tried to kill me by now. This place just seems desolate and sad."

"Then let us explore further and see if we can find you such a monster."

The two of them began going building to building but found not even a trace of life until finally there was but one home to check. It had been obvious, really, but it had been important to check the rest for fear of missing a vital detail.

"I don't know what exactly we'll find in here but if anywhere will let you understand the cause of this nightmare it will be here," Erebus informed him yet put out an arm to stop him going inside.

"You know something, or at least suspect," Pheus observed.

"Two good people died here. This is the home he can never return to. What the two children have in common, the loss of a home, the loss of their parents."

"And the reason I can't go inside?"

"You can but I suspect Alec will be there, I'm worried about the effect someone might have on his nightmare if they were to burst in."

"I thought you weren't an expert on dreamscapes?"

"I'm not but I know Alec, possibly better than he knows himself."

"Really? A boy you just happened to rescue on your travels, who's village you just happen to have a near intimate knowledge of."

"You know," Erebus whispered tiredly. "Please don't tell the boy."

"If he's as smart as you say he'll figure it out for himself. He won't thank you for not telling him."

"You almost make it sound like you care."

"Or I just enjoy watching you hurt. Can I go in now?"

"Yes. Dining room and kitchen the doorway on the left, both bedrooms in the back, and the door opens onto what is essentially a living room or parlour."

Pheus gave his unsought partner a curt nod before pushing the door open, striding in as if he were still a god amongst men.

His first impressions of Alec's home were poor. No gold, no marble, nor even the simple stone he was forced to tolerate these days. The place smelled strongly of earth, and the furnishings were simple, if well made, oak. The kitchen had a similar motif; the crockery possessed of a certain deciduous air, each bowl, plate and cup made of many thin layers of various woods, bent and carved into shape and held together with strong resin. Pheus turned his nose up at the lack of jewels.

Both rooms shared another additional theme; they were devoid of life.

His next target was the boy's room, surprisingly fully furnished, though it had been a theme of the entire town that the children all had a small writing desk in the corner of where'er they slept, courtesy of Alec's first mentor, the monk. What it was missing, however, was Alec himself. With an annoyed scowl marring otherwise perfect features, he moved to the final room, Alec's parents' room.

Even at the door, he could tell. There was a tension to the air, a charge of power still potential. A fact only further confirmed when he got hit by a static discharge strong enough to make his knees weak when he touched the smooth worn wood of the doorknob.

He drew his hand back sharply, cautious to a fault. This would require a gentle touch, he decided.

The child's power was a strong one, he could

certainly survive an outburst from him, but to do it nestled this deep in the boy's psyche, the measures he'd need to take would likely leave the boy unable to even feed himself.

Carefully he drew back out of the house, standing in front of the patiently waiting Erebus.

"Well?"

"He's stronger than I expected. A lot of natural power, none of your borrowed nonsense."

"Envy ill becomes you," Erebus replied dryly. "And my borrowed power has its advantages."

"If the rumours are true that's a lot of advantage."

"You know how rumours are, people exaggerate." The necromancer smirked slightly.

"I also doubted them, until I found out how you overcame all that null.

"Lifeforce, over a decade of impure vitae. Which is shocking considering I know your bloodline hasn't a trace of daemon in it."

"This borders very close to stalking."

"No it is stalking, I did tell you we were taking an interest, you and your merry band are the best entertainment since your lot stopped warring with your nearest neighbour."

"Back to the matter at hand please. What can you do to help Alec?"

"I'm no longer sure," Pheus admitted begrudgingly. "This is going to take a day; minimum. You used to be a full-time healer as I recall?"

"You need me to keep them stable."

"Correct. Is this a problem?"

"Quite a large one," Erebus confessed, expression deep and drawn. "I don't have very much in the way of reserves right now. The process of warding alone is going to tap those. Nearly everything I have has been going on growing new heart cells and fixing our dear patron's botched heal."

"A little ungrateful aren't we?"

"Not even mildly, he saved my life, but he also left me with a section of my heart that is likely to tear itself slowly apart without constant supervision. As it is I'm barely surviving through the night."

The ancient creature gave this due thought, "How long until you finish healing?"

"Without risks? Six months. Myocardial cells are a pain in the ass to make, not high energy, just technical."

"Myocardial being heart cells? I lose track of the terminology you mortals bandy about."

"Yes it's heart cells," Erebus growled, "the point being that I am very limited in what I can do right now. Too much energy and my 'stitches' burst."

"Can you bring in someone to handle the healing then?"

"Not a chance. In Seruatis I could find at least one of any brand of battlemage you'd care to name even the illegal ones… make that especially the illegal ones. But most of them don't even have basic triage training."

"Why didn't you stop the paladin?" Pheus demanded, sharp and sudden, jolting the mage from his line of thought.

In other circumstances, Erebus would have applauded the ambush, nice and private where the answer would be unheard, but with his thoughts in disarray, he opted reflexively for defence. "Why do you want to know?"

"Because you're too important to show weakness. Because I want to know this fragile little world is in safe hands and because I like knowing things others don't. Pick whichever one appeals to conscience and ego."

Erebus stared at him studiously for long enough that the silence grew deafening until, at last, "He wasn't worth the price. Now, if you will excuse me, I have a patient to attend to." With that, the mage vanished, withdrawing from Pheus' mind as gently as he'd arrived.

"Interesting," the old god mused before getting back to work.

From the safety of his own body, Erebus took a few precious moments to plan. The situation was, from the information available, hopeless. It was a matter of hours before Holly's body, and then Alec's shut down, and the only chance was for a madman to create a spell of what even he admitted would be of dubious help. Normally he'd have been able to hold the pair of them at the cusp of death for days, or if he were prepared to delve deep into the few forbidden arts, he could hold them there indefinitely.

As things stood, he might hold for an hour, maybe two if he approached it aggressively, predicting and addressing failing organs as they happened, but that was optimistic in the extreme with no equipment beyond his travelling staff.

The spells would have to be cast on Alec and then hopefully mirrored across the link; dryad biology was just too unknown to him to heal on the fly. What he needed was an edge, desperately, and he knew exactly where to find one.

Against his better judgement, Erebus permitted himself a moment of self-pity before he put his plan in place. "You're getting soft old man." The lie slipped easily from his tongue by virtue of practice.

Soft had been thirty years ago. Soft had been foolish

promises to a dying friend and a daemonic contract made in haste and rage.

Soft would have killed Lutan without a second thought.

Self-pity over with, he made his way to the door, unsurprised to find only Saiko outside.

"You said something innocuous and she lashed out," he surmised. "Not your fault sellsword, she would have been looking for any reason to go on the offensive ever since I involved Pheus."

"How did you-?"

"It's my job to know. Also their antagonism is infamous." Erebus smirked, at a passing thought, fast as a trout rising for a mayfly and then gone. "Now I need you to do two things for me."

To his credit, at least in Erebus' eyes, Saiko didn't protest at his co-opting, merely looking briefly bemused, "What do you need?"

"Go to Dus, she'll be in her room at the library, top floor, can't miss it, tell her I need her to see me immediately, not I need to see her, I need her to see me. Make sure she knows I insisted on that wording, she should be able to figure out my plan. After that I need you to sprint to the cafeteria, get a warding expert to come here, I don't care how you do it. Then to the Confluence's meeting hall. Tell The Swordsman that I urgently request access to the Seruatis' vault and require temporary use of the Temporis Vitae hourglass. Understand?"

"I'm not sure Dus will be very-"

"Just tell her it's to save the boy, she has a weak spot where youngsters are concerned."

"And The Swordsman?"

"Enjoys every bit of mischief and intrigue he can manufacture within the rules he's bound by."

"Very well," the mercenary conceded, taking off at a reasonable jog which rapidly accelerated to a sprint as he rounded the corner.

With peace assured, Erebus allowed his mask of confidence to slip. He was taking a risk involving the Temporis Vitae hourglass, whilst magic that altered the perception of time was allowed, magic that actually altered one's path through it was strictly forbidden to mortal kind, with immortal kind only allowed it because no one had been brave enough to take it away, and whilst he bent that rule many times, often to the point it was practically a knot, requesting the hourglass would make it a matter of public record. A situation previously avoided by the phrase 'no survivors'.

Still, the chance that future necromancers might stumble upon his misdeed was one he was prepared to take; the Temporis Vitae was an invaluable device, allowing a mage to throw a single spell up to an hour into their own future, literally as long as the sands lasted. An extra hour he could buy and then once more into fate's less than gentle hands. If it came to that, he'd ask Dus to gaze the boy, Alec, to become yet another stone patient, their lives on a permanent hold until a cure for their ailment was discovered. Holly, with a body of magic, would be less fortunate, dryads immune to a gorgon's gaze.

Dus was first to arrive, the gorgon almost silent in her approach as she took station by the door, facing the wall as her voice rang quiet but clear through the infirmary, "My mask is off." And then she stilled, much like a statue herself.

"Thank you," Erebus replied quietly, one hone over Alec's insensate form as he ran some low energy diagnostics on his patient. "The plan is to stonegaze me while I channel a high energy panacea spell into Alec. Hopefully the spell will carry on whilst, being a stature, the resultant wasted magic won't tear my stitches."

"I'm hoping there is more to this plan because all I'm seeing is Alec unable to die until you run out of magic, and it can't be your magic powering it."

"I have some daemons contracted to supply me in times of need."

"I bet that cost a pretty penny. What did they want?"

"Nothing I'd miss." Erebus assured her.

"Well as delightfully perverse as I find using daemons for a healing, this still leaves you even more stone-faced than usual come the end."

"That has been accounted for," he promised. "Hopefully our dear patron can be persuaded to loan me the Temporis Vitae."

"And if he doesn't?"

"Either I spontaneously replicate the effect of an advanced artifact who's magic is not only nuanced but who's construction took thirty years without even seeing the device in question. Or I can look forwards to a highly successful career as a lawn ornament."

"It's not worth it," Dus said softly. "I like Alec, truly I do, but this world needs you."

"I'm rather relying on that to be given the Temporis."

"Manipulative," the gorgon observed approvingly.

"Is it really manipulative when the person you're manipulating actually wants to be manipulated?"

"Yes."

"Then yes it's manipulative. Still unless you and the merc finally got past your sexual tension enough to gaze lovingly into each other's eyes," he already had his own shut for Dus' inevitable reaction, the shocked gorgon spinning around unmasked as she rallied to defend herself, "then the hourglass will be here shortly."

"I would never-"

"Then there's no need to be so angry, my lady," Erebus interrupted with consummate calm. "Just stop being so spiky around the poor child."

"He's a grown man Erebus, accountable to his own choices," she snapped.

"Maybe. But after so long they all seem like children."

"And there lies the doom of mages. Everyone's a child who can't be trusted with responsibility, so you make sure no one else ever has any. You know there's a word for that, it's called tyranny."

"And the alternative? This world hangs by a thread. We dare not risk another war 'tween mages, not for ten thousand years. Too many wounds in the world, easy to inflict hard to heal. And too many chains still lingering in the mind, warping our natures towards conflict."

"And is that really yours to decide?"

"No. But I'm doing it anyway," Erebus declared. "And yes my hypocrisy is breathtaking."

"Then why do it?" Dus demanded, greater heat and greater ire venting from her than she'd ever directed at Saiko, such strength to it that for a moment, he feared violence.

"Because no one's principles are an unassailable fortress, everyone has to compromise them somewhere, or force others to do the same to accommodate them."

"I've never-"

"Your situation is unique Dus, and cruel, and your

principles revolve entirely around revenge and staying alive. Everyone else has to compromise under certain circumstances, maybe their life is threatened, maybe a loved one's life is threatened, maybe they are faced with torture, starvation or the condemnation of their peers, or perhaps their principles conflict and they have to choose which one they compromise. Such is the fate of all who wish for more than to have their enemy dead at their feet and to spit on the corpse. My personal point of compromise is the destruction of all life."

"A cruel fate."

"They seem to enjoy it."

"And what of your fate young necromancer?"

"I had it told once, a true telling from one driven mad by their spark of divination, she told me my destiny, told me that while most such fates can be escaped with effort and foresight, mine was bound tighter than chains. Naturally I rebelled against such a proclamation, but alas she was correct."

"Cursed to eternal happiness, joy and success?" the gorgon asked sweetly, almost sing-song in her speech.

"Nothing so cruel as that. I will simply always arrive too late."

"A nebulous statement, your victories are great, the fate false," Dus argued.

"No, any victory I ever had came from battles I stopped from happening, or from battlefields rendered lifeless before my arrival. Necromancy at least benefits from tardiness. I could not escape it, so I subverted it, embraced it even, I joined a first response team, tried to use my fate to my advantage, later second response, and still the fate was cruel."

"So all you've done is because you're trying to outrun fate. A pity. I thought there might by hope for you."

"No." And there was iron in the necromancer's voice, a cold fury that flared brighter with each bitter word. "Everything I've done I did because someone had to do it. My fate, true or not, is not something I've run from; I turned it into a blade to be wielded against those I call enemy."

"Good. Now… go back to saving Alec's life," the order undisguised and resolute.

"Of course m'lady," Erebus answered amiably, his hand never having left Alec's shallowly rising chest. "But I can't maintain this forever."

"You seem perfectly fine at the moment."

"That just means I'm good at seeming m'lady. One of the spells on my heart just gave way."

"Wonderful," Dus observed dryly.

Erebus shrugged, a slight strain creeping into his voice, "It is what it is. Now I need you to face the wall again; if Saiko bursts through those doors right now I'm going to have to explain to a very good friend why his apprentice is doing his best impression of a rockery."

Silence reigned after that, one irritated at their dismissal and the other increasingly struggling to even stay on his feet.

By the time the mercenary arrived, cradling a brass hourglass the size of a pub stein, Erebus was on his knees, eyes closed not from concentration but agony and fatigue, the necromancer slumped against the bed, a single-arm limp across Alec's chest as his mind raced to keep them both alive with the limited magic he could avail himself of.

As quickly as he could, without risking the artefact entrusted to him, he roused the necromancer with a gentle nudge.

Erebus turned half-focused eyes upon him, taking

precious seconds for his pupils to sharpen, focusing upon the hourglass in the mercenary's outstretched hand. "Thank… you… you need to leave."

"Well there's gratitude for you."

A hand gently came to rest upon his shoulder as Dus whispered to him, "It is." The grip tightened as he tried to turn. "Don't turn around. My mask is off. Eyes to the floor, crawl out. There is no time for consideration."

Saiko complied, eyes not leaving the floorboards until he reached the door, gaze raising in time to see the vibrant green-yellow flash of the panacea being cast, the excess energy of the spell rattling the windows and raising the ambient temperature from muggy night to lacklustre sauna.

Seconds later, everything that was Saiko was forced from his body, mind-expanding to encompass the world and everything in it, then wide, a perfect sphere of awareness encompassing next the moon then the world's fellow planets and the star they faithfully orbited.

Then wider, the local star systems, wider still until he could make out a spiralling arm and then the galaxy it was attached to. More information than any mind was meant to hold.

Then more, the local group, out and out until he could not even have pointed where he started from, whilst at the same time his focus narrowed; every grain of dust, and smaller. He didn't have the words to describe what he saw as his vision shrank, molecule then atom, all of it down to the space between space. A meaningless expanse of infinite information.

When Saiko came back to himself, he became aware someone was screaming, ragged, reedy and hoarse; seconds later, he recognised it as himself.

"There's a reason some spells are banned," Dus said from behind him; fortunately her mask was on again, the merc lacking the presence of mind to close his eyes — if he were honest he'd probably struggle to count his fingers right now.

Unsteadily the gorgon slithered past him, managing to make it to the grass before retching copiously; moments later, Saiko joined her in feeding the flowers.

"What was that?" he gasped once there was nothing but bile left and precious little of that.

"Spell backlash," Dus answered weakly, wiping her mouth clean with the back of a hand before wiping that clean on the grass.

"Bullshit," the mercenary replied. "Spell backlash is a bit of heat and a few sparks, not… whatever that was."

"That's because you have never been near a time spell before… and that the energy required was enough you'd need to destroy reality itself to cast it."

"Then how did he do it?"

"By destroying the universe." She paused to enjoy his disbelief, "Well in potential. The hourglass axes entire lines of causality, carefully selecting ones where the spell fails, or where the spell backlash is expressed in a fatal manner. That potential powers the spell."

"How can you know all this? I can't see ancient magical artifacts coming with a book of instructions."

"Well I could say that logical deduction states that that's the only way that such an obscure branch of magic could be used by anyone, or that I had the pleasure of meeting the designer before her execution, but in actuality I'm just a good librarian, and there's a copy of her notes in the library."

"Why was she executed?"

"Time altering spells are completely forbidden, for most people even knowing there are time altering spells is completely forbidden."

"Then this ring The Wanderer gave me…" Saiko began, fishing it from his pocket.

"Is sufficient to sign your death warrant many times over if anyone outside Seruatis learned of it."

"And the Immortals have them why?"

"Death penalties have historically proven ineffective against them," Dus quipped. "So as long as they restrict themselves to spells that don't threaten to violate causality they're given some leeway."

"And if they do violate causality?"

"Steps are taken," the gorgon replied, finality etched onto every word, her jaw clenched at the end of it.

"Steps?" Saiko answered, unable to take the hint in his spell-stunned state; presumably Dus was in a similar mind-altered state given she didn't sound like his continued existence was a deathly insult.

"Steps. That which cannot be killed can at least be severely inconvenienced."

"Wonderful," The Swordsman grumbled. "Life sentences when you can't die."

"It serves as an effective deterrent… most of the time."

"Why are the Immortals given so much leeway? It can't just be a power thing."

"They're a deterrent for threats from elsewhere, daemons, fae and suchlike. Anything strong enough to give a lich heart palpitations turns up, one of them gets a message. It's one reason they meet so infrequently, entire swathes of the world are undefended right now."

"I can't see The Ancient being up to fighting a daemonic horde."

"You'd be rather surprised. Daemons are his specialty. Daemonic bindings are effectively legal contracts, given enough time there are few daemons he can't banish or bind."

"I've never met a daemon that was inclined to give much time to people they're trying to kill."

"True enough. That's why he's only wheeled out when a major threat makes it to the mortal realm."

"Why would such a being agree to leave?" Saiko demanded, struggling with the concept of a demon-duelling lawyer and quietly allowing a thousand jokes about 'conflict of interest' and 'professional courtesy' die unsaid.

"Well sometimes they don't, an unbound daemon doesn't have to do anything it doesn't want to, including accept a binding but most are just too happy to negotiate terms. It's usually why they invade at all. To force a concession which strengthens their position back home and they know if they push their luck too far we'll arrange for someone with the raw power to banish them to send them packing, that or have allies in the infernal realms attack their holdings while they're away." Dus paused as a snippet of gossip came to mind, "Didn't you have a daemonic girlfriend? You should know all this."

"One clingy succubus is hardly a magnum opus on infernal political theory," Saiko groused before adding more quietly. "And we didn't really uh… talk much."

"You pig," Dus snarked, shaking her head in condemnation.

Scarlet shame spread across Saiko's gaunt cheeks as he changed the topic, or rather returned to the initial one, "One thing I'm still not getting, if we've got people who can just dismiss a daemon lord from our world… why bother negotiating at all? Actually I've got other questions on those lines but I'll stick to this one for now."

"Well firstly," The librarian began, delighting in his discomfort, "A banishing and a dismissal are two very different things. A dismissal is between a summoner and a bound daemon, reasonably low energy and usually mutual. A banishment is far more difficult, by definition the daemon is unwilling and usually will have great magical reserves of its own to bring to bear. Lesser daemons actively seek out contracts with very few exceptions but the greater daemons and the lords tend to be far too prideful to bend the knee to a mortal. So you've got to be both stronger willed and have more magical strength that it to forcibly eject it from our reality, people like that don't come around very often. People that could survive doing it even less so."

"What about him?" Saiko demanded, indicating the infirmary where Erebus laboured in stony stasis.

"Without any help? He probably could but even if he lived through it he'd be a hollow shell of the man he was."

Saiko let out a long, low whistle, "That's a lot of power."

"And they know it," Dus agreed. "Most of the time a banisher charges more than the demon. Hells sometimes they go so far as to collude to drive the price up. Bastards."

"You make it sound like being mercenary about the fate of the world is a bad thing," said the mercenary.

Even through the mask, Saiko could feel the force of her glare as if he had gotten close to a campfire but abruptly, the intensity dulled as Dus barked out a dark peel of laughter, "You truly are unapologetic, aren't you?"

"What should I be apologising for exactly?" Saiko asked, not having to feign the confusion in his voice.

"All the harm you've caused over your lifetime. All the lives taken. All the monsters you've helped escape, whose plans you have enabled and carried out."

Saiko scowled, expression borderline thunderous, but his voice was steady, "I'm a mercenary. That's the job. You do what they pay you to and don't judge until afterwards. Why? Were you planning on a sudden bout of repentance yourself?"

"I have no idea what you're-"

"I know who you are. Who you were. It took me a while to put together but I managed it last night. And I am amazed that you have the sheer brass neck to talk to me about lives taken. About repentance. You who blazed a trail of destruction through war after war, friend and foe alike!"

Dus scowled, "Were we anywhere else in the world I would strike you down for that."

"Case in point," Saiko observed dryly. "You're a thug Dus, an exceptional thug but no more than that and you wear your pain like armour and shield."

"You bastard!" The gorgon snarled, hideous venom and fury frothing forth, "I am going to-"

"Attempt to threaten me into submission again." He cut her off with a sharp wave of his hand, "I know I'm not the smartest man in the world but I do figure things out eventually. You can't actually hurt me."

Dus scoffed, "Whilst I'm thrilled you've found your spine if you insist on following this line of argument I will take great pleasure in removing it."

"No. You won't. I mean you're more than capable but you'd be kicked out of here."

"And you would be dead," she pointed out frostily.

Saiko's smile was either enlightenment or madness, "I told you I figured it out. You know I asked around. Got to know people here. And not one of them could remember a time you weren't here. Killing is against the rules, threats aren't and your threats are empty and hollow."

The gorgon scowled, anger boiling off her in near-visible waves before she tensed, calming herself with an effort that left her shaking until she finally mastered herself, suddenly calm, and with a voice like a human stiletto said, "I finally see what he sees in you."

"I wish I did," he muttered, not quite quietly enough.

"Then again maybe not. What are you prepared to pay?"

"For?" He tried not to sound too interested.

"The knowledge of what he sees."

"Or what you think he sees," Saiko observed.

"You're bargaining," Dus observed in kind, "trying to talk my price down."

"Maybe. Is it working?"

"Until you asked that question, yes."

"I haven't got much to pay you with. I didn't exactly plan on an extended stay, so I've only got my emergency stash on me, unless you desperately need a nullsteel ring."

"What about your sword?" Dus asked, soft as velvet and smooth as silk.

Saiko glanced briefly down at the blade at his hip then back up to the eyeless mask. "Why exactly would you want an immortal slaying blade?"

"Why would you?" the gorgon countered.

"You're deflecting. But if you want the honest answer… I think at this point to stop people who want it from having it."

"Hoarding or is that a glimmer of conscience?"

"Oh I wouldn't go that far…" Saiko mused, "but…

I never had any illusions I was a heavyweight when it came to magical nonsense, but I did think I was a bloody good swordsman and with enough nullstone I could take just about anyone."

"So it's wounded pride?" Dus interrupted. "How terribly disappointing."

"I haven't made it to my point yet," Saiko growled. "My point is… my point is.. that I'm now surrounded by people who could take me out if they sneezed at the wrong moment. But with this sword I'm a threat to any of them and the last thing any of these people need, including you, is more power."

"I see." Dus smiled, quickly covering it with a hand, "So you want to act as a deterrent? And you think that the sword will let you? It's not an awful idea, but the bad news is that I just killed you." As she finished, the hand darted up, removing the eyeless domino mask.

Saiko tried to turn away, to close or cover his eyes, but not in time to avoid seeing Dus' closed eyes.

After a few seconds Dus would say, "It's safe to look now. But I trust the point is made."

Turning back with more than a little glare, "Stone me you stone the blade too, probably."

"And if my intent were to remove it permanently from circulation?"

"Then I'd be a dead man, you're still not having it."

"Fortunately I don't want it. My price is one favour, to be called at my discretion."

"You must think me an imbecile. I'm not going to write you a blank cheque."

"I'm prepared to give you a guarantee that I'd never ask you to do something you weren't capable of, physically, mentally or morally."

"The answer is still very much a no."

"Suit yourself." Dus shrugged, "But be aware that you're little gambit is very much a double edged sword, as you said as long as you have that sword you're a threat to everyone, most of the other retired monsters aren't as kind hearted as I am."

Saiko withheld a chuckle, "I find that more than mildly doubtful. So how long until we get worried about how long it's taking?"

"The spell lasts an hour so after an hour," Dus said, rolling back her shoulders as she moved to recline against the walls of the infirmary.

"And so far it's been?"

"I don't know. Ten minutes? Quarter of an hour tops? I'm a librarian, not a clock."

"Do people actually enjoy your wiseass remarks or do you just enjoy being regarded as a complete bitch?"

"Maybe I'm not the one who has trouble making friends?"

"Maybe I don't need friends?"

"Spoken like every lonely outcast in history."

"So is this really how you're planning to spend the next forty-five minutes? Trading insults?"

"Unless something better becomes available."

Saiko let out a long sigh, "You sure love a captive audience huh?"

"I'm hardly holding you hostage drama queen."

"Honour is holding me hostage, I gave my word that I'd retrieve the artifact as soon as Erebus was finished with it."

Dus shrugged, "I suppose I can hold my tongue awhile. Still I will probably need to go in first, to gaze young Alec."

"You don't think this is going to work then?" he

asked, shocked; not once had it crossed his mind that this could fail.

"No," she admitted, sad and soft. "The chance was good at the beginning, but now? It would take a miracle."

"Well according to you we do in fact have a god on our side," Saiko pointed out.

The old gorgon forced a small chuckle, "Oh Pheus is the best for this sort of thing. I'd happily feed him his own entrails before saying it to his face but no one else would have a prayer. But still… I suspect this battle is lost. And perhaps it's for the best… oh don't look so shocked. I want the boy to live, but Erebus is… important, and Alec is a distraction. We don't need Erebus here playing nurse, we need him out there, stitching up the wounds in the world. His childish feud with the paladin has cost so much I could slap him at times."

"That's pretty cold," he pointed out. "And I can't help feeling that you're being dramatic, I can accept that the necromancer is powerful, but not that he's vital. No matter how much power he can bring to bear he's still just one man amongst many other very strong mages."

Dus gave a sad smile, "You're not wrong, in truth even a middling magician could rise to the same heights through the same methods, but they don't. It requires an act of madness to commit oneself to an apprenticeship in the hells."

"So that's what this is all about? That he knows a lot?"

"It's… more than that. You know how the Immortals are all bound, how liches are contained, and all the elder races have bargains constraining their power. That's what makes him special, that he has all that knowledge and strength whilst skirting the bounds of such controls. He is bound by but two things, his word and his conscience," the gorgon sighed. "Now if only he'd stop letting the latter lead him astray."

"You say that, but power without conscience would be worse," Saiko said levelly. "You're talking about him as if he were a weapon rather than a person."

"He is a weapon," she snapped. "In the last thirty years he's cleared up threats that have plagued the mortal realm for centuries. Demon lords laid low, old curses lifted, lost artifacts found, scars in the fabric of reality itself finally faded, two of the aetheric chains broken! And yet he insists on indulging in petty sentiment."

"And thank the Veil he does," the mercenary replied softly. "You've been here too long I think. What you're calling his flaws I'd call saving graces."

"Then you'd better grow up if you wish to keep wielding that blade."

"Yeah that's not happening, you already condemn me for my lack of morals yet you say I have to become even less so?"

"Such is life. You wanted to be a threat to the great powers of the world, this is the price."

"I refuse to pay it," he said simply.

Dus shrugged, "Then you accept the consequences."

Saiko decided he could live with that. Or die with that if it came to it.

Chapter 17

The Lord of Dreams stalked the silent streets of Respite. It was not a true dreaming, or even a true nightmare, were it so he'd have been able to unravel it with little more than a thought. But the human psyche was still a playground he knew well. It was just a matter of changing the right thing and doing it delicately enough that it wouldn't radically change his subject.

Of course, this time it was more complicated, he'd expected, coming in, for the dryad's mind and trauma to be in dominance of her mortal host, even with Alec's rather large latent magical potential a being of pure magic like Holly should have suborned him entirely, foisting her own brand of horrors upon him.

That hadn't happened, the two were apparently too alike, in trauma at least, and so he was having to handle two separate dreams, one of which he couldn't directly access. He knew what he had to look for, a commonality, something shared between the two that would resolve for both at once. Which was doubly a problem because he knew next to nothing about them beyond a brief conversation with the thrice-cursed necromancer.

He suspected he knew where the answers lay, in the locked bedroom in Alec's erstwhile home, but with the barrier on the door, he was loathe to go for the direct route. Sure the necromancer had agreed to his price success or failure but there was pride at stake here, and more than just a little bit of it.

It had been so terribly long since he'd had a chance

to do what he was good at; the idea of failing was grotesque, not just the loss of face but a significant blow to identity as well.

So for now, he lurked through the streets, well-worn cobbles that were almost frictionless if one weren't careful, or a superlative being like himself, hoping for some hint or sign that would help him figure this out.

Respite was an old enough village; he'd at least been aware of it, and had remained a small village for that entire time. Old bargains lay thick on the ground here, and even in memory, there was the potential for mishap, made all the more deadly because he didn't know the details of this Bargain. And it was a Bargain, ancient if not terrible, a pact betwixt man and monster worthy of the capital letter.

What Pheus did know was the broad strokes, that a village would be permitted within the borders of the forest and that it would go unmolested by malevolent flora and ravenous fauna; the residents would be permitted to retrieve deadwood from the forest but could not take an axe to a living tree without reprisals, but the finer details had eluded him, and there had to be finer details. Little else would explain why, after so long, the village had stayed so small or how it had consistently been able to survive on little more than hunting and expensive food imports.

Not that the wood it exported was cheap, Von Mori's trees were a breed apart, tougher, harder to burn and inheriting a small fraction of their matron's resistance to magic and null alike, they were a beloved purchase of both paladin, the village's backer in the modern era, and magician, on the rare occasion they could get their hands on some. Artificers, in particular, were obsessed with the wood, its mutual resistance to null and magic meant it was hard to make it take a spell, but when it did, the spell stuck and stuck hard, working in null-heavy environments and able to stand up to magical assault, a real favourite in defensive objects. A Mori-oak shield properly enchanted was better in almost every way than its steel equivalent, and rumours had even reached Seruatis that the Necropolis was stockpiling Mori-yew battle staves for the next Paladin-Necromancer war.

But whilst Respite's food situation could be explained by expensive exports by a generous viewer, its population could not. The village's lack of growth reeked of magical compulsion, but the how of it eluded Pheus, and the how was important; such details were the tripwires of a Bargain.

The old god (not Old God, that was a different class of being entirely, albeit one that had gone extinct long before even Pheus' time when deities had slung the primordial forces of creation around as if it were so much soil, not that there had been soil back then) needed those details to be entirely safe, though he doubted he could trip over them. Von Mori was not careless in her dealings with mortals, and for a Bargain to last this long it was probably airtight. Still it was possible that, even in durance vile, a violation of it would allow the dryad of the forest to lash out and Pheus had no illusions that Von Mori liked him enough to stay her hand, or at all in fact.

So caution before all else, he'd checked the bakery, there was no mill, so the flour must also be an import. A windmill would have been almost out of the question, there was no elevation to make use of the wind so they'd have had to build up pretty high to get past the windbreak the forest provided. A waterwheel was also out of the picture, the nearest river was many miles away, Respite's water coming from a single well that had mysteriously never run out of water in all its many years, much like Seruatis. He'd also searched what appeared to be a carpenter's, a cobbler's, a small tavern and all the various other tradecrafts that kept a village alive.

They were the most likely to give hints as to what ailed Alec's mind, the god presuming his patient had expressed at least some interest in a trade. Afterall everyone wanted to do something with their life and whilst searching the forest for deadwood was lucrative, it was hardly interesting. Hunting certainly held excitement, a bit dangerous in the Forest Von Mori where the wildlife tended to hunt back and Alec hadn't had the array of scars he'd associate with such a person. But there was nothing out of place there either.

Pheus rubbed at his eyes, massaging away the tiredness. It was looking more and more like he'd have to force the door and just hope his patient would be able to feed himself afterwards.

Still, there was one place to yet go over with a fine toothcomb, one place he knew for a fact Alec had spent time and had perhaps left impressions of himself.

The monk's residence was on the very outskirts of the village, and it was… not shabby, but lacked the solidity of the dignified ageing stonework of the rest of the village. There was a roughness to the stone, and the mortar was already beginning to show signs of flaking.

The inside was modest, no true bed, just a well-padded mattress, straw rather than the more expensive stuffings. A very small lap-jointed writing desk and bookshelf took up most of the rest of the space alongside a small travel pack in the opposite corner, the wood used would cost a fortune anywhere else in the world. Still it was easy enough to get pieces large enough; it was only once one graduated from furniture to architecture that appropriately sized timber grew scarce. They'd have been better off importing the wood than hoping something of sufficient size passed away in the forest.

He checked the desk for hidden compartments; for all it seemed too small for it. He didn't really expect to find anything, this was built from Alec's memory afterall, and he highly doubted Erebus would have left anything significant that could be discovered by inquisitive teens, or at least anything he didn't want them to find, but he checked anyway, just in case.

Next, he perused the bookshelf, the poor thing full to creaking with texts that he'd flick through just in case; many of the books blank except for the title, showing that Alec had never read them, and again no hollowed-out books or bewildering cyphers.

"You could just ask you know," Erebus said from behind him.

Pheus whirled around in something close to panic, one hand raised to throw power at the necromancer before he stopped himself, "I didn't notice you approach."

"That was rather the idea," The magician pointed out. "So any progress?"

"Very little," Pheus admitted glacially. "I've seldom encountered a mind so… uncluttered. And no that's not an insult, there's just surprisingly little of himself here, unless I'm missing something truly obvious he could use a lot of encouragement, I've seen larger egos in automata."

"Automata?"

"Before your time. And after your time too I suppose, if things develop at their current pace." The god looked a touch amused at the prospect, "A pity really, it's always fun to watch how a society copes with artificial sapients. So many wonderful ways it can go wrong."

"Delightful. So what will you do now?"

"Well first I'm going to ask what in the hells you're doing here, I thought we had a plan."

"I was able to spare a bit of my attention," Erebus said as if it explained everything. "I thought you might need the help, and clearly you do." He leaned against the wall only to stumble as part of it seemed to collapse into splinters and dust at his weight. "Okay, that definitely cannot be good."

Pheus scowled darkly, "It isn't. It means the boy's mind is starting to decay, probably, I mean it could be an aspect of the nightmare representing the preference of memory compared to real life and childhood's end, but if so I just don't understand it. Do you know how many nightmares I've spectated? How many I've crafted? This place makes no damned sense, it's a hideous hodgepodge of half-ideas. There's no unifying theme that would translate to the dryad."

"Holly," Erebus said helpfully.

Pheus didn't rise to the bait, "My point is that I know what the solution should be, I just can't find it."

"Keep going…"

"Desolate streets usually means some kind of monster giving chase, something that represents all the boy's problems, but besides us there's just nothing here. By now something should have tried to grab me, stab me, drag me screaming into the shadows, something, but there's just nothing. The door he's protecting, I should have been jumped just reaching for it if this were that kind of nightmare."

The necromancer nodded along, "So when is a door not a door?"

"When it's a jar," Pheus replied deadpan. "That joke wasn't funny when it was first invented, it's not funny now, and its continued survival is a blight on comedy everywhere, though I do take the point." The old god began to mutter to himself, "Edge cases… edge cases…"

Erebus watched from the increasingly crumbling wall, keeping his own counsel to let the expert work. Unusual in Pheus' eyes given the antagonism, but he clearly cared for Holly and Alec, or at the very least felt a responsibility for them.

Inspiration struck. "Holly and Alec," He said aloud. "That's the key. It's not two similar nightmares, it's one nightmare shared between them."

"Which means we're in the wrong place… I presume the boy spent some time in the forest, if not very far in?"

"One would presume so." Erebus nodded.

"And the dryad would never have entered the village, nothing's happening here because nothing can happen here. It's not a shared perspective, one monster, one nightmare, it would have to be something they're both afraid of… smart money is on your paladin, probably three feet taller than in real life and with glowing red eyes."

"So we head to the forest?"

"We head to the forest. Carefully."

There was little more to be said on the subject, not that either would have felt much like talking in the oppressive gloom of the perpetual twilight Respite was frozen in. Normally Pheus would have a suite of supernatural senses to puncture the darkness, but Alec didn't know such things existed, and so here they didn't, he had to despair for the state of education, sure the very existence of gods was one of the most deeply held secrets on the planet but right now it was inconveniencing him, and thus he despaired.

The line between forest and village was old, it had been a wall once, a collection of stones stacked together probably about waist high but that had been a very long time ago. Now it was a verge overgrown first with moss and now with grass, the original stones buried somewhere near the centre. Just beyond it, the first trees loomed, and they did loom, ancient imposing and pillars of wood. This late in the year the boughs were barren of leaves, looking more like talons aimed at the heavens than branches. Every single one was an oak, the guardian dryads absent from the dreamscape — Alec had never known they were there — though whether they were there to protect village from forest or forest from village Pheus doubted anyone other than Von Mori knew.

As leaves crunched underfoot, Pheus and Erebus gazed around with the furtive caution of the hunted. In the real world, almost nothing corporeal would be able to walk through the leaf-littered ground in silence. Still the rules of reality didn't apply here, and in a nightmare the monster could jump out from anywhere, possibly somewhere they'd just checked… especially somewhere they'd just checked in fact.

No phantom paladin was in evidence and after ten minutes Pheus was starting to get really frustrated. "Don't tell me that we have to go into the heart of the forest? The boy would never have gone so far surely?"

Erebus merely shrugged, "If that's what it takes, that's what it takes."

The god of dreams' eyes narrowed at the necromancer as he mused aloud. "No. It has to be a shared location, a shared fear. That's the only way any of this makes sense! So if not the paladin… Von Mori? She's certainly a nightmare when she wants to be and she has the metaphysical weight that her death could… affect things…"

"Want me to try calling her?" the necromancer volunteered. "She seemed to respect me."

"I'm not sure it would help," Pheus said. "Though there is one more person the two have in common…"

"Which is?"

The only reply was a beam of fire so hot as to be moving from blue to white aimed squarely at Erebus' chest, the torrent of fire splashing ineffectively against the mage's barrier of will.

"Ah. Me." A slow smile spread across the mage's face. "I did wonder how long I could keep this going."

Pheus cursed, the real Erebus would have been carved in half by that beam, or at least he would have against a mere mental shield. That was both good and bad, the real necromancer, weighing in at nearly two centuries of putting down major magical threats and who knew how much tutelage in a demonic realm had a nearly bottomless bag of magical tricks. Against the real mage, he could have expected anything from a precognitive counterspell to a point-to-point teleport or a full arcane barrier to stop the flames. On the bright side, the boy and the dryad didn't know any of that really existed, or if they did, how it was actually used in a fight.

The bad news was that the boy's impression of what

Erebus could do was quite a bit stronger than the real thing, and worse, the dryad would have a decent grasp of magic and very little idea of how mages actually thought so he could look forwards to a lot of…

As the thought occurred, the god leapt high into the air, using a circle of compressed air to stand on when outright levitation failed as the earth turned liquid at a gesture from Erebus.

…a lot of terrain control, he finished the thought.

So blasts of elemental force way stronger than the mage could actually manage, ditto for spell shields and probably superlative hand to hand fighting combined with masterful control of the environment, because of course he'd taken so long to figure it out that he'd been drawn into the forest. Lovely. And to top it all off, he was fighting with a restriction to start with.

He couldn't use any magic that Holly or Alec couldn't understand, well, he could, but he'd have to force it and making his patients bleed from the eyes and ears probably counted as a failure.

That was a problem in its own right; when dealing with an experienced enemy magician, the first thing anyone went for were their esoteric magics; gravity, magnetism, entropy, time, stranger things if they knew them. Things that were hard to conceptualise and even harder to block.

"So what gave me away?" Erebus asked, the slight shimmer of his shield dropping.

"The real Erebus knows Von Mori isn't dead… that and a bunch of other things. But that one clinched it."

"You say the real Erebus, but I'd argue I'm just as real. I'm Erebus as seen through the eyes of those who were lucky enough to survive him."

Just what Pheus needed, a mental construct with

self-awareness. Still, he gave the best answer he could; a series of sharp, resounding cracks as he lifted a bunch of pebbles from the floor and accelerated them past the sound barrier to leave slowly spreading concentric circles of light on the necromancer's shield. Sure enough, it covered all directions, including down and up, but it had been important to check.

"Except when the actual Erebus was here you weren't. Too afraid to confront yourself?"

Pheus dived behind a tree as the counterattack carved through the trunk, a blade of air that no shield he could muster would have stopped, the invisible scythe passing inches above his head as it carried on deeper into the forest and only a frantic piece of telekinesis kept the tree from falling on him as well.

"It's how I work, isn't it? Only stepping in after the danger is past?" The voice came from behind him; Pheus whirled and let loose with an actinic flash of lightning, following up with a burst of decay and rot, but it was no use, the shield blocked both.

It blocks everything, he realised belatedly, the child never once saw it fail. He could hammer on that barrier of will until he ran out of breath, and it wouldn't shake, bend or break. It was immutable in here, inviolable.

But there were ways to kill the unkillable. There had been a lot more gods once upon a time.

If he couldn't go through the shield or around it, he'd simply have to bypass it entirely, attack the person maintaining it.

"Danger's still here. Dryad's dying. Kid's dying," he said, backing away as he fielded a few rocks on his shield. They were slower than his own shots but much larger, solid stones rather than the handful of pebbles he'd sent. He didn't even bother trying to stop them outright, deflecting them with just enough telekinetic force to send them past him. "The real Erebus cared about them."

By his grandmother's pitch black soul, but that stung, to say something complimentary about a necromancer, still as long as the actual Erebus never heard about it, he could cope.

"I'm the reason they're dying. I roped Holly into this in the first place, I dragged Alec from the ruins of Respite. I let Holly be tortured!"

"Erebus doesn't believe that. Hells, I'm not sure even the boy believes that," Pheus said dryly as he braced for the next attack. He'd had air and earth, there wasn't enough water here for an attack, so he was expecting fire.

He didn't get it, or at least not yet, as roots began twining around his ankles instead, revealing another weakness. He was rusty. What had it been since he'd last been in a fight, ten thousand years? Twelve thousand? Long enough that a threat he'd known to watch for was bogging him down.

He survived the fire, though barely, leaning back out of the way as the crimson stream went over him, trusting to the very roots holding him in place to keep his balance, at least until a quick gesture, and two blades of air, freed him. The god's back hitting the floor for just a moment as he rolled away, not staying still long enough for them to pin him to the floor.

He'd flick out more airblades as he got to his feet, cutting down roots, ivy and grasping branches. "What are you getting out of this huh? You're smart enough to know you're just an avatar, if they die, you die."

"If they live I also die," Erebus pointed out, not yet unleashing another elemental assault. Pheus allowed himself a moment's hope that he was getting through to the half-baked impression rather than that he was just building up for a really big spell.

"True, true, then why are you here? Why claw for each desperate second of life when it's so very hopeless?" The god's voice was sweet to the point of poison, not stopping there. There was enough of the real thing here that defiance was second nature, "When you could do something meaningful with your death I mean. In the end we're all going there, it drags you down… you think you're tired… that you're hopeless… I can tell you it doesn't get easier. That desire to just give in grows like a cancer, gnawing, consuming, devouring, it never tires, always hungers… so why stay when you're one of the lucky few who gets a good reason to give in…"

Doubt appeared in the necromancer's eyes, and Pheus rejoiced, folding his arms behind his back, trying to seem confident and non-threatening. Alec had built a picture of Erebus in his mind, the power, the intelligence, the defiance in the face of a hopeless situation, and maybe, just maybe, the sheer world-weariness.

"I-", the necromancer began uncertainly, dropping his shield. The god didn't wait to hear it, one of the hands behind his back curling up to raise a stone behind Fauxebus and then pulled it to him. The necromancer gave out a gasp, the soft sound of surprise out of place in the sudden silence; the stone hadn't slowed even with him in the way and had taken him in the throat.

He brought his hands up to heal the wound, not panicking, but it did no good; Pheus was already on him, hitting him around the waist a running tackle and bringing him to the floor. Perhaps the real Erebus could have healed it anyway, kept fighting even as his lifeblood poured into his lungs, but this one couldn't, the muscles in the god's forearms like adamantine as he strained to keep his wrists pinned whilst the necromancer thrashed, slowly stilling to twitching… something faded in his eyes and a panting Pheus rose slowly from the corpse.

It hadn't been as satisfying as he'd hoped; sure, it wasn't the real thing, but he'd expected to feel a thrill at snuffing out a necromancer's life, a taste of long-sought vengeance after so long, but it wasn't there. Just a quiet relief he'd survived and the gentle pleasure of a job done… if not well, then at least done.

It was surprisingly loud. That was what Erebus first noticed, raucous voices apparently coming from all directions as feeling returned to his limbs. He carefully didn't move, de-petrification spells were a roll of the dice at the best of times, and there was a very good chance parts of him were still stone as the spell did its work, obviously nothing immediately vital like the lungs, heart or brain, but having to live without a stomach or a liver would be something of a problem if in a moment of impatience he tore it free of arteries before it could return to normal.

There were too many voices to really make out any words, but he didn't try to cast anything to isolate some of the sounds, that could have been worse than moving. Still, he held his nerve for a good few minutes before he finally opened his eyes to find himself staring into the unblinking eyes of Holly.

"Oh good, you're not dead," she observed dryly, moving back to sit on what had been Alec's infirmary bed; the teen himself not immediately apparent, which given Alec's nature meant the necromancer could safely conclude he was somewhere else.

"Fairly sure that should be my line," he quipped weakly before covering his mouth to cough. Fortunately, no stone dust was there when he pulled his hand away. "How are you feeling?"

"Not in pain. Which is nice I guess. Irritated and wondering where I am though, no one wants to answer me, they keep saying I need to wait for some founder guy to tell me but he's busy."

"You're in Seruatis. Guessing your memory's a bit spotty, what's the last thing you remember before waking up here?"

"That infernal collar going on, after that, nothing," she said bitterly, rubbing at the phantom memory of it on her neck. "We made it then… that's good."

"For a given value of made it," Erebus replied bleakly. "You've been comatose for best part of a month, Alec for a day, and I'm still recovering from a botched healing. Just be glad dryads don't get muscular atrophy."

"I don't know what that is," she admitted. "But sure, glad I don't have it."

"So where's your host? And why are we surrounded by people?"

That wasn't entirely true; since he'd opened his eyes, people had begun leaving, to general grousing and complaint.

Holly's eyes unfocused a moment as she concentrated, "Alec's eating, don't know where. And everyone was here because of you. Some kind of spell you were casting, I saw someone's leg grow back so that was interesting."

Erebus rubbed at his eyes, there would probably be

consequences to that, but he couldn't really begrudge Seruatis' residents taking advantage. High-grade panacea spells were hard to find even here; if he hadn't been running the spell off borrowed power and a statue to boot, he'd have collapsed in minutes from the strain.

Still, he didn't say any of that, it wasn't Holly's problem, and besides, there were more interesting developments, at least to his mind, "You couldn't do that when we last spoke."

The young dryad forced a smile, "It helped he said he was starving before he vanished. We agreed one of us should stay with you to thank you, and I don't eat or sleep so…" she trailed off awkwardly. "It's good that he found food though, I was starting to get hungry. Got to say I don't like it."

"We agreed, or he agreed?" Erebus pressed gently while mentally signing Alec up for a few more lessons on emotional control.

"We," she replied firmly. For a moment, he considered pressing further, but he was tired, and his two charges not fighting with each other wasn't the sort of news he was in the mood to get to the bottom of, just this once sleeping dogs could lie.

"Well, I'm afraid I'm going to have to leave as well, might be worth your time tracking down Alec, some people will doubtless want to talk to me, and things might get… heated." The necromancer stretched a slow, languid motion as he checked that he still had a full range of motion in each limb. Mages certainly weren't stereotyped as athletic, but battlemages bucked the trend, far more energy-efficient to dive out of the way of a spell rather than shield or deflect it and thus the dryad was treated to the near-paper white face flushing a deep red as he managed, with some effort, to press his forehead to his feet.

She waited a few more moments, but apparently, the conversation was at an end, and so she sidled out of the infirmary with the last few stragglers as they admired the fact they were now sans scars and wrinkles, and in one case sporting a few more fingers than when they'd entered.

Now to find the cafeteria… Holly considered just asking someone but wasn't sure how to approach them. Her experience with non-dryads (who weren't openly hostile) so far extended to a grumpy ghost, a distraught teenager and an eccentric mage; for all that she was inexperienced she knew that wasn't much of a sample when it came to talking to people.

Besides, she'd been raised on horror stories about what humans did to dryads… well, to trees at least, the dryad tended to be something to stab their way past to get to the timber, but either way, it hadn't exactly endeared mankind to her.

So instead, she fell back on magic; it was, if not easier, then at least more familiar. She quickly hurried out of sight of anyone, not quite breaking into a jog, and then focused inside herself, going a little bit cross-eyed in the process.

The bond had grown a lot during her convalescence, much like a muscle it had grown all the stronger through constant, but not excessively strenuous, use, though the last couple of days had put a strain on it, a few strands of it frayed, but it had held.

In her mind's eye, it was a blue cable extending from her out into the ether, carrying a veritable cornucopia of information to her from Alec, very little of it that she could make sense of. Holly trees didn't come with colour vision, or vision at all, nor taste, and though there were analogies to the other senses, they didn't translate even approximately. It would be a very long time before she could fully understand it. Presumably, Alec, if he was in a receptive state, would get a similar deluge from her.

For now, she took a deep calming breath and got to work narrowing the focus, a tree might not have eyesight, but she did, and she soon identified the strand of the bond sending sight, letting it consume her thoughts as with her eyes closed Alec's vision easily superimposed over her own. Hopefully, with enough practice, she'd be able to process her host's vision as well as her own, but before Erebus had de-petrified, she'd given that a try and the resulting headache had forced her to sit down.

He was still in the cafeteria; she didn't know what a cafeteria was really, but along with the image was the word. And going by the plate of food, now being mopped clean by a rather fluffy white type of food with a brown edge, it was somewhere to eat. Though she'd already figured that out when the hunger pangs that most definitely weren't hers had stopped.

Still, none of this was particularly helpful when determining location with respect to other buildings.

Out of the corner of Alec's eye, she could see a set of stairs leading downward and a door, as well as natural light filtering in from windows at the same level, though the windows had metal grills over the top of them for some reason. Underground then? Or a bizarrely fortified second-floor balcony. Both should hopefully be visible from outside.

'*You could just ask you know?*' Alec pointed out with a mental chuckle.

The only reason Holly didn't scream was that she got a hand to her mouth on the inhale.

"Alec?" she squeaked back. There was no reply.

It took her a few seconds, but she managed to send it across the link as a thought.

'*Who else?*'

'*How are you doing this?*' she asked, still incredulous. Just how much had she missed last month?

'*Erebus had me doing meditations for a month, as well as some limited mental contact. Sensed you in my thoughts, thought I'd try to reply. Looks like it worked.*'

'*Looks like it did.*' Holly agreed, impressed despite herself.

'*So what were you rummaging around in my head for? I sensed you had a question but not much more than that.*'

'*Erebus dismissed me from the infirmary, he thinks there's going to be an argument, no idea why, but didn't want me hearing it so probably secret necromancer stuff. I was told to find you, but I don't know where you are.*'

'*In the cafeteria.*'

'*I know that,*' which, in sheer frustration, she yelled aloud as well.

'*Where is it?*'

'*Oh… uh where are you?*'

'*I don't know!*'

'*Well can you get back to the infirmary? I can guide you from there.*'

That, as it turned out, was something Holly could do. No more than a few minutes later, she found herself opposite her host as he wolfed down an unconscionable amount of fish stew, which raised all sorts of questions that she decided not to ask. She knew her knowledge of the local geography was subpar, but she was fairly certain Seruatis wasn't coastal, and the river that ran through Von Mori was miles away.

"You're looking… better," Alec said carefully, taking a break from inhaling stew.

"Thank you, I think," Holly replied stiffly.

"You know what I mean, more mobile."

"It would have been hard to be less mobile."

"And yet somehow we nearly managed it," he pointed out, pushing away a now-empty bowl. "So… now what?"

"What do you mean 'now what?'" she replied, the question too vague by far.

Alec took his time with the answer, "I mean now what should we do? What are our plans going forwards? I know our options are limited unless we can get an escort out of here to civilisation, but you are ultimately a partner in this… I'd value your input."

Holly gave him a doubtful look, just sitting there staring at him.

"Too stilted?"

"Way too stilted," she agreed. "Still thanks for saying it. As to plans… I don't have any, I did this to see the world, and like you said we're stuck for now."

"Yeah, as much as I'd like to blame it on circumstance you've definitely been handed a raw deal." The teen sighed, "Still for my part I plan to keep working on my swordsmanship while I've still got people willing to teach me, after that who knows."

Holly smiled, enjoying the quiet moment of agreement with her host. Things were looking up.

Erebus would have been lying if he'd said he wasn't nervous. It didn't show; he'd been trained too well for that; he'd been trained well enough not to even show that he wasn't letting it show, probably. Unfortunately, some of those present knew him and knew him well.

One didn't show fear to predators, and as he stared back at the assembly of powerful beings about to decide his fate, it was hard to think of them as anything else.

It was a nice little bit of theatre certainly, a small amphitheatre with elevated seats and him in the middle at the bottom, the sparse candlelight making it suitably gloom-some whilst also massively overplaying their hand — he could see the inactive light crystals on the ceiling.

All the melodrama meant one simple thing, he was going to live; there was no point intimidating a corpse.

There were a few denizens of Seruatis in attendance as well as the Immortals. Dus, naturally, Pheus and his two brothers, alas. Dragonlady Memra and Alamaya the Elder Wraith as well, the two sat together in what he had to presume was some form of political statement so obtuse he couldn't parse it. And finally, someone lurking at the back, opposite Alamaya and rendered an unrecognisable blob by the weak candlelight. Perhaps fortunately for him, none of them got a vote on Immortal matters, though they were allowed to add their own views to the issues presented.

"Master Erebus, stand for judgement," The Swordsman ordered with a voice like granite.

That was interesting. The Immortals seldom stood on ceremony when they met and perhaps ironically cared little for titles. Erebus doubted it was for the benefit of the peanut gallery either, so it had to be for him. The only question was, what was the message. Don't rock the boat perhaps? Be polite?

With these musings running circles in his head, the

necromancer rose from his chair slowly; it wasn't purely for dramatic effect; he was exhausted and frankly in need of sleep. There were spells to transcend such things, but tragically he didn't trust himself to cast them whilst this tired.

"On the matter of whether you should be classified as immortal, and thus bound by our laws, you should know the Confluence has voted four to three, with one abstention, that you are not in fact immortal."

Erebus didn't allow himself to feel relief, but for the Enigma's staunch refusal to take a stance on anything that could have gone very, very badly. He was too defiant by nature to bend the knee, but he was also under no illusions as to his chances. Even if he were not carrying a major injury and thoroughly exhausted, mentally, magically and physically, he'd only have even odds of being able to take out an Immortal — not kill but cripple or contain — and some of those in the peanut gallery whilst lacking in defence compared to their noble patron had an offence order of magnitude above Erebus' own.

"I am grateful for the Confluence's decision," he replied, keeping his tone level and calm; it wasn't technically a lie after all. "But would question why I am present given this finding?"

The Huntress answered, taking over, "Other matters were raised. One remains unresolved."

The Swordsman shot her a look, but his counterpart ignored it blithely. Well, at least from that, he had some idea of how she'd voted.

"However, before we get to that matter, I suppose I should present the other matters for your awareness and consideration. Your recent injuries may have swung the vote on your mortal status, a fact a more suspicious mind might have questions about, they do however raise the question of reprisals to and from the Paladin Protectorate." She allowed her gaze to flick swiftly from Erebus to the shadow in the back.

"Was there a question there?" the necromancer asked sweetly, trying not to relax too visibly now he knew, or at least thought he knew, his role in this charade.

"Merely enlightening you to the broader context. Now as to the matter of whether you pose a clear and present existential threat to the sapient peoples of this world, we have, after much pleading on your behalf by interested parties", she gave a quick nod to Dus and then Pheus of all people, "voted five to three against."

Another surprise, the Enigma, one of the younger Immortals, was renowned for abstaining on votes, or at least votes where there were even numbers, guaranteeing there wouldn't be a tie at any point, for them to have forsaken that stance then Dus and Pheus must have been impassioned indeed.

Erebus shrugged, "Again I would question why I need to be here for this. As delighted as I am not to be summarily murdered it's something I could happily have found out about in a missive or memo."

"Don't push your luck necromancer, still I suppose what remains are lesser matters, we shall embrace brevity and move to the unresolved matter. Ambassador if you please?"

The woman in the shadows stood up, taking a moment to stretch and ease the stiffness from her limbs; Erebus could sympathise, the chairs had far too little in the way of cushions, which was to say none.

Elder beings tended to see comfort as a fleeting distraction, at least those who hadn't engaged in a full-time embrace of hedonism. It was for this reason the Necropolis had long ruled that the undead were not, under any circumstances, to design anywhere where the living were expected to spend more than five minutes at a time. There were still a few dingy private studies, long lost libraries and if rumour held true, two airless, lightless and possibly even gravity-less alchemy labs deep in the Wraith Vaults that had never been sullied by mortal touch and likely never would.

As she stepped into clearer lighting, which was to say into the small, well-lit circle at the centre, Erebus took in his newest adversary, or at least their newest incarnation.

She was a broad-shouldered woman, despite her scribe's robes' best efforts to hide it, and Erebus could well imagine she had once gone so far as burly. A borderline pugnacious jaw and an aquiline nose framed by what was almost a brow ridge, all softened by advancing years and wiry steel hair that still held the occasional hint of copper. What hadn't softened were the eyes, a deep blue if a touch rheumy and burning with the fiery zeal of a fanatic, whether to the faith of the old order or the byzantine bureaucracy of the new was irrelevant, they'd do their duty as they saw it and damn the consequences.

If it hadn't been written in her eyes, then it was written all the more clearly upon her robe's heraldry. Patches from a dozen campaigns, at least twice as many patches for valour, courage and meritorious conduct in the field, all of it not quite hiding or distracting from the bulge of chainmail beneath the robe — old habits died hard.

Erebus knew what this was, an old soldier past their prime and being forced to spend their twilight years behind a desk.

He could scarcely imagine someone more dangerous.

She couldn't turn him to stone with a glance or move at speeds the eye could barely track. She couldn't manipulate the very forces of reality against him or shatter his psyche with a telepathic strike. She couldn't beguile the senses, inflame emotions or numb the body. But if anything, that was what made her very presence terrifying, because she had survived decades in a game where everyone she'd be facing off against could do those things, and she was still here, and they weren't.

"Janiah Vorthame, ambassador to Circulus Seruatis for the Holy Paladin Order," she introduced herself, voice even and entirely unintimidated as she took a sheaf of papers out from a satchel bag at her left hip, next to her sword. "I have here a joint warrant from the Holy Paladin Order, the Council of Mages and the Necropolis for the arrest of Daniel Vorthepe on charges of high treason, impersonation of a Paladin officer, impersonation of a Paladin monk, the murder of a Greater Forest Dryad and the indiscriminate slaughter of the village of Mori's Respite."

That got something of a confused silence from those gathered.

"The criminal also goes by the name Erebus," she stated without missing a beat.

Now there was a quiet susurration, nothing so coherent as words, but fragments of conversation muttered lowly.

Erebus permitted himself a frown, "My name is Erebus, fourteenth of that name, I cast aside the other name when I took my vows."

"The same vows you are being accused of breaking Daniel," Janiah pointed out. "As I understand the matter the name is a title assumed with the oath, no oath, no title."

"I forswore nothing."

"That is not for you to decide."

"Nor for you," the necromancer pointed out archly. "Unless I have been tried in absentia, which I doubt given this is the first I have heard of these charges, then officially my vows are unbroken, and my name stands."

"Good, then you will have no problem submitting to my arrest so the matter can be settled."

"In a paladin court?" Erebus asked, "or a fair one?"

"I resent the insinuation," the ambassador replied evenly; though the smile was strained enough it had to be making her jaw ache.

"I wasn't insinuating anything. I was stating it," he growled, dropping diplomacy entirely. "Let me be clear, you have more chance of opening a ski resort in the hells than getting me in front of any court where Allister Lutan holds sway."

"Fortunately that is also not something for you to decide," Janiah replied, a smile spreading slowly across her face as she turned to address the room. "I ask the Confluence to honour this warrant and release Erebus into my custody."

"I decline," The Swordsman declared fast enough for it to count as a reflex.

"I ask the Confluence, eternal one, not you," she replied, words carefully formal if not quite respectful.

"The Confluence has no power over Seruatis. They will not grant you your request because it is not theirs to grant," the patron of the Protected Circle pointed out, heat creeping into his voice.

"But they have power over you. You are free only as long as the rest allow it."

The Swordsman chuckled at that, "Such arrogance, do you truly believe my friends would turn on me just because you asked?"

Janiah's smile was a terribly cold thing as she fished briefly inside her satchel for one more document, producing it with a flourish, "Because I asked, and because I have here a revocation of Seruatis' status as neutral ground within Paladin territory, again agreed by both the Paladin Order and the Council of Mages as well as warrants of arrest for all of you. Pending your decision on this matter, naturally."

"We will not be blackmailed!" Edward wheezed, fury in his eyes as he managed to yell, the sheer effort of it forced him to dissolve into a coughing fit. "We are-" another brief hacking cough, almost reminiscent of a cat bringing up a furball, "eternal. And we will be here long after your precious Order and Council are forgotten tales even historians would question the validity of."

As the eldest, at least in terms of flesh, of the immortals subsided, mostly because he couldn't speak further, The Smith would lay a gentle hand on his friend's shoulder in support, "What he said, but louder. Who are you to tell us what we can and cannot do?"

Janiah kept smiling, "The people who actually have to live and die in these lands. And frankly this has been a long time coming, how can we expect people to obey the laws of the land whilst we allow the likes of you to flout those laws merely because you have power?"

Erebus could only sit back in admiration as he saw the ancient personages assembled caught entirely flatfooted. Internally he was agape, though he refused to let it show in front of an enemy, the necromancer finally realising that he was not the real prey Janiah was hunting. And as the logic cascaded down in his mind's eye, he had to question if he ever had been hunted in the first place. Was it possible that Lutan's grudge had been a thing of artifice, a careful guise to bring him to this place, in this manner?

Had it all been for this? He knew the Immortals fulfilled a vital role in the defence of the world, but for all he held them in high regard he had to admit they held themselves above those who toiled and died in their tens of millions every generation. The Swordsman, for all he was a paragon of empathy and close personal friend, held himself aloft and aloof even to him, and Erebus was as close to immortal as a man could be without crossing that line irrevocably.

Could it all have been for this moment? To finally bring the strongest amongst them to heel. The immortals were strong (an understatement by any measure), but for all their incredible force at arms, they, when faced with the unified strength of the two greatest powers on the continent, would have little choice but to bend the knee.

The High Paladin, or Gregor as Erebus had the rare privilege to call him, or Greg if he was trying to be annoying, was a good person or at least tried hard to be, but he'd also seen the man when he was deep in his cups, and the Immortals, and other great powers of the world, rankled him. They were a scab he couldn't stop picking, an itch that couldn't be scratched and a wound that just wouldn't heal.

As far as Gregor was concerned, no one person should have that kind of power, and as a holder of that sort of power, if at the lower end, Erebus didn't disagree, but what could anyone do? When one man could slaughter an army? What option was there but to train and send a similarly dangerous individual against them? Knowing they were beholden only to their word, that should they ever choose to turn that same power against their benefactor, there was nothing that could stop them.

That was the entire reason for the Paladin Order in the first place, as a counter-balance to that kind of power. And they'd come a long way from the days when the best answer mankind had to hostile magic was a good bow-arm and fervent hope, first with defensive rune-work then the discovery of null, but it had never been enough to bring down the truly powerful. Daemon lords, immortals, lost gods, rogue dragons and rampaging elementals had remained the purview of the very mages they were trying to keep in check, and that barely.

To get those whose power placed them outside the law to conform to it, it was in many respects a noble goal, one his friend would be more than prepared to sacrifice one village and a personal friend to achieve. Gregor had always been good at that, dissociating his principles from his personal life.

The cascade of logic continued in his mind's eye; the play here was Gregor's, Janiah was his agent. But there was a flaw in the plan. To know the method was to know the man, and to know the man was to know the method and whilst Lutan would as gladly see the Immortals humbled and brought to heel, his was a far more tempestuous mind, no matter how lofty the goal vengeance would always supersede it. And Lutan knew him too, all too well.

Right now, through the slowed time of adrenaline-fueled realisation, he was about to watch the very balance of power on Contemnere, perhaps the entire world of Reath, shift. Possibly for the better, probably for the worst.

More than even the Immortals, Erebus knew what lay out there, beyond the world, beyond its many fragmented parallel planes, beyond the Hells and out in the Silence Beyond.

What waited there, in hunger and in malice. Why demon lords and fairy queens both sought so desperately to get to this one small world when they had the power to rule thousands, and if the Immortals had to bend the knee to mortal kind, to be beholden to mortal laws no matter how noble the sentiment, then they would come, with all their terrible power as they fled that which was most terrible in all the worlds.

He'd never been able to get Gregor to understand that part. For all their might and majesty the Immortals only saw themselves as guards against demonic aggression; none of them had gone further than the near Hells and only then in times of great conflict. Lutan, of all people, had understood, back when they'd still been on speaking terms and not so many mistakes had been made, and he'd used that understanding for this moment. Aided Gregor in his scheme and made it his own because he'd known his foe well, and there was just one thing to be done.

"I submit myself to the justice of the Paladin Order."

Epilogue

Three days alone in the dark, dank cold of a cell. Well, perhaps not that dark, a lighting crystal emitted a steady sterile glow from the ceiling, powered off of Erebus' siphoned and shackled magic. And not really dank either; it was dry and indeed warm in truth. One didn't get thrown into one of Seruatis' hidden cells in the hopes a sharp shock could reform an errant soul. Still, the loneliness gnawed.

The thought galled him, a foe thought long-vanquished returning at this hour to challenge him.

At least it gave him something to do, something to fight, even if it was just himself. It had been a terribly long time since he'd been so idle or so powerless.

Not powerless in that he lacked magic, Seruatis' cells were exceptionally good at draining magic, but there was no siphoning enchantment in the world that could fully cope with a sudden surge, and there was always power to burn if one was prepared to pay the cost. Powerless in that he was here by his own free will, his captor was the best gaoler he could imagine, himself.

He'd received food and water each mealtime, and not poor food either but some of Agh'zak's finest, teleported directly into the cell, an extravagant waste of power, but they'd siphoned at least thrice that off of him in just the first day. But no visitors, no contact, no real evidence the outside world continued to exist in his absence.

Until now, at least, the clipped echoes of boots on stone slowly approaching, almost certainly not a guard

— the prison beneath Seruatis was large but not so large it would take days for a guard to walk their beat. If it had guards.

There was the sound of a turning key in an iron, or at least iron adjacent, lock that hadn't been oiled in far too long.

"So do you want me to bring you a ball or something to throw at the wall? Maybe take the chance to finally learn to play an instrument?" Saiko asked as he swung the door wide to grin at him, though it didn't stop the Spellbreaker in his hands from being levelled unerringly at Erebus's throat, the merc not stepping past the threshold.

"You weren't who I was expecting."

"Yeah well Dus' kinda loathe to come down here, too many familiar faces I guess, and the head honcho's been barred from his own prison on account of playing favourites. Didn't even know this place had a prison."

"Few do."

"Thought you'd be more nervous," Sai observed coolly.

"Well I considered it but you're not carrying either cigarette or blindfold so I think I'll see another day."

"He's absolutely furious with you you know?"

"I know," Erebus assured him.

"So how are you planning to get out of this?" The mercenary decided to just directly ask about the issue of the day.

"I'm not. It's not what I wanted to happen but this is the best outcome I can currently see."

"Yeah well, circumstances change, you could always claim asylum here."

"And that would just start this exact same fight again in a couple of months."

Saiko chewed briefly at his lip before replying, "I'm not much of a philosopher, but maybe that just shows the fight needs to happen?"

"No," Erebus replied, definite and definitive. "Because it can only end one way. The Immortals cannot be allowed total freedom from law, if they pushed this issue they would find themselves opposed by almost every nation not just on Contenmere but on the face of Reath itself. They would have no choice but to concede, and then they would be bound, their capacity to act curtailed. It would be the beginning of the end."

"The Swordsman doesn't believe it will come to that."

"The Swordsman is an optimist," the necromancer retorted, "I'm a realist. I cannot escape while in immortal custody, and I doubt I will be given the opportunity once outside of it." He gave a shrug, "Could be worse, I've had a fairly good life I believe, and I'd like to think I've done a lot of good with it as well."

Saiko frowned, "Well, I'll go tell him your mind can't be changed." He reached out his hand, and to his surprise, Erebus shook it.

"I'd consider it a personal favour if you looked after the kid, ideally get him somewhere he can live a normal life if that doesn't interfere with your apprenticeship."

The merc merely nodded before leaving with a final clang and creak of the elderly cell door.

"I don't see why I can't visit him," Alec stated for the umpteenth time that day, arms folded rather petulantly though there wasn't much point given his audience.

Dus' sigh was long and heart-felt, as it always was when he said it, having been appointed, by fiat, to care for the teen in Erebus' absence.

The gorgon wearing a full face mask rather than her usual domino-style blindfold. Aged silver, gorgeously carved to show a crying face, the only concession she'd really made to the events of the past few days. Unfortunately, her patience had not held in that time; there was only so many times you could have the same conversation without it devolving to a simple:

"Because you're not." It was perhaps to Dus' credit that she didn't snap it, speaking calmly if through gritted teeth, "and it's not in my power to grant you access nor grant you access to the person who can, who also won't give you access."

The teenager glared at her, not that she noticed, "That's nonsense and you know it. He listens to you."

"Yes. That's why I don't have access either," the gorgon pointed out, her serpent hair dangling limply as they echoed her mood. "I can't tell you to stop worrying… well I can but I know it won't work, but you need to stop worrying. Swordsy's got this."

That at least broke through her charge's malaise, "Swordsy?"

It turned out a grin could, in fact, be audible. "He must never know."

"You have my word," Alec replied, suppressing what an uncharitable, or perhaps realistic listener would describe as a titter. "But I want to help. To do something. Anything!"

"What you can do to help is the hardest thing I could imagine asking of you, do nothing, just trust that those who can help are doing all they can to ensure his safety and his liberty."

"And if they can't?" It was very much an Erebus question, and one Dus didn't have a good answer for. There was no good way to say what she was thinking, that Lutan had thus far had a counterpunch for every trap evaded and that even if Erebus escaped the noose, there was probably something else waiting in the wings, that she barely dared think of the ways to free her friend (irritating as she found him and his thrice-cursed hero worship) for fear that something might pluck the thoughts from her head and close down any such opportunities, that The Swordsman, stalwart and noble as almost any she'd met in her long, long life might decide discretion to be the better part of valour and honour his friend's choice to preserve the same status quo they all chafed at.

"They will," she settled on, reaching out to ruffle the teen's hair and smiling as he pulled away. She was going to miss Alec, especially when he left; it had been far too long since youth had dared trespass on Seruatis. "You should focus on being ready when the time comes, unless you wish to stay here forever?"

"I've thought about it," the teen admitted, "asked around, as has Holly, we're both resolved to go. With Erebus that is. It could be years before we get another chance to leave."

"Yeah that's Seruatis, lots of arrivals, very few departures." Dus shrugged, "Well make sure you say goodbye before you leave. I know I've got a present for you and I'd imagine there's a few others who would like to wish you well."

"I will Dus, promise."

"Good, now go find someone else to annoy."

"He's resolved sir," Saiko said quietly, sat down opposite his boss, the desk between them festooned with a pile of paperwork that certainly hadn't been there when he'd left.

The Swordsman nodded, not looking up from a rather familiar slim black volume, "I expected as much."

"Would you actually have helped him escape?"

"He's my friend," the immortal replied simply.

"And to hell with the consequences huh?"

"I honestly don't care where the consequences go. One day that fight's gonna happen, I'll probably be there for it, doesn't matter to me if it's today or in a hundred years."

"Some of us here now might prefer it not being today," his apprentice pointed out.

"True, and the people in a hundred years would probably prefer it had happened a hundred years ago," he said, finally putting down his book, laying it open on the desk to reveal the small and precise handwriting of Seruatis' newest prisoner.

"For someone who was prepared to overturn civilisation as we know it if he agreed you seem surprisingly relaxed that he refused, if you don't mind my saying."

"That's because the game's not over."

"Seems pretty over where I'm standing, we hold him for a few weeks, during which he'll outright refuse to escape. The escort arrives to take him away, null cuffs, draining runes the works, he gets tried in a paladin court, dances the hemp fandango and that's it."

"Yes but the escort has to arrive, because my friendship with him puts any guards I might choose from here in a less than trustworthy light." The Swordsman smiled, "And outside Seruatis the sort of elite soldier who would be trusted to contain someone of Erebus' prowess is rare indeed."

He handed Saiko a list of names, it wasn't an especially long list. Twenty names at the most.

"And I have here," he indicated Erebus' personal journal, "a complete list of everyone who owes our favourite necromancer a favour."

The immortal's smile was positively vulpine, "How many names would you want to bet overlap?"

ACKNOWLEDGMENTS

I would like to say thank you to all those who have helped bring this novel into being:

Karen Carrington, my secondary school librarian for encouraging me to write and listening to my endless rambling;

Deborah Griffiths, for talking me through the publishing process and editing the book;

My parents, Colin and Gaynor, for being nothing but encouraging even when I was at my lowest;

Christopher Paolini, Eragon showed me you're never too young to write and was one of the major deciding factors in doing so. Though it may have taken me a lot longer to finish than I expected;

And to my good friend Kye Ottley for a magnificent job on the front cover.

About The Author

Bristol-born and bred David was an avid reader from a young age with the works of Tolkien being a particular joy even before the age of ten; it was almost inevitable he took up writing the fantasy genre himself as his passion for reading continued to carry him through his formative years until, as a rather calcified elder of fourteen and newly certified Aspie (now referred to as Autistic Spectrum Disorder) he took to writing fanfiction (which he sincerely hopes never sees the light of day).

Eventually, he grew bored of exploring worlds built by others and moved on to creating some of his own; many of these live on in the form of plot synopsis of the generic and uninspired quality acceptable only to creative writing exercises and Hollywood scriptwriters.

Upon leaving for university to study physics at Swansea, writing was forced to take a back seat and he wouldn't go back to writing until leaving, sadly with just a diploma rather than a degree due to a long bout with depression.

Since leaving university he has rebuilt his confidence, finally finishing his debut novel alongside building a second-hand goods business both of which he hopes will put something worthwhile back into the world.

Printed by Amazon Italia Logistica S.r.l.
Torrazza Piemonte (TO), Italy

41407831R00185